One Year to

Forever

Halos & Horns : Book Four

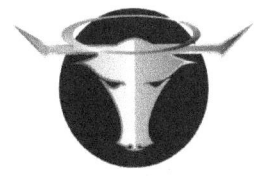

BY
LORI LEGER

This is a work of fiction based loosely
upon real occurrences, as told to the author.
It is not meant to be a biographical account.

ISBN-10: 1940305063
ISBN-13: 978-1-940305-06-6

Cajunflair Publishing
P.O. Box 641
Kinder, LA. 70648
www.CajunflairPublishing.com
http://www.facebook.com/CajunflairPublishing

Praise for Lori Leger's La Fleur de Love series…

"Lori Leger pens a novel with charming characters that you cannot help but relate to. The secondary characters are fun and feisty."… "If you are looking for an easy and charming read, then pick up SOME DAY SOMEBODY by Lori H. Leger."

(4/5 Stars) Romance Junkies reviewer

(On LAST FIRST KISS) "Lori Leger pens a romance that will break your heart and then leave your heart leaping for joy." "…a sweet romance that will warm your heart…"

(4/5 Stars) Romance Junkies reviewer

(On HART'S DESIRE) "This beautifully written, heart-wrenching short story has well-developed characters that reach out, grab the reader and draw them into their conflict…Exquisitely done.

(5/5 Stars & Crowned Heart) InD'tale Magazine Reviewer: *Carol Conley*

"BROWN EYED GIRL is a sweet romantic story, with a scrumptious love triangle between Tiffany, Tanner, and Red! … Lori Leger is a master at great romance, though, and the one between Tiffany and Red is a perfect example.

(4 ½ Stars/Crowned Heart) InD'tale Magazine reviewer: *Victoria Z. Burg*

(On HEAVEN IN YOUR EYES) "A thrilling read…After reading this story, I immediately purchased the rest of the books, and cannot wait to read them."

(5 Stars) Romance Junkies Reviewer

Praise for Lori Leger's Halos & Horns series…

"GREEN EYED TEMPTATION (Halos and Horns)" by Lori Leger is a modern romance with a lot of punch in it." "The author's style is conversational and easy, with a humorous touch." … "She creates sensual situations as skillfully as she builds tension and intrigue, and is a polished, accomplished author."

Readers' Favorite Reviewer: *Stephanie D.*

(MEAGAN'S MARINE) "… Ms. Leger has an exceptional way of developing the characters. … This is a truly lovely story of a military family getting a fresh start. It is sweet, it is charming, it is wonderful. Kudos Ms. Leger!"

(4 ½ Stars/Crowned Heart/RONE Award finalist) InD'tale Magazine reviewer: *Julie Caicoo*

(ONE YEAR TO FOREVER) ". . . Positively swooneriffic! "One Year to Forever" renews one's faith in true romance and the kind of love that lasts a lifetime. Ms. Leger's devotion to this story shines like a bright new penny. The plight of military relationships and life while deployed is raw and real, garnering greater appreciation for the sacrifices of our military men, women, and their families. "One Year to Forever" proves that chivalry is very much alive, and a warrior's heart fights for love just as fiercely as it fights for freedom. Thank you, and Ooh Rah, Ms. Leger!»
~ InD'tale reviewer, Sofia St. Angeles~ (5 Stars/Crowned Heart)
Winner of the 2015 Romance Novel of Excellence award for Contemporary Romance in Cops, Jocks, and Cowboys category.

Praise for Seasons of Love series…

HEARTS, HEARTHS & HOLIDAYS: Is a wonderful compendium of romance reads to ring in the holidays. Romance is the order of the day, and Seasons of Love does not disappoint.
(5 Stars/Crowned Heart) InD'tale Magazine Reviewer:
Victoria Z. Burg

SPRING PROMISE: These very talented authors have written four stories that will entertain and delight any reader looking for love! Each one is unique and just long enough…take one away without spending the day!"
(4 Stars) InD'tale Reviewer: *Rose Mary Espinoza*

SWEET SUMMERTIME LOVE: "Still Loving Cat"(by Lori Leger) captivates die-hard romantics and fans of the friends-to-lovers theme. Readers will adore the sigh-worthy Zach, and his steadfast love for Cat."
InD'tale Magazine Reviewer: *Danielle Hill*

CHRISTMAS BY CANDLELIGHT: This Christmas anthology would be a wonderful addition to the stack of books to be brought out each holiday season to be read over and over again. The stories are reminiscent of a relay race. Lori Leger's "Baby Blues Christmas"—the best of the bunch—rockets out of the block like a shot and it's amazing how she fits what feels like an awesome, full-sized novel into such a small package. ... Way to go ladies, high five!"
(4 ½ Stars/Crowned Heart/RONE Award finalist) InD'tale Review Magazine Reviewer: *Sofia St. Angeles*

DEDICATION

To Ben and Haley.
The beautiful couple whose stories of Afghanistan,
Hawaiian islands, barrel racing, stretch limousines,
roses on Mondays, candlelit hotel rooms,
strawberries, champagne, chocolate hazelnut spread,
and rose petal trails leading to handwritten words of love,
inspired this novel.

May you always be as in love
with each other as you are today.
I don't think my heart could take it, otherwise.

ACKNOWLEDGMENT

To my husband for keeping the house from falling down around me during my all-consuming, deadline induced, sprints to the finish line. Your housekeeping and cooking skills are much appreciated, as is your ability to supply me with fresh coffee prepared exactly the way I like it. I love you, babe.

To my friend/ex-co-worker/book club member/Photographer Joan Granger of Simple Memories Photography In Welsh, LA for the fabulous cover shots of Ben Bonin and Haley Broussard. Thank you for making it difficult to choose a cover image. Thanks also for the better-than-I-really-look bio shot of the author. I wish I woke up looking that good!
www.simplememories.org

Sean and James Gayle of Patti's Book Nook in my old hometown of Gueydan, La.
www.pattisbooknook.com and
Christy Lepretre of Java Joltz in Jennings, LA
http://javajoltz.wix.com/javajoltz

Thanks to Matthew French, of militaryflighttravel.com for the informative phone conversation on chartered military flights and routes generally taken. I hope your wife approves.

Thanks to Ben Bonin, for your dedicated service to your country, and also for opening up a world I knew nothing about. I hope you didn't get too tired of the endless questions, texts, emails, phone calls, and any other method I may have used to pick your brain. I did give you fair warning.

Thanks to Haley Broussard for 'keeping the home fires burning' by waiting faithfully for Ben at home. If you hadn't, there would have been no story, or one not nearly as satisfying.

Thank you Monica Chapman, for 'volunteering' your son as research material. Seriously, *you* made this happen.

Other books by LORI LEGER

Table of Contents

Chapter 1

Never say Never

"Stop that!"

Haley Broussard slapped her dance partner's hand off her boob. He promptly moved his hand to her butt. She sent him an icy glare as she turned on her heels. He jerked her back around.

"Aw, don't be like that, honey. We haven't finished our dance yet."

The creep seemed to have eight hands, each one simultaneously trying to cop a feel at whatever part of her body he could reach. Once more, she tried to escape, only to have him pull her back, this time disgustingly close to him. She averted her face, overcome by the stench of beer, bourbon, and stale cigarettes on his breath, then shuddered from the feel of his hardness against her hip. He was ready for her second attempt to pull away, and she barely managed a step back before he reeled her in. She slipped both hands between them and pushed with everything she had to give herself a little breathing room. "Look, what'd you say your name was?"

"My friends call me BJ." He grinned drunkenly at her. "Cause there's nothing like a good BJ."

Haley cringed. "Well I'm not your friend, and—Ew. So, you need to back the hell off. I accepted a dance, not a grope session." With both hands trapped between her body and his, Haley's panic set in for real. Even under normal circumstances, she didn't like her arms or hands confined. This was far from normal.

Craning her neck, she scanned the room for Matt, her brother, with no luck. She was near to succumbing to a full-blown, hyperventilating, panic attack when a hand landed on her partner's beefy shoulder. A masculine voice—rich and ominous with barely contained anger, cut through the music.

"Excuse me, but is this asshole bothering you?"

Too relieved to speak, she somehow managed a nod at the straight-backed man who stood a good half head taller than her partner, but without the bulk. Maybe she couldn't speak, but she could stare—at the clean-shaven line of his strong jaw, sexy eyes, and nice lips. What he lacked in bulk he made up for with broad shoulders and well-developed biceps that screamed of some kind of workout regimen— all in all, a well-rounded package for a much appreciated knight-in-shining-armor.

"I think the lady has had enough of you for tonight."

Her captor used one arm to shove hard at the guy, while keeping a tight grip on her with the other. "Back off, ass-wipe."

"Let her go man, you don't want to do this tonight." Her knight spoke with steely determination, totally controlled.

"What I want to do tonight doesn't include you, so why don't you buzz on outta here before you get hurt...*junior*."

Haley winced from BJ's iron grip on her forearm, knowing she'd have a bruise to explain to her irate father later. Her would-be rescuer must have seen it, because his next move was to situate himself between her and the asshole that refused to release her arm.

"Let her go, man."

Meagan, one of the bartenders working that end of the room, pushed her way between them, obviously hoping to ward off trouble before it started.

"You." She pointed to the troublemaker. "Let her go, and then get on out. If you don't want to be barred from this place forever, you'll leave without another word."

BJ glared at Meagan as though he was about to turn on her, but seemed to think better of it. Instead, he swiveled his thick neck toward the knight and stuck one finger in his face. "You don't want a piece of me, bro. You Louisiana boys don't know dick about messin' with somebody like me." He shoved hard at the man's chest, surprise registering clearly on his face when it barely budged..

The bouncer pushed his way through the gathering crowd's nucleus, packed tight with onlookers. "Break it up, now."

"Mickey, that's the one causing all the trouble." Meagan pointed to the jerk still clutching at Haley's arm.

BJ's drunken gaze narrowed, seconds before he let go, but only to take a swing at Haley's knight. Instead of taking one in the face, he grabbed BJ's fist, twisted the man's beefy hand neatly with his own and whipped it around. In one quick, graceful, and somewhat familiar move, he'd pinned both BJ's arms behind his back.

Haley's heart skipped in a mixture of admiration and distress over the suspicion that her knight was probably military. As a matter of fact, she was sure of it, as sure as she knew her horse's favorite treat was apples.

He held BJ in position as he spoke to him. "I'm going to let you go, okay buddy? Go on home now and leave the lady alone."

"Yeah, okay," BJ hissed. Haley decided he'd already traded in what little brains he had for bravado, because the instant BJ was free he took a healthy swing at his captor.

She cringed, and heard the empty whoosh of a swing and miss, then a trio of lightening quick jabs that spun BJ around, sending him into the waiting arms of the bouncer. Not a bad turn of luck for him, considering the alternative would have been to land face down on the hard floor.

The bouncer shook his head, grumbling, as he half-carried, half-steered the punch-drunk BJ off to the exit. "Can't say you weren't warned, asshole."

A large, but gentle hand pressed against Haley's lower back, ushering her away from the scene. She glanced back and upward at the man escorting her. The no-nonsense expression on his face had the lingering crowd parting easily to let them pass. She slumped in an empty chair at Meagan's end of the bar and turned to him. "Thanks for that, but who *are* you?"

"I'm Ben. Are you okay?" He examined her arm. "It's not broken, but you're going to have a nasty bruise later."

Meagan pushed her way to the two of them, her face a mask of concern. "Haley, are you all right? Did that guy hurt you?"

"She needs ice on this."

"Right away." Meagan scrambled off, leaving the two of them alone.

"So, Ben." Haley smiled at him. "Do you have a last name?"

He returned the smile, answering in James Bond fashion. "Bonin—Ben Bonin."

"Well, thank you Ben Bonin. I'm Haley Broussard." She stared into beautiful hazel eyes, found herself admiring his smile. "What branch of the military are you in, Ben?"

He cocked his head. "Marines. How'd you know?"

She laughed and gestured at his head. "The short hair is always a sure sign, and then, there were those moves back there. My brother, also Marines, tried to teach me that same slip once, but I couldn't get the hang of it." She laughed and shrugged one shoulder. "He says I'm unteachable."

Ben's right brow lifted adorably. "Maybe you need a different instructor."

Haley smiled and sucked in her breath, praying he no longer served. "Are you out, by any chance?"

"No, I came in this morning for my pre-deployment leave. My last deployment. Why?"

Uh, because even if you were St. Benjamin of Good Deeds, I don't believe in long distance relationships? "No reason."

He examined her arm closer. "Are you sure you're all right? Do you need me to call someone for you?"

"No." Haley scanned the area around them. "My brother's here . . . somewhere." She turned to face him again. "Really, I'm fine." Her breath caught as one corner of his mouth lifted in a sexy as hell half-smile.

"That's obvious, but do you want me to find your brother for you?"

A light snort accompanied her laughter.

His right brow lifted curiously. "What's that about?"

"I was thinking if that was a line, it was a damn good one."

The corners of his eyes crinkled with laughter. "I didn't think I had any lines, but if it worked . . ."

Meagan approached with an icepack wrapped in a dishcloth. "Here you go, sweetie. Try this out for size."

Ben took the pack from her and laid it gently against her arm, using his large hands to hold it in place. "How's that feel?"

Fabulous, but was it the ice or the gentle touch of his hands on her? She fanned her face, slightly flustered from the nearness of him.

He leaned forward. "Haley? Does that feel okay?"

She blinked once and shook herself out of her stupor. "I'm sorry, I thought I answered you. Yes, that feels good." *And you smell wonderful.*

He shook his head, frowning. "It always blows my mind when guys treat women that way."

"Unfortunately too many men in the world think that kind of behavior is acceptable."

Ben pinned her with his gaze. "No real man thinks that." He removed the ice pack and towel and began to make some adjustments. "Hang on, let's try something." Within minutes, he'd used the dishtowel as a wrap to tie the ice pack securely to her arm. "How's that?"

She flexed her elbow, immediately missing the touch of his hands on her. "I think that'll work. Thank you, Ben."

He jutted his chin toward the makeshift wrap. "You think that thing will hold up for a dance, or are you too upset to go back out there?"

She cocked her head. "I guess that depends on who's asking."

"I'm asking."

"I'm accepting."

Ben led her to the outer edge of the dance floor, his hand placed at her lower back, a reminder of the masculine presence he personified. Her heart set up a heavy thud at the feel of one of his hands covering hers, while the opposite rested almost protectively at her waist and back. One Chris Young ballad later, and she regretted leaving his arms.

Halfway back to the table the band picked up a quick country jitterbug. He leaned in close. "Can you dance to this?"

Haley gave him an enthusiastic nod. "I love to dance."

"I'm not real good at it, but if you don't mind me stepping on your toes, I'm game."

She accepted, thrilled that he was willing to try for her. Several minutes later, she headed for the bar, breathless, both from laughter at his comical antics on the dance floor, as well as trying to keep up with him. A gentle tug on her hand had her spinning around to face him. The piano introduction announced the song *Wanted* by Hunter Hayes. His eyes issued a silent command: *Dance with me*. Without a word, and oh so willingly, she returned to the welcome cocoon of his arms.

Within seconds, he'd tucked her hand close to his chest. A minute later she looped her arms over his shoulders as he wrapped his around her waist. Resting her face on his chest, she released a long, slow sigh at the feel of his fingers gently caressing her back. She lifted her face to stare up into his. The look on his face, along with his next comment, took her breath away.

"I want to see you again, Haley. Is that okay with you?"

Game over. End of story. Any, and all free will she'd possessed at that point, had flown out the window like her cousin's pet canary. She blinked several times and swallowed. "Absolutely."

A dozen dances later she fidgeted nervously, waiting for Ben to return with their drink orders. Common sense told her she needed to get a good night's sleep for the next day's racing competition. All she wanted to do was cancel and spend all night talking to this man.

"Here you go." Ben set the bottle of water she'd requested before her. "How's the arm?"

She touched the ice pack and gave him a nod. "It's good." She checked her phone for the time.

"You gonna turn into a pumpkin at midnight, Cinderella?"

She glanced up into eyes sparkling with laughter. "No, but if I don't get some sleep my race will be a bust."

He nodded. "I can respect that. Why throw all that practice away with one crappy night of sleep?"

"That's right." Haley smiled, and then took a deep breath, releasing it slowly as she shot her brother a text saying she was ready to go. Seconds later, Matt answered, saying he'd meet her at his truck. She slipped her phone in the back pocket of her jeans and pouted at Ben's expression. "I *really* don't want to go."

Ben took command of the situation, almost as though he were trying to make it easier for her. Taking her hand, he nodded toward the exit. "Come on, I'll walk you outside."

Halfway to the door, the DJ kicked off the band's break with a song request for a couple celebrating their wedding anniversary. Ben pulled Haley to a stop as the mellow sound of Keith Urban's *Making Memories of Us* flowed through the sound system.

No words were necessary. She nodded, and let him lead her to the rapidly filling dance floor. Obviously, they weren't the only fans of the song. She turned in to his embrace, sucked in her breath as he took both of her hands in his, and slowly lifted them to his broad shoulders. His arms encircled her waist, pulling her tightly against his torso. The two of them danced slowly, swaying in time to the tune Haley had adored from the day of its release. She avoided his gaze, half afraid of what she'd find in those somber pools of hazel.

Ben had other ideas. He brought one hand forward slowly to cup and lift her chin, until their noses practically touched.

"There you are," he said.

Haley stared into the handsome face that was a good combination of hard and soft, seriousness and humor. She had to wonder if this would be the last she'd see of this man who, from what she could tell, projected all the qualities of a good Marine, a good man. He'd said he wanted to see her again, but did he mean it? He'd be leaving for Afghanistan in about three weeks for a seven month stretch. Seven long months . . . and wouldn't be out for another five months afterwards. A year—an entire year. Was he really interested in keeping up some kind of long distance relationship? And even if he was, was she up to that? She'd spent all of her adult life worrying about her brother through several years of Middle Eastern deployments. At least, she had, once she was old enough to realize what was going on.

The song drew to a close and he leaned in to place a soft kiss on her lips. "Thanks for one last dance, Haley."

She had the strongest urge to pull him back for more, but that's not how she was raised. She stepped back and let him take the lead, pulling her along behind him with a soft grasp of her hand. She placed her free hand on her stomach, reliving the kiss from seconds ago. Said kiss may have seemed totally innocent from anyone else's viewpoint, but Haley suspected that if there was a way to physically *see* pheromones, they'd be rolling off the man in waves.

He reached the door, held it open for her to exit first. The outdoor breeze stirred the delicious scent of his cologne, fresh with a touch of spice, carrying it directly to the part of her brain in charge of sexual appeal.

As she passed him, he lifted one hand to brush his fingers gently along her cheek. Her body's reaction to his subtle touch was a head to toe shiver that took her by surprise. Haley turned to meet the gaze already locked onto hers, caught the tenderness in his eyes.

Pheromones. Waves of them. All locked and loaded, and targeting her girl parts like a bull's eye on a rifle range. Every single one of them dedicated to turning her insides to mush.

Holy. Crap. If he ever discovered the effect he had on her, she'd be done.

Suddenly she caught the slight wink, revealing the hint of mischief in his eyes, and knew the warning had come too late.

She *was* done.

Haley tried to concentrate on what she had to do to bring in the best barrel races of the day. She chided herself for thinking about Ben, fantasizing he was somewhere in the crowd, watching her. He'd asked about her race times, seeming interested, but she knew he had family obligations. Without a doubt his parents, siblings, and friends all had claims on his time off during the next two weeks. Hope flared when hands covered her eyes from behind.

A masculine voice whispered. "Guess who?"

She turned, hoping to see Ben. The sight of Trevor, a guy she'd dated briefly, distinguished her hope in a flash. "Oh, it's you."

"Well hell, Haley girl. That's a fine greeting."

She arched one eyebrow. "Now you know how I felt when I caught you kissing up on that chick during one of our dates."

He rested his hand on one hip and waved his index finger in front of her nose. "One time. One time you caught me. Are you ever going to let that go?"

She shook her head. "That's the point, Trev. I only caught you once, but there's no telling how many times you got away with it." She turned her back on him to rub her hand along Dakota's satiny nose. "What are you doing here, anyway? I didn't think you were competing anymore."

"I'm not. I was here with a friend but sh—uh, he had to leave." He got closer and slipped his hands around her waist. "Are you finished here?"

She gripped his hands and pushed them forcefully away from her. "Not quite, but I'm not alone, if that's what you're wondering." Haley looked purposely at a spot behind him. "You remember my big, *big* brother, Matthew, don't you, Trevor?"

Trevor faced the man, and seemed to shrink as Matt approached, towering above and well beyond him in all directions.

"Uh, yeah. Hi, Tex, I remember you." He stuck his hand out. "Trevor Campbell. Remember me, bro?"

Her brother's eyes narrowed to angry slits as he bared his teeth, growling his reply. "Yeah, I do, unfortunately for you." He ignored Trevor's outstretched hand. "I ain't your bro, and only my friends call me Tex. *You*, little man, can call me Matthew—or sir."

Trevor pulled his hand back and wiped it on his pants leg, stammering his reply. "Y-y-es-sir."

Haley had to cover her mouth to keep from laughing as Trevor ducked when Matt stuck his finger in his face.

"Don't think I've forgotten you sneaking around on my sister, asshole. You aren't worthy to lick the horse shit off her boots."

"Yes sir—I mean, no sir—I mean, I know that, sir." Trevor lifted both hands. "I'm only here as a friend."

"Humph, I'd say that's up to her, but with friends like you . . ." Matt grunted, sent Haley a wink that said he'd had enough fun for one day, then turned and walked away from them. Trevor took a deep breath, Haley assumed, in order to re-inflate his testicles.

"Well shit, is your brother always that intense?"

She turned her back on him and tended to her horse. "Nope, he's usually a barrel of fun. Must be you bringing out the worst in him."

He looked over his shoulder to make sure Matt wasn't within ear shot of them. "You need me to hang around to help out with your horse? Which one is this, anyway? Is this Blue Montana, or whatever the hell you named the damn thing?"

"Her name is Miss Red Dakota and she was already named when I got her. And no, I don't need any help with her. If you want to hang around, I guess it's okay."

"Cool. Are you, uh . . . going home tonight?" He threw his arm over her shoulder.

Before Haley could shake Trevor's long, lanky arm from her shoulder, Dakota swiveled her large head around. She nipped at his elbow, almost as though she sensed her mistress's annoyance with the man.

"Shit!" He jerked his arm away and rubbed at his elbow. "She bit me."

Haley grinned, thinking her girl had earned a couple of extra apples tonight. "Yep, she does that every now and then." *Especially to people who rub her the wrong way.* "Horses are very astute judges of character, you know." She hugged Dakota's neck as she gave her a gentle pat on the shoulder.   "So far, you haven't made very good impressions on members of my family." She turned to face him. "And not that it's any of your business, but no, I'm not going home. Matt and I are staying at the house of an old military buddy of his."

"Army . . . huh." Trevor snorted. "A man's gotta be a damn fool to serve in the military these days."

Haley turned for the sole purpose of giving him a verbal reaming. However, the sight of Matt approaching from behind had her yearning for a little more payback, courtesy of big brother. "You think so, huh?" She sent him a brilliant smile, in hopes he'd keep talking long enough to hang himself.

"You bet your ass. They couldn't pay me enough money to join the Army, Navy, Air Force, National Guard, and Coast Guard . . ." He guffawed loudly. "And sure as hell not the Marines—I heard those dumb jarheads don't have minds of their own. They couldn't think for themselves if they had to."

"The hell you say." Matthew's deep rumble of condemnation sounded disturbingly lethal.

Haley stared, totally transfixed at the sight of Trevor's Adams Apple bobbing up and down rapidly as his shoulders hitched upward toward his neck. If he shrank any more, she'd have to enlist Matt's help to pull the poor guy's head out of his own ass.

Trevor turned slowly toward Matthew, and to his credit, attempted a little bravado through his obvious terror. He made a slight attempt to redeem himself, but his ignorance ultimately did him in. "Yeah, you know what I mean. You always hear everything about the Marines, like they're all that. It must be ass-chapping to an Army man, like yours-s-e-l-f-f."

Haley held her breath. Judging from the hitch in his breath and the distinct stall in his speech pattern, he'd caught sight of the tattoo on Matt's enormous, flexed bicep.

"Tell me what you see, ass-wipe."

Haley found herself thanking the stars Matt was her brother. Otherwise, the ominous growl he emitted would have had her shaking in her Ropers.

"I-it s-says S-Semper Fi-fidelis—sir."

Matt nodded, lowered his arm, and then raised the opposite bicep. "And here?"

Haley couldn't hear Trevor's swallow over the background noise, but that Adam's apple bobbing up and down was proof enough. She stifled another laugh, thinking she almost felt sorry for the guy. *Almost.*

"USMC—sir."

Matt threw a heavy hand on Trevor's shoulder and leaned in so close their noses nearly touched. "I bet you're wishing right about now you'd been a little more observant, aren't you, ass-wipe?" When Trevor kept his silence, Matt straightened and looked at his sister.

"I'm going to get a beer. You need anything, little sister?"

"No thanks, I'm good."

He nodded, looked at Trevor and made a half-assed lunge for him before he jerked back—enough to make

Trevor flinch and take a step in the opposite direction. Matt turned and walked off toward the nearest concession stand, his massive shoulders shaking with laughter.

Haley kept her silence as Trevor collected himself and finally turned to face her again, trying to look as though he hadn't come close to soiling his own Wranglers.

"Now, what were we saying?" he said, attempting to get back some of his macho facade.

Haley crossed her arms and took a step back before letting her gaze trail down to his crotch.

He puffed up like a rooster and lowered his hand to adjust himself. "Ah, I see you eyeing the merchandise. Think you might be interested?"

She met his ridiculously smug gaze and gave her head a slow shake. "Nope. I was checking to see if you'd peed yourself."

Remarkably, Trevor stuck around for the rest of the day. For the life of her, she couldn't figure out why. God knows, she hadn't given him one iota of encouragement. She'd even mentioned Ben's name several times in conversations with her brother and Mitch, who'd shown up to meet them at the arena. Mitch had urged her to let him get rid of her shadow, but she actually didn't see the harm in him being around. Her parents hadn't raised her to be out and out rude to anyone, whether they deserved it, or not.

He must have overheard Matt and Mitchell's conversation about how they should finish in plenty of time to make it to Red's club by seven o'clock. She'd waved him off as he left the arena the same time they had, around 5:00. They'd gone to Mitchell's place to take care of Dakota, and she jumped at the opportunity to rid herself of the smell of horse. By the time she, Matt, and Mitch reached the club that night, Trevor was waiting at the door.

"Well, shit. Look at that, would you?" A groan of disbelief accompanied Matt's comment.

"He's a persistent little son of a bitch, isn't he?" Mitch leaned over to her. "You should have let me get rid of him for you, Haley."

"Yup, one little accident and he'd be out of your hair, sis. For good, if need be."

She grabbed both of their arms. "Be nice, you two. It's a free country, and he can go anywhere he likes. Besides, he's a friend."

"Fine, but that doesn't mean I have to talk to him." Matt proved his point by totally ignoring Trevor's presence.

Trevor strutted forward. "Hey, I was hoping I'd run into you here tonight."

"Well, looks like you did." He followed her inside the club, which vibrated with a driving bass beat.

Mitch took the lead, and they painstakingly made their way over to Meagan's end of the packed bar.

The barmaid looked up at their approach, and grinned. "Hey, I'm glad to see y'all back."

Mitch pointed his thumb at Haley. "She's coming to collect her birthday shots."

"Ah, that's right, Miss-21-year-old gets a bottle of her choice. If my memory serves me, you wanted to think about it. Have you made your decision?"

Haley smiled and slapped her hand on the bar. "Actually, I believe I've decided to support the Louisiana sugarcane farmers and try the Bayou Rum. Ben said it's really smooth."

Meagan beamed at her. "*Ben* would be correct. It's fabulous mixed with cola, but smooth enough to shoot straight. I highly recommend it. You want the Silver or Spiced?"

"Let's start with the Silver, please."

Meagan set out a large plastic tray, placed the bottle in the center and added a few cans of Coke and four shot glasses for their corner table.

Within minutes she'd spotted Ben. Haley's stomach flipped pleasantly when she saw him speaking to Meagan, and then shaking Mitchell's hand. When Mitch used his beer bottle to point in her direction, she averted her gaze, not wanting him to know she'd been watching the exchange. She waited another minute, and no Ben. She'd begun to think he'd changed his mind about approaching her, when he called out to her. She whipped her head around at the sound of his voice.

"Hey, there—I thought you weren't going to be able to make it tonight!" She didn't even attempt to stem her excitement at his presence, no matter how cool she should have played it.

"I didn't know for sure until this afternoon. I cancelled some plans to be here."

"Did you?" She laid a hand on her chest, thrilled that he'd thought enough of her to do that. "I'm honored. Now, come shoot a round of birthday rum with me."

He smiled, his eyes sparkling with amusement. "I've already had a couple of beers, so I'll pass on the rum. But how about if I watch you shoot and offer to hold your head when you're hugging the porcelain throne later?"

Trevor, with his impeccable sense of timing, stepped up and threw an arm possessively around her shoulder. "Uh, excuse me, but that's what I'm here for, buddy."

Wondering why she hadn't let Mitch get rid of him when he'd offered, she jabbed Trevor in the side with her elbow. "Don't be a jerk, Trev. You don't own me. Trevor Jameson, this is Ben Bonin. I met him here last night. I ended up dancing with a human octopus and he rescued me." She heard herself speaking too quickly, practically rambling. She turned away to pour some shots, and tried to relax.

Haley turned with the tray, in time to see Trevor and Ben shaking hands. She tried to ignore the crackling vibes of clashing male testosterone in the air. She pretended not to notice Trevor flexing his hand as though he was in pain. She lifted the tray before her. "Here's to being twenty-one."

Matt appeared, handing her a shot as he took the tray. Mitch approached in time to clink his beer bottle with her glass. "And all the fireworks that go along with it."

Trevor reached for a shot glass. "Here's to free booze."

Matt growled at him as he pulled the tray out of his reach. "Go buy your own damn drinks, you pain in the ass."

Ben clicked his own beer bottle to Haley's shot glass, and gave her another brilliant smile, his eyes brimming with sincerity. "Here's to you, Haley. I hope you have nothing but great birthdays from here on out."

Haley smiled at the toast that certainly seemed sincere. "Thank you." She barely had time to throw her first shot back before Trevor grabbed her arm.

"Come on Haley, you love dancing to this song."

She nodded, recognizing Blake Shelton's *Sure be Cool if You Did.* "You're right," she said, pulling her arm from him and looking expectantly toward Ben.

She didn't think the man's chest could have gotten any broader than it already was. But his pecs seemed to swell before her eyes as he reached for her. She placed her hand in his and he led her to the dance floor.

He laced his fingers through hers and pulled her close with one arm around her waist. He lowered his mouth to her ear and spoke over the music. "You know, I've been kicking myself since you left here last night. I forgot to get your number."

"But you knew I'd be here."

"I know, but I kept thinking you may not show. Sometimes things happen . . ." His voice trailed off.

She smiled, keeping the fact that she'd run home and found him on Facebook to herself, both a personal account, as well as one from the base at Kaneohe Bay, Hawaii. She'd barely kept herself from sending him a friend request. "But I'm here."

He nodded. "Didn't stop me from worrying about it."

"Aw. I hope you didn't lose sleep over it."

"As a matter of fact, I did." He shifted his head slightly, and looked down his nose at her. "As soon as this song ends I want that number."

"Okay." She stared straight ahead into the huge expanse of chest, hoping to hide the huge Cheshire cat grin she wore. "I'm on Facebook and Twitter, too," she said, loud enough to be heard. His instantaneous "I know" had her grin widening to a face-cracking level. "You looked me up?"

"Sure did."

"I didn't receive a friend request from you."

"I wanted a face to face request."

She nodded, tapping her fingers lightly on his shoulders in time to the music.

"What are you thinking, Haley?"

She let her head drop back to meet his gaze as the music started drifting to a close. "How much I like being your reason for losing sleep." Ben lifted one hand to caress her face gently as he leaned in for a kiss that had her toes wanting to curl.

He pulled back and spoke, the sound of his deep voice carrying over the fading music. "That's good, because I doubt it'll be my last sleepless night over you."

Sweet Jesus.

Haley let Ben lead her back to their table, and then excused herself. She made her way to the ladies room, more to collect herself than anything else. She stood before the mirror placing the palms of both hands on her flushed cheeks. Within seconds, Meagan entered the space and caught her gaze in the mirror.

"Girl, that's some serious sparks flying between you two out there."

Haley turned to face Meagan, using both hands to fan her face. "Oh God, is it that obvious?"

Meagan's eyes widened. "Uh, yeah. You look like you need a cold shower."

"I know. He's so . . ." She waved her hands frantically. "Full of potential, you know? Nobody . . . I've never . . ." She stopped, not having the slightest clue how to express her feelings.

Meagan took a step toward her, placed both hands on her shoulders. "I do know. I know exactly what you mean. But Haley, you can't let this thing move too quickly."

"I know," she groaned. "I'll try not to, but there's something there, Meagan." Her eyes widened as the realization hit her. "I really think he could be the one, Meagan."

Meagan's eyes darkened as she grew more serious. "Listen, I adored my son's father, and I wouldn't trade having Buck for anything in the world. But I'm raising him alone, and it's been difficult."

Haley brought one hand to her mouth. "Oh, I didn't know."

"Well, I'm not ashamed of it, but it's not something I advertise. I didn't find out I was pregnant until Christopher had already returned to Afghanistan. What's worse is that I didn't get to tell him about the baby before he lost his life over there. It . . . it haunts me to this day."

Her words had the effect of a polar plunge. "I'm so sorry, Meagan. I hadn't heard that." She gathered her new friend to her for a hug. "Thank you for worrying about me. I can handle this, I promise."

The two of them exited the ladies room together before going their separate ways, Meagan back to working behind the bar, and Haley, heading back to Corporal Bonin.

Before she reached him, Trevor grabbed her arm and pulled her aside to speak to her.

"Haley, what is this?"

Annoyed at his intrusion, she turned to him. "Excuse me?"

"So . . . what? Are you *with* that guy now?"

She stared at his incredulous sneer, recognized the self-absorbed attitude he'd displayed so many times, and wondered what the hell she'd ever seen in him. She faced Ben, who watched their encounter with an eagle eye. Although he kept his distance, she suspected he'd be there in a second if he thought she needed him.

Haley met Trevor's gaze. "Oh God, I sure hope so."

He let go of her arm and stepped back, his face a mask of shocked disbelief.

She turned and made her way back to Ben.

He stood at her approach. "Everything all right?"

"Sure is. But it'll be better once you get me back out on that dance floor."

Throwing back the last of his beer, he set the bottle on the bar and grabbed her hand. He led her out to dance to the band's cover of Easton Corbin's *Clockwork*. He tucked her hand close to his chest and held her close.

He jutted his chin toward Trevor, standing alone at the bar. "Has your friend given up, or do I need to have a talk with him?"

Her heart fluttered at the sound of concern in his tone. "I think I got the point across to him."

He nodded. "Good."

"But, for the heck of it, if you did talk to him, what would you say?"

"I'd tell him you're going to be busy for the next couple of weeks." Before she could respond he finished. "But first I'd have to ask you."

She pursed her lips. "Ask me what?"

In the middle of the dance floor he stopped, taking her chin in his hand. "Are you with me, Haley?"

Haley swallowed the lump in her throat. "Do you want me with you? I mean, you're a Marine." She suddenly found herself smoothing his shirt, straightening his collar, touching his buttons, anything to indulge herself with the feel of him. In her opinion, everything about the two of them seemed to click. But what did he think? "I mean, maybe you aren't the type to want to be with one wom—"

His mouth came down on hers, silencing her words. One hand moved to the back of her head, as the other gently cupped her chin. The kiss lasted for several seconds, would have lasted longer had a familiar voice not interrupted them.

"Why Haley, what would your mother think?"

She pulled away from Ben and stared, wide-eyed, into her brother's smug, grinning face. Refusing to look flustered, she paused a moment to collect her thoughts then sent her brother an equally smug grin. "She'd probably understand that I'm *with* someone now." She looped her arms around Ben's neck. "Aren't I, Benjamin?"

Ben sent Tex a big grin and nodded. "Roger that."

Tex grinned and sent his sister a wink. "Never say never, Haley girl. Never say never." His guffaw of laughter carried across the space as he swung around them with his own dance partner, a petite redhead with a too-big smile, and too-big boobs to match.

As with the previous night, Ben had proven to be a willing participant at the faster dances, even though he was a novice. But his exceptional ability to slow dance thrilled her, giving her hands ample opportunity to explore his upper torso. It would have to suffice, especially when she had the urge to explore every inch of him.

When Matt was ready to leave around midnight, Ben offered to take Haley home so she could stay. Two hours later, Ben parked his truck beside her brother's in Mitchell's driveway. And still, they talked. It took another hour before they reached a long enough lapse in conversation to realize the lapse in time.

Haley placed one hand on the door handle, stuck somewhere between knowing she should exit the truck and not wanting to leave. "I'm sure your family has a full day planned for you. I should let you leave now."

He reached out to cover her left hand with his own. "Please don't go, yet. At least not until you say you'll spend the day with me."

Her chest tightened as she considered her options. "I live in Beaumont, Ben. I have to go home and stable Dakota in . . ." She stopped to check her phone. "In a few hours, actually."

He leaned over the truck's console to get closer to her. "I'll follow you back to Beaumont, pick you up and bring you home tonight. I don't care what it takes."

"That isn't necessary. I have my own car."

His eyes widened. "Are you saying you'll spend the day with me?"

She nodded. "If you're sure your parents won't mind."

Ben shook his head. "My mom will say the more, the merrier. Believe me, I know her. But you have to let me pay for your gas, at least."

Haley tapped her fingers on the armrest, contemplating her plans. "My grandparents live ten miles south of Jennings, and they've been asking me to spend some time with them. I'm sure they'll be glad to put me up for a few days."

"Are you serious? That's only ten minutes from my house in Lake Erin."

"I'm warning you, they're kind of old fashioned. You'll have to pass my Paw Paw's twenty-one point inspection, or he won't let you anywhere near me."

He rubbed her hand between his. "I'm not worried."

She cocked her head to contemplate his answer. "You aren't, are you? Do you worry about anything?"

"Only that I won't get to see you every day for the rest of my leave."

"Ben . . ."

He pulled her closer, framed her face between his two hands. "I mean it, Haley. I want you with me."

She stared into his eyes, knew that he meant it. Trying to still the butterflies in her stomach, she inhaled deeply, and released a slow breath. "I know we've only met, but . . ."

"This is different, right?" He dipped low, cocked his head to one side. "I mean, is it me, or do you feel the potential here, too?"

"I feel it too, Ben. And something's telling me to spend every minute I can with you." She gave him a shy nod. "So yeah, I'll be there as long as you want me around."

He narrowed the distance between his mouth and hers. "Hell, that's good to know, because something's telling me that's gonna be a long . . . *long* . . . time."

Haley had experienced a few kisses in her previous twenty-one years. Even so, she found herself not quite prepared for the kiss that followed. It began innocent enough. Somehow, he managed to fool her into thinking the first whisper-soft touch of his lips would be the end of it. One slight adjustment, and subtle shift of his head later, he went in for the kill, proving that this particular Jarhead knew how to make a lasting impression. A warm glow started in the pit of her belly, spiraling outward as a sweet heat infiltrated her limbs and torso.

He pulled back, sucking in his breath as he touched his forehead gently to hers. "Oh, man . . ." The words came out in a hoarse whisper.

"Oh man . . ." she countered, before he targeted her mouth again for another kiss, this one filled with the promise of many more to come.

Chapter 2

Learning to Let Go

Haley unloaded and stabled Dakota, cooing softly to calm the animal. She filled the trough with feed, watching her mom's approach from the corner of her eye.

"Hey Popcorn, Matthew says you've had an interesting two days."

Her mom's rare use of Haley's childhood nickname put a smile on her face. "Yeah, I had a good race."

Angie Broussard grinned. "Well, I'd already heard that. What I want to hear about is this new young man you've met . . . and want to spend some time with?"

Haley covered the feed container and took a deep breath before turning to her mother. "Mom, he's only in for two more weeks, and I want to spend as much time with him as I can."

"Haley, you're twenty-one years old. I can't stop you from doing what you want. But I'll still worry about you. How much do you know about this boy?"

"He's not a boy, mom, he's a twenty-two year old Marine."

Angie gave a low chuckle. "If you're trying to make me feel better, you're not." She lifted her daughter's chin and stared into her eyes. "Look, I'm not too old to remember those feelings. That's why I'm having this talk with you."

"I know, but . . ." Haley paused to pull her buzzing cell phone from her pocket. She checked the screen, seeing a text message from Ben, asking for her home address. She sent him the information along with a double question mark. She waited for his response and grinned at his immediate reply.

On my way, already at the state line.

"Would it help if you met him, first, Mom?"

"It might. I guess that depends on what kind of impression I'd get from him."

Haley lifted the phone, showing her mom the text Ben had sent her.

"Awe, that'll do," Angie said, and gasped, along with her daughter at the follow up text he sent.

I can't expect your parents to trust their beautiful daughter with me for the next two weeks unless I meet them first. Don't you think?

Angie nodded and exchanged amused grins with her daughter. "That'll do nicely. Tell your young man he's off to a good start."

Ben spent the next two hours with Haley at her parents' place, assuring them his intentions were honorable toward their daughter. He followed her back to her grandparents' home, arriving a little before noon to meet the older couple, both in their late seventies. Within the hour, Ben had charmed her grandmother, and impressed her grandfather with his sincerity.

Haley slipped into the passenger side of Ben's truck and buckled her seat belt, then watched as her Paw Paw shook Ben's hand and waved at her through the window. She waited for him to situate himself into the driver's seat before speaking.

"So, is that part of your job description with the Marine Corps?"

He started his truck and turned to her. "What's that, babe?"

She smiled, deciding she liked the endearment coming from Ben's lips. But then, she had a feeling she'd like pretty much anything that came from those lips.

"Charming old people into accepting you enough to leave with their only granddaughter."

His laughter filled the cab of the truck, low, but not lacking in confidence. "To my knowledge that's never been part of my MOS."

"What was that?"

"My MOS—Military Occupation Specialty—my job description."

She shook her head and pulled her gaze from him to keep from climbing over the console to get to him. "Hmm, maybe it should be. You sure made easy work of it."

"It's not that difficult. My mom knew something was up before I even mentioned you this morning." He leaned in close and Haley met him halfway for a kiss. "And now, it's your turn to charm the pants off of my family."

Haley placed a hand over her stomach, nervous at the prospect of meeting his rather large family. His parents had both remarried, so he had a slew of step relatives thrown in with the blood relatives.

She needn't have worried. As it happened, his family was every bit as warm and welcoming as hers had been, despite there being so many of them.

By the end of their time spent in almost constant company, Haley had thoroughly meshed into Ben's family. As for she and Corporal Bonin, the two of them had grown close—closer than she could have imagined in such a short amount of time.

Two days had turned into one week, and one week into twelve days. In those twelve days, they'd learned about everything there was to know about one another, in every way—except for one. As badly as they both wanted it, and boy did she want it, Haley kept Meagan's words of warning close to her.

Just as she wasn't the type of woman to sleep with a guy so soon after meeting him, Ben wasn't the type of man to coerce her into doing anything she didn't want to do.

Twelve days of spending every possible minute together led to precisely the predicament Haley had never wanted to face. She had to find a way to let him go. To Afghanistan, a good eight thousand miles away from her— on the other side of the world—where people she knew nothing about would like nothing better than to see him dead.

How can I let him go?

Haley clasped his hand tighter, not wanting to break contact with Ben one second sooner than she had to. How had she gotten herself into this predicament?

I will never fall for a man in the military.

Her proclamation of less than two short weeks ago returned to haunt her, like the Ghost of Christmas Past in the Dickens novel.

Had she really said that? Absolutely, and as she'd spoken those words she had meant every flipping one of them. It seemed fitting that Ben entered her life on that very night, as though God's sole purpose had been to make a mockery of her determination. Her brother's words— *Never say never, Haley girl*—echoed in her mind, also mocking her previous stance on dating a Marine.

Her eyelids drifted shut as she leaned her head against his chest, turned her face toward the source of warmth and comfort—breathed him into her. The delicious scent of Ben, mingled with Dolce & Gabbana's Light Blue cologne for men, always managed to make her a little weak at the knees. His arm tightened around her, letting her know that he didn't want to let go, either. Haley slipped her right arm around his waist, reveling in the feel of taut, hard muscles under her hand as she struggled to get closer—knowing she could never be close enough.

"I know, babe. I know." His deep voice, accompanied by a soft kiss to her crown, seemed to reverberate in her skull, echoing in the crisp, stillness of the fall air. The soft sounds of music surrounded them, courtesy of someone's I-tune list. At the present, Keith Urban strummed the heartbreakingly mellow guitar and crooned *Making Memories of Us.* The song had somehow turned into *their* song in the time they'd spent together.

The fire pit on his mom and step-dad's back deck glowed with warmth on this unusually cool fall evening, hissing and spitting sparks at their shoes. They sat before it, in a two-seated glider, moving slowly back and forth. Neither of them wanted to leave their comfortable positions, lest they break the mesmerizing spell of being one with the other.

He'd be gone in thirty-six hours. Overwhelmed at the thought, Haley's heart constricted, forming a lump in her throat. She swallowed painfully, unable to keep the quiet sob from escaping.

He wrapped both arms around her, hugging her close. "Please don't, babe. Please don't cry. I'll be back before you know it." His voice, whisper soft in the air, still managed to sound so strong, so controlled.

"I'm sorry, Ben. I'm trying."

"Don't apologize for not wanting me to leave. That's a good thing."

She knew he was smiling as he spoke, which made her smile, too. "It'd be great if I could be as strong as you, but I'm not." She tried to loosen her grip, but when his hand tightened around hers, she brought both up to wipe her tear-streaked face.

"Sure you are, Haley. You just don't know it yet."

She let the weight of her head fall back against his shoulder as she met his gaze. He lowered his lips to hers for what she thought would be a quick, innocent kiss. It turned deeper, his tongue mingling sweetly with hers as his arm tightened around her. It wasn't the first time he'd kissed her like that, but it had never happened in front of his family.

She pulled back enough to whisper a mild reprimand. "Ben, not here."

He grinned and kissed her again before pulling back. "Why not? You think these people don't think I've kissed you before?" Snickers from around the deck accompanied his statement.

Ben's sister, Kristy, chimed in. "Don't worry about it, Haley. We know. Every chance he gets, boy do we know."

"Yeah, but that doesn't mean he has to subject the rest of us to it—constantly, I might add," his brother, Zeke, threw in. "Go rent a room somewhere, for Christ's sake."

Ben's mother, Monica, jumped to her feet. "No. No room. Whatever you two want to do, you can do right here."

Ben's right brow lifted as he looked up at his mom. "We can?" He stood, pulling Haley up alongside him. He bent at the waist and lifted her like a sack of potatoes over one shoulder in one smooth movement.

"B-e-e-e-e-n-n." Haley's screech of horror filled the air. "What are you doing? Put me down." She gasped for air, craning her neck to see what was going on. When she realized he was heading for the doorway she beat on his back with both fists. "Put me down, Benjamin—*now*." She stiffened, as a sharp whack from his large hand landed on her butt. At least she thought it was Ben's hand. From her disadvantaged viewpoint, it may well have been someone else's hand. She could only blame the blood-rush to her brain for her next comment. "That better be your hand on my butt, Benjamin Bonin." Ben's laughter combined with several other snorts and snickers to complete her utter mortification. Haley issued a low groan. "That's not what I meant."

His mother stopped him at the door. "Where do you think you're going?"

"You said we could do whatever we wanted right here—we're going to my room." He swung around and waved at the rest of his family. "See y'all later."

"Put me down *now*, Benjamin." Haley's voice came out in a low, furious hiss.

Monica's laughter rang out as she forcefully pushed her son away from the door. "You know what I meant, smart ass. Now put that poor girl down before she dies from embarrassment."

Ben chuckled as he set Haley gently down on two feet. "Hey, it didn't hurt to try."

Haley covered her face with two hands, at a complete loss for words.

"Now see? Look what you've done to her." Monica gave her a one-armed hug. "Don't worry, sweetie. We all understand. I guess shame kind of flies out the window when you spend time cooped up with a bunch of Marines. We've met some of his buddies, you know. Believe me, when they get together, they're nothing but a bunch of goofballs."

"Hey." Ben lifted Haley's chin and kissed the tip of her nose. "I'm sorry if I embarrassed you."

"Oh please." Her voice came out in an indignant huff as she pushed playfully at his hands. "You've been doing it the entire time we've been together, so don't start lying now."

His shoulders shook with laughter. "I know, right? I thought you would have been used to it by now."

She put her hands on her hips to send him a hard glare, trying to retain at least a little of her anger. His beautiful smile cut through her pout, and had her shaking her head. "Nope, you're too adorable to stay mad at."

"Really? Tell *that* to the hadjis." He pulled her close to plant an innocent kiss on her mouth then pulled back to stare adoringly down at her.

Haley laughed as one fat raindrop landed on Ben's nose, then another, and several more, giving them all enough notice to scramble into the house before the skies opened up in a heavy deluge.

"Anything on the tube?" Ben grabbed the remote, settling on a rerun of Iron Man. He occupied one end of the couch, pulling Haley next to him to watch the movie as his step-dad, Big Ben, got the room's fireplace going for the first time that year. Haley wasn't crazy about cold weather, but figured she didn't mind it so badly if it meant spending the evening with Ben in front of a nice, warm fireplace.

By eleven o'clock that Friday night, everyone else had hit the sack except for him and Haley. He turned off the flat screen and stared into the crackling fire. They sat, with her back to his chest and both stretched out on the length of the overstuffed sofa. His chin rested on her head, both arms wrapped around her as he curled a lock of her hair around his right forefinger.

A long, low sigh escaped from her to grab at his attention. He leaned over, pulling her hair back to get a better look at her. "You all right, babe?"

Silence permeated the air, interrupted by a pop and hiss of a log on the fireplace. Delectable aromas filled the air . . . a combination of oak logs and a faint trace of the gumbo he'd requested earlier, coming from his mom's kitchen. "Haley?"

The telltale shaking of her shoulders alerted him to the tears he knew she'd held back all night. He lifted her, turning her in his arms so that she faced him. At first, he tried to stop her, but once he realized the futility of his attempt, he held her tighter and let her cry. He knew she'd find the strength she needed to see him off at the airport on Sunday morning. But for tonight, he sensed she needed this release—needed to purge her heart of the overwhelming fear of losing him. He'd known that fear once. That was before he'd faced it head on, and then mastered it—kicked its ass into submission. He'd traded it in for the distinct rush of adrenaline that appeared during a mission with his team, cut off from the rest of his platoon in the Afghan desert.

Suddenly he understood. She wasn't him. She wouldn't get to feel that rush, have her days too full to think about him being on missions, or getting blown up by an IED. All she would feel back here, once he left her was . . . alone.

"I'll be back, Haley. You know that, right?"

She nodded, managed to sputter something that he took for "You'd better, dammit—" and continued to sob into his T-shirt.

"I'm coming back for you, babe. I promise." He'd always told himself he'd never make that promise. Too many people had died out there, Marines as well as other military personnel, who'd made promises they couldn't keep. But here and now, he promised himself, as well as Haley, that he would do whatever it damned well took to come back to her.

Suddenly, as sure as he embraced the sweet weight of her in his arms, he sensed he'd succeed. He would be back for her, if she still wanted him.

That was his only fear. The one thing completely out of his control.

Would she still want him by the time he made it back? Some women couldn't take being alone; he'd damn sure seen that happen with other guys. Would Haley be willing, or able, to wait for him?

He realized he had one year to make sure she would.

Ben held Haley close, letting her cry until she passed out from exhaustion, her face planted on his chest.

While she slept, he plotted. He came up with ideas, plans to lessen her pain of having him gone. Tomorrow was Saturday, the only day he had left to do what he needed to do. He set his watch alarm to make sure he got up early enough to get a good start. He'd need to make two important stops in the morning, and hopefully he could get it done before Haley woke up.

He laughed inwardly at himself. Here he was, a U.S. Marine, making plans—*romantic plans*—to make sure the exhausted girl asleep in his arms wouldn't forget about him. Better yet, that she would have a reason to smile at least once a week.

He buried his face in her hair, inhaled the scent, a mixture of shampoo, mixed with smoke from the fire pit outside—then into the crook of her neck for a whiff of the perfume that drove him nuts when she was anywhere near him.

How the hell did he get into this predicament?

She shifted slightly, settled even closer to his chest than she was before, and sighed in her sleep.

He smiled down at her, thinking he might actually owe something to that asshole who had tried to paw her on the dance floor of Red's club weeks earlier. Maybe he should thank him if he ever saw him again.

He pictured Haley as he'd seen her that first time; angry, but her eyes wild with helplessness and panic.

Then again, maybe he'd break the bastard's nose one more time, for good measure.

Chapter 3

Thanksgivings and Thanks for Nothings

Haley entered the room, looking about as cheerful as a Golden Retriever with a dead duck tied around its neck.

Tex put his paper aside. "What's going on, sis?"

She flopped down on the couch; her laptop tucked under one arm and holding a family size bag of Skittles in the other. She dug around in the bag and came up with a handful of orange ones, but still didn't answer.

"Why the hell don't you go to the mall and buy bags of orange ones?"

Eventually, Haley graced him with an irritable glare. She picked up the remote and began flipping through the stations, finally landing on the Thanksgiving Day Parade.

"You know, little sister, your boyfriend may be dealing with something that requires a higher priority than keeping a phone date with his girlfriend."

Haley turned to him, her eyes wide and filled with threatening tears. "No. Really? That thought never crossed my mind. Jerk."

"Hold on, now. I doubt there's a hell of a lot going on where he is right now. He's in the north Helmand Province, isn't he? He's probably spending most of his time on the base, being bored out of his mind."

"He's in the south this deployment, and I should have heard from him by now." She pulled her phone from her pocket and waved it at him. "He said he'd call or email or message me first thing this morning to wish me a Happy Thanksgiving." She dropped her phone on the couch beside her and popped a couple of candies in her mouth. "He always calls when he says he will. Wherever Ben is, he's sure as hell not sitting around being bored."

Tex folded and rolled up the Beaumont Enterprise as he'd found it on the doorstep of his parents' front porch this morning. He swatted his knee a couple of times, and then stood suddenly. "You need a change of scenery, Haley girl. Get yourself dressed, because you and I are taking a little road trip."

"Where to?" She let him pull her up by the hand.

"We're going to Louisiana. Mom and dad taking the trip to Colorado doesn't mean you and I can't have a decent Thanksgiving."

"We'll be back by tonight, won't we? I've got to be here to take care of my horses."

"Nope. Pack a bag for the night. Give 'em a little extra hay, they'll be fine until tomorrow evening."

"But I hate leaving Dakota."

Tex stared down at his petite sister. "For Christ sake, she's a twelve hundred pound horse, not a child. I think she can handle one night away from you without succumbing to separation anxiety. Besides, she has three other horses out there to keep her company. She'll be fine." He grumbled under his breath. "God knows their stalls are all nicer than my own house."

"That's only because you live like a slob. Bachelor pads are supposed to be welcoming to women, but yours is disgusting." She shivered. "You can't set foot in that place without having to step over take-out cartons, empty beer cans, or dirty laundry." She tucked her laptop under her arm and scooped up her phone. "You really should hire somebody to clean once a week. I thought Marines were supposed to be neat and organized."

"Little sister, I had to be neat and organized for twenty years. Now I can be as sloppy as I want to be. Besides—" he slapped one of his biceps. "Once the ladies get a hold of this, they're too mesmerized to see anything else."

Haley walked away from her brother, snorting with laughter. "Yeah, Stud, you keep tellin' yourself that."

Tex watched his sister slip her boots on and head outside, thankful he'd been able to pull her out of her temporary depression. There were a few good reasons for a Marine not to contact his favorite girl on Thanksgiving Day. Worst-case-scenario would be her guy lying dead from a Taliban bullet or an IED. The possibility was plausible, though slightly less so at this point in the war. Other reasons were injuries, which were also a possibility, a lack of signal or a SAT phone, or wanting to dump one girl for another. From the sickly-sweet phone conversations he had witnessed on occasion between Haley and Corporal Bonin, he figured that was highly unlikely. Chances are he was busy with supply runs or on patrol, and lacked the equipment to phone home. Both included an element of danger. She'd have to wait it out. In their parents' absence, he figured the least he could do was to make the waiting less painful for her.

He pulled out his phone and found the contact he was looking for. He punched in the number and waited through three rings before Mitch Hebert answered with a jovial "Happy Thanksgiving shit brick."

"Same to you, jerk wad. Are you up to a visit from your two favorite Texans?"

"Mom."

"Hang on, Buck, I'm coming." Meagan topped the green bean casserole with the last of the French fried onions and slipped the dish back in the oven for the last 10 minutes of baking time.

She wiped her hands on her jeans and went into Buck's room. He sat on his bed trying to dress himself, but without much success. She laughed at his half-dressed predicament, one leg in and one leg out of a pair of oversized sweat pants, and one arm and his head through a #8 Texans football jersey.

Meagan finally succeeded in getting his brace through the second leg of the sweats. She sat back and groaned at his choice of shirts. "Son, you have other shirts, you know. Nearly three weeks of the same football jersey is getting old."

"But the Texans was my daddy's favwite team, and Mitch gave it to me." He looked at her with pleading eyes as he kicked his good leg against the side of his bed. "Please mom?"

"Okay, but once this cast comes off, I don't want to see you in jerseys for a while. And you *will* be dressed up in an adorable little suit for Christmas if it kills me." She finagled until she finally got the cast through the arm of the jersey. "You want me to carry you in the living room?"

"No, I want to go in the kitchen with you and Niki." He got his crutch and hopped to the kitchen as if he was born using the darn thing.

Niki passed him in the hallway and groaned. "God, I can't wait until he gets off of that thing. It's like having our own little Tiny Tim from that Dickens novel."

Meagan laughed as she placed the buttermilk pies on the snack bar next to the pumpkin pie. "I know, but it's so much better than the alternative, right?"

"Definitely. Hey did you remember to pick up whipped topping for the pumpkin pie?"

"I'd forgotten, but Mitch is bringing it."

"Are you sure? Because, I only have pumpkin pie once a year and it's not the same without it."

Meagan looked up at the sound of knocking at the front door. "There he is, go ask him yourself."

Niki jerked on the handle and held the door open wide as Mitch entered, carrying a large roasting pan. "Good Lord, that smells awesome." Her gaze followed the roaster as she pushed on the door. "But where's the whipped topping?" Something large stopped the door from closing. She turned to see Tex Broussard in the doorway, wearing a shit eating grin.

He pushed his way inside brandishing two cans of whipped topping and a twelve-pack of domestic beer. "Ask and ye shall receive, madam." He bowed gallantly at the waist before holding the cans out to her.

His younger sister, Haley, pushed her way around him. "Yeah, yeah—Mitch already bought the topping, you just carried in the cans. Hey Niki, how are you?" Haley reached out to give her a hug. "I hope y'all don't mind that Mitch asked us to come along. Our folks went to Colorado and it sucks being alone on a holiday with only *him* for company."

"Not at all, and I'm good, Haley. More importantly, how's it going with your Marine?"

Niki watched expectantly as Haley's honey brown eyes lit up with barely concealed excitement. "Ben finally Skyped me before we left the house. He was supposed to call first thing this morning and I was so worried. God, I miss him so much. He sends me a rose every single Monday, Niki. Isn't that the most romantic thing?"

Tex groaned and made a show of rolling his eyes. "Jesus Christ, that's all I hear lately. 'Ben said this,' and 'Ben did that,'" He shook his head. "Give me a break, would you?"

Haley surprised her brother with an effective punch to his gut. "Shut up, big brother. You know, it's not a sin for a guy to be romantic. From what I hear, you could take a few lessons from him in the consideration department." She winked at Niki before heading to the kitchen and leaving the two of them alone at the door.

Niki stood with her hands fisted on her rounded hips. "Well, I sure as hell didn't expect to see you here."

Tex stepped closer for a kiss. What he got was a barely-there brush on her cheek as she spun away from him. He stood to his full height, looking somewhat shocked at her reaction to him. "We spent two fabulous nights together, Nicole. But you look a little disappointed to see me."

She smiled at him, showing her dimples. "I was disappointed weeks ago, when you didn't call after aforementioned nights. I've moved on since then. Now, I'm simply shocked that you're here." She batted her eyelashes at him. "Thanks for carrying in the topping though. That was surprisingly—considerate—of you."

She made a show of checking her watch as another knock sounded at the door. "Oh, hang on, that must be my dinner guest." She swung it open, greeting the newest arrival with squeals of delight at the gorgeous basket of fall flowers in one hand and two bottles of wine in the other. "Hey, sweetie, come on in." The tall, good-looking man leaned over and she threw her arms around his neck to kiss him soundly on the lips.

"Happy Thanksgiving, Niki. And thanks again for inviting me to this dinner." He held out the bottles of wine. "This is for the two lovely hostesses, but the flowers are all yours. And uh, there's a little surprise inside for you, but you'll have to look for it."

"Oh, you know how much I love surprises." She took the wine from him and placed the bottles in the fridge to chill, before placing the basket on the table. Remembering her manners, she turned back to the two men. "Oh, Bo McAllister, this is Tex. Tex Broussard, this is Bo." She left it to them for any further introductions, but kept an eye on them as she began her search for Bo's surprise. Each giant of a man seemed to size up his equally large competition.

She smiled to herself, suspecting that Tex hadn't encountered too many men who could meet him eye-to-eye, in the literal sense of the phrase. *It's time he learns he's not the only stud in the pasture.*

Tex was the first to step forward and offer his hand. "Matthew Broussard, but everyone calls me Tex."

"Bo McAllister. It's nice to meet you man, and Happy Thanksgiving."

"You t—"

Niki cut off his reply with an ear-splitting screech as she jumped up and down. "The ballet? You got tickets to the ballet? I adore The Nutcracker. Oh thank you, thank you, Bo!"

Bo caught her easily as she jumped in his arms. The room resonated with his deep laughter as he spun her in a circle. "You know I aim to please."

Tex stood by, watching the display with a growing sense of alarm burning in the pit of his belly. Mitch approached his side.

"What's going on in here?"

Tex looked at his friend and cocked one eyebrow. "He scored some tickets to the *ballet*…something about cracking somebody's nuts. Looks like it could be his. Who is this guy, anyway?"

Mitch gave him a friendly shove into the kitchen once Meagan joined the noisy melee in the living room. "He's Red McAllister's first cousin, and he's a hell of a nice guy, so don't even think about giving him a hard time, or I'll have to pull both Niki and Meagan off your ass."

"Thanks bro…semper fi to you too," Tex snorted at his friend.

Mitch gave him a casual shrug. "Hey, I told you to call her, but you had more important things to do. You remember, like that blonde pole dancer in Beaumont?"

Tex hooked his thumbs in his belt loops and cocked his head. "Dude, do you have any idea what kind of muscles those girls *use* to hang upside down from those poles? That is some serious stuff, man, I shit you not."

Mitch raised one hand to shut him up. "Whatever, man, but you screwed up. Meagan warned you about her roommate's low tolerance for jerks and assholes. She told me she even *called* you to let you know Niki was getting tired of waiting for you to call. You blew it."

"Well hell, I guess I did." Tex leaned his shoulder against the door and crossed one booted foot over the other as he watched the adoration fest in the other room.

Within seconds, Bo freed himself from the women and came over to meet the men in the kitchen. "Damn, something smells good in here. Did you deep fry that turkey?"

"Sure did," Mitch said, shaking Bo's hand. "How you doing, man? You two been introduced?"

"Yeah, before he brought out the big guns—the ballet tickets," Tex snorted.

Bo grinned at him, his McAllister blue eyes sparkling with mischief. "Oh that?" He jerked his head toward the women, who were already making plans. "Merely a diversionary tactic. I told them I'd watch Buck if I could get them tickets for that ballet. I also knew the ballet was scheduled for the same night as the heavyweight prize-fight in Vegas. I figured while they're at the ballet, we can be at my place watching the pay per view fight on my 70" flat screen. I ordered the fight today."

Mitch slapped him on the shoulder. "Good plan, buddy. Excellent plan."

Tex nodded, hating to agree, but unable to think of one damn reason not to.

Corporal Ben Bonin sat on his bunk at Forward Operating Base Delhi, shoving gear into his duffle for the early morning drive to one of many Patrol Bases in their Area of Operation. Setting the stuffed pack aside, he dropped back onto the mattress and stretched out his long legs.

He closed his eyes and took a deep breath, releasing it slowly. He pictured Haley as he'd seen her during last night's Skype call. He'd finally managed to squeeze in a session to tell her Happy Thanksgiving, a few hours later than he'd planned to. Holidays were hell on the calls home. The room had buzzed with the activity of other jarheads waiting their turn to Skype. The hours of waiting paid off in spades.

His first glimpse of her always took his breath away— big brown eyes sparkling with laughter, her luscious rose lips parted invitingly as she smiled to reveal adorable dimples. He could practically feel the soft silkiness of her hair gathered in his hands, cascading loosely between his fingers.

Ben groaned, remembering again, that he wouldn't physically see her for another six months. That is, *if* he saw her again. He had to face the fact that not all girls were willing to wait for their Marine to return from deployment. He'd already seen it with some of his buddies, heard them, witnessed them blowing off a little steam after getting a call or message from a girl who'd moved on. Or worse, hearing the news from someone else, because some girls didn't have the nerve to call off the relationship themselves.

No thanks for serving your country—just a thanks for nothing.

He whispered the prayer that Haley would wait for him—the same one he'd uttered no less than fifty times since meeting her.

Damn, but he had it bad for that girl. Quick witted and intelligent, she was easy as hell to talk to about anything and everything. During his time at home, he'd seen her every day, no less than sixteen hours a day, and sometimes more, thanks to her staying with her grandparents.

They'd spent days together . . . fishing, boating, and kayaking at the river, and nights filled with everything from late night bonfires to clubbing and dancing. He knew more about Haley than any other woman on the face of the earth, including his mom and sister. Ben couldn't believe how well he'd come to know her during his short time off.

And he still couldn't believe his luck. Maybe God, or maybe his own intuition, he couldn't be sure, but something told him he'd met Haley at the exact time he was meant to.

The thought sliced through his mind like a double-edged blade, calling to mind a conversation he'd had with his grandfather before his first deployment. He'd been full of bravado, talking about kill shots and Taliban captures. His Pa Pa had given him this look, brimming with a combination of tremendous pride and absolute terror.

He'd placed a hand on his grandfather's shoulder. "I'll be okay, Pa Pa."

The old man had nodded, blinked several times to clear his eyes, and pulled his grandson close for a hug. "I know you will, Benjamin. But I can't help wishing you had a girl waiting for you at home while you're there."

Ben had searched his grandfather's face for clues for the totally unexpected statement, came up completely dry of any kind of answer.

"It might keep you more grounded. Keep you from taking any chances with your life." He'd reached out to place a hand on his shoulder. "Or maybe keep you determined to come home . . . alive." Donald King, the man Ben had spent so much time with over the years, had given his head a slow shake. "Because I can't even imagine what I'd do if . . ." He'd stopped then, unable to finish.

Ben imagined himself and his team in some life or death situation. Would knowing he had Haley waiting for him at home keep him more focused, make him more determined to come home to her—and not in a body bag?

He pictured Haley's face as he'd left her at the airport. Trying to be brave, trying not to cry in front of him, even though it crushed her when he left.

He'd had always looked up to his grandfather, had nothing but the utmost respect for the man who'd taken him fishing as a kid, loyally supported him in the stands through seasons of pee wee through high school sports. The man had always been there with advice, whether Ben had asked for it or not, and unconditional love. He'd taught him so many things throughout the years. Even at his advanced age, and with Alzheimer's disease beginning to curl its ugly claws around him, Pa Pa Don was still teaching him.

Ben realized his Pa Pa had hit the ball out of the park on this one. He'd do whatever was humanly possible to go home to Haley.

So yeah, maybe she'd entered his life to keep him strong, focused, and determined to walk out of that shit hole, alive and well.

The tension suddenly eased from his shoulders as he spoke in the semi-darkness of the tent. "Thank you," he whispered to the God who'd seen fit to put her in his path.

Chapter 4

Mental Meanderings: A Girl and Her Marine

"Looka here, Haley. You'll get a kick outta this shit."

Haley looked up from her math homework long enough to glance at the television station her brother had stopped on. She narrowed her eyes and released a huff of disgust. "Really? Women barrel racing wearing bikinis?" She shook her head. "It is sad the crap they're passing off as reality television these days."

Tex snorted. "Well, I don't know if the show qualifies as part of the *Arts*, but I'm willing to bet it'll provide plenty of *Entertainment*."

She dropped her chin to her chest and quirked her right brow. "Please tell me you aren't considering watching that trash."

He shrugged. "If they're willing to ride a horse in a bikini, who am I to denounce their efforts to entertain the male species?"

Haley sent her brother a disappointed glare. "Your brain cells are disappearing as we speak."

He frowned. "You're mighty quick to judge, especially being you've never seen the show."

"When does it play?"

His features lit up in a grin. "You want to watch it? See how you compare?"

She flipped her hair and turned back to her homework. "No—to make sure I'm not home."

"Hater," he snorted, as she buried her nose in her book again.

Another thirty minutes of laboring over her Ultrasound Physics book had her muttering barely audible curses at the people responsible for this particular subject. She slammed the book shut and rubbed her throbbing temples. Any more cramming would be useless in her frame of mind. Yet another three weeks with barely a word from Ben had her edgy and irritable, making it difficult to concentrate on much of anything.

She pushed off from the sofa for a glass of water. Haley popped a pain reliever then stood at the window over her mom's kitchen sink. Staring out into the back pasture, she watched her horse enjoying the few days of unseasonably warm December weather. It had actually gotten into the low 80's the previous day, and the temperature wasn't supposed to dip lower than the mid to high 70's today. The horse ran back and forth along the fence line, kicking up her heels and flinging bits of mud as she ran.

"I see you girl." Haley headed out the back door, deciding that if she didn't know what she needed to pass that test by now, she never would. This weather was too perfect not to take advantage of the opportunity to wash the muck from her horse.

Minutes later, she gripped the curry brush tighter, running the bristles over her mare's thick winter coat, and then smoothed it down with the opposite hand. "There you go, girl. That feels good, doesn't it?" She laughed as her horse closed her eyes and released a deep breath, standing stock-still. Dakota always seemed to be meditating during her beauty treatments.

"You know, you'd stay a lot cleaner if you'd stop running through those patches of mud, you crazy horse." Almost as an apology, Dakota lowered her head enough so that horse and owner touched foreheads for a moment. Haley laughed and smoothed Dakota's muzzle. "Yeah, yeah. I know. You're real sorry—until you go out and do it again thirty minutes from now." She jumped slightly at the sound of a throat clearing from behind her.

"You know, one of these days, that animal will answer you back, and you're gonna shit yourself."

Haley turned to her big brother. "She answers me back all the time, and it's easy enough for me to translate." Tex's chuckle carried through the cool, damp December air of southeast Texas.

"In horse talk, maybe, but as much as you pamper and converse with that animal, I'm surprised she hasn't learned to speak English by now."

She kissed the soft nose of her four-legged friend and smiled. "Maybe one day, huh girl?"

"Heard from your Marine lately?"

Haley's stomach flipped familiarly, as it did at any mention of Ben. "He called me yesterday. He leaves for a mission tomorrow night—or whenever the hell that is, our time." As always, the thought of Ben facing danger thousands of miles away, filled her with a deep-seated dread. The ten and a half hour time difference unsettled her, drove home the fact that he was on the opposite side of the earth. She hated feeling useless, but there wasn't a damn thing she could do to change the situation.

"Now you see."

She stopped brushing Dakota long enough to face her brother. Haley didn't have to ask. She knew he was referring to the fact that Matt had never committed to a steady girlfriend during his entire time in the Corp. She'd dogged him mercilessly, but his answer had always been the same. *"What good is it to have one extra person back home worrying about me? It's bad enough when my family has to."*

She nodded. "I do see, but I'd rather be worried about him here, than have him over there thinking there's no one waiting for him to come home. Besides family, I mean."

Tex answered with a nod, accompanied by a low grunt. "Whatever works for you, sis. Have you met any of his family?"

"Yes, I have." She smiled, thinking of the entire network of supportive family members Ben had in Lake Erin, Louisiana and the surrounding areas. His mom and dad, two stepparents, his siblings—both blood and step, and that's not to mention the myriad of grandparents and cousins in the area. "I spent a lot of time with him over there at family functions—barbeques and fish fries—when he was in." Haley thought of his mom and sister, with their bubbly personalities, and caught herself smiling. She glanced up and found Tex's gaze zeroed in on her. "What?"

Her big brother graced her with a surprisingly sincere smile. "They must be good people to share him with you during his trips home. I know that time is precious to them."

"They are very good people. I've even met his mom and sister for lunch at the Lake Coburn mall a few times since he left. We did some Christmas shopping together. His mom is so funny and sweet. She could barely talk about him without crying the first couple of weeks after he left."

He rested his large hand heavily on her bare head. "And you? How are you handling it?"

She hitched one shoulder. "I'm okay. Trying to stay busy, you know? I mean, I only met him a little over three months ago, and he's been gone for most of that time. But Matty, the time we had together. . ." She paused, not sure if he'd understand the point she wanted to make. "It was special. I feel as though I know him so much better than if I'd known him for years. I can't explain it."

"You got the super-condensed Rosetta Stone version. The kind that packs this much information about a person—" He spread his arms wide. "—into this amount of time." He brought his hands a few inches apart.

"Yes." She sent her brother a grateful smile. "I'm a little shocked you got that."

"I'm not as much of a moron as you think I am."

"I don't think you're a moron. First cousin to the missing link, maybe, but not a moron." She laughed at her brother's grunted reply as she put the finishing touches to her horse.

"I don't want you to get hurt, Haley girl. Lots of things could go wrong for him over there. I've seen it often enough."

"I know that, Matt, but I figure Ben and I have been thrown together for a reason. I've decided not to question it, and instead, focus on the positive." She stored her grooming tools inside the hinged box her dad had built for that purpose. "I've got faith that he's going to come home to me."

"What if he comes home with parts missing, Haley? Have you thought about that?"

Haley whipped her head around to send him her best have-you-lost-your-freaking-mind glare. The look on his face stopped her from the verbal ass-whipping she'd had in store for him. She snapped her mouth shut instead and gave her brother a long, hard perusal.

Having Matt home again, alive and healthy, with all his body parts intact, had dulled the not-so-pleasant memories during his deployments. Any news reporting the loss of a Marine brought on a nightmare of worrying for her and her parents. Until recently, Haley couldn't remember a time when her much older brother hadn't been a Marine. Through the years, she'd fallen asleep so many nights praying for his safe-keeping. Her parents, on the other hand, would greet her at the breakfast table, wearing the haunted expressions of people who had spent another sleepless night worrying about their son.

Over the years, they had met several of his Marine brothers. Some had walked into their home on two legs, some had rolled in by wheelchairs, missing one limb or two, and one, in particular, had to be pushed in because he'd lost both legs and arms trying to rescue an Afghani child from what they suspected was a car bomb. Later, they'd met his wife; one of the nurses who'd cared for him during one of his stays at the hospital. She'd fallen in love with him as he was, with no limbs, but still holding on to his faith, and a sharp sense of humor. Haley had only recently discovered that she'd been his second wife. The first had abandoned him, unable to take being married to a handicapped ex-Marine.

She gave her brother a slow nod, knowing he asked, not only for her sake, but for Ben's, as well. "I think about it every night, Matty, as I did for you. I can't imagine not wanting him in my life, whether he comes back with all his limbs, or none. I suppose that depends on him."

Tex displayed the killer smile that had always made other women drool. He pulled her to him for a big bear hug. "You're a winner, kid. I hope Corporal Bonin realizes that."

Haley kicked at a rock with the tip of her boot. "If he doesn't, that's his loss." Matty released a low chuckle of agreement and they began the trek back into the house.

"The protected can't begin to understand the price paid so they and their families can sleep safe and free at night."
— Gen. John F. Kelly

Ben readjusted his position, laid on his back in the dirt, his backpack acting as a pillow that he'd propped against a stack of wooden pallets. The pallets, remnants of the resupply dropped off by helo two days earlier, provided little shade but did keep the majority of the sun's rays off his face. As far as resupply was concerned, all the "good" MRE's had been raped from the stash early on. Not that it mattered—he'd eaten them so much, they all seemed to taste the same now. Like shit.

He tapped the screen on his new e-reader, ordering it to proceed to the next page. He'd recently received the device in a care package, an early Christmas gift from Haley. He'd mentioned once that he loved to read on deployments and she'd sent him the reader, pre-loaded with several books for him. As if her looks and awesome personality weren't enough to hook him, she had to be thoughtful as hell too.

"Stop it, you fucking assholes."

Ben glanced up from his screen to see their corpsman trying to sleep, despite a bombardment of pebbles. He chuckled under his breath. Poor Doc was navy personnel stuck with a bunch of crazy-ass snipers for a whole seven months. Fortunately, for all of them, he meshed well with their group and had proven, on more than one occasion, to be the go-to guy with any medical problems. The low rumble of a motorcycle passing their Patrol Base overrode the laughter of Doc's torturers.

The PB was an old abandoned Afghan compound. All that remained of the original building was a thick, 7-foot tall mud wall encompassing the area. It wasn't much, considering it was their only means of cover in the event of an attack, but it was sure as shit better than nothing.

Marines with automatic rifles stood at each corner holding security so everyone else could get a little downtime. Each Marine stood post for a couple hours until his relief showed up. Personally, Ben detested standing post. He'd done enough guard duty during his first deployment. This time around, his sniper team's single task assignment was to hunt the insurgents attacking the PB's. So, no post for him, thank God.

He released a sigh and tried to focus on the words floating on screen. As usual, one thought of Haley and his concentration turned to shit for anything as trivial as reading. He'd finished his Skype calls home with hours to spare before departure for the PB. A good thing, too, since he'd received word that he wouldn't be back for close to three weeks. That meant a quick word to her on the sat phone every now and then, but no glimpse of that gorgeous face. Well, shit.

Tired of not being able to concentrate, he shut down and slipped the reader into his duffle before heading over to his team leader's tent. Hopefully, his TL would have the mission info ready so Ben could start working on his billets, or jobs. Ben had three billets on this team: point man, assistant team leader, and sniper. As point man, it was his job to get them from Point A (patrol base) to point B (FFP or final firing position). This particular Point B is where they set up their hide site, which is basically, a hole they dug under cover of darkness, large enough to fit the entire four man team inside. If done correctly, it could be very effective. In the desert, with vegetation transplanted around the edges, it's almost impossible to see. Unless a hadji walks on top of them—if that happens, of course they'll see, and the team is compromised. Then it's an RTB—Return to Base. Shit happens.

As it happened, his TL had the info ready. Once they'd discussed the mission, Ben grabbed the map and GPS to input the coordinates his team would need over the next three days.

Job 1: Done.

He left his team leader and made a B-line for his own spot in this God-forsaken home away from home for the next three weeks. He prepped his gear and cleaned his rifle—his baby. As Assistant Team Leader, it was his job to make sure the other guys were also ready to rock and roll. Ben walked over to meet Badgett, the radio operator, or RO, to make sure he was packed and ready. He made another stop at the second sniper's digs to do the same.

Job 2: Done

As soon as the sun sank low enough, he lined up with the other three members of his team. They all wore chest rigs that held sapi plates, ammo, grenade, and a 153 radio. Ben adjusted his pack, filled with an ungodly amount of shit, and held his baby close, waiting for the okay to leave the patrol base on foot. He knew he was ready and took several seconds to pray that this three day mission would be a success and earn them 24 hours of R&R—Rest & Recover. Hopefully, he'd have a good enough signal to give his folks and Haley a quick call when he got back.

They stood, tense and silent, as the team's Radio Operator, or RO, requested permission to leave friendly lines. Once he got clearance, the TL gave Ben the hand signal to lead them out. Within two hours he'd led his team to the proper GPS location. By sunrise, they'd set up their hide site on elevated terrain, and established a base line on the local village. For the next 72 hours, it'd be the four of them against the Taliban, who did a good job of blending in with the local populace. All that was left was to sit and wait until they caught one of them setting an IED. As soon as they did, take him out.

Ben used his scope to scan the area for insurgent activity.

Kill the asshole trying to kill me . . . I bet I win.

Job 3...To be determined.

Chapter 5

Nut Crackers and Pole Dancers

The door to Bo McAllister's apartment flew open before Tex could even knock. He stood there with his fist in the air, staring at Mitch Hebert.

"Shit brick. Glad you could make it." Mitch leaned in closer. "Glad you didn't let the old green eyed monster override your good sense to keep you away. It's gonna be an awesome fight, man."

"Me? Jealous? Of what?" Tex hefted the cooler carrying a couple of chilled six packs and a bottle of Louisiana distilled Bayou Rum he'd picked up as an afterthought.

"Of the fact that Bo's still hot and heavy with Niki, and you're not." Mitch lifted his hand to stop Tex's comeback. "Don't even try to deny you still want her, man. I know you better than that, remember?" He grabbed him by the arm and pulled him across the threshold. "Come on in here. No use you standing out there and freezing your nuts off."

Tex entered the apartment and looked around, immediately noting the lack of mess. "Damn, what does this guy do for a living? Clean houses?"

Mitch grabbed the cooler from him and placed it along the wall with two others. "You mean because he doesn't live in his own filth, like some people? Seriously man, I've seen your place, and I understand Haley's comment about needing a tetanus shot to walk inside."

"Whatever, man. Where is Miss Merry Homemaker?"

"He brought Buck to the store to pick up some kid friendly snacks. Which reminds me; you need to watch your mouth tonight. I know how a few beers get your creative juices flowing when it comes to cussing. I'd appreciate it if my kid doesn't go back to his mom with any new phrases added to his vocabulary this time."

"I would never—"

"You already have. Meagan caught him calling his pancakes and syrup 'shit on a shingle' after your last visit."

"I sure as hell didn't teach him that."

"He overheard you, apparently. He hears everything, man, I'm telling you."

Tex hung his head. "Aw, for fucks sake, man. I'm gonna have to apologize to Megs."

Mitch cringed and slapped his hand on Tex's chest. "Keep quiet with that stuff. That didn't upset her nearly as much as him suggesting that Niki should take up pole dancing because it would build up her thigh muscles."

"Oh . . . are you shi . . . kiddin' me?" Tex would have found it a hell of a lot funnier had the kid asked anyone but Niki. "Please tell me she doesn't suspect where he heard that."

"She doesn't *suspect* a damn thing. Buck told Niki to ask you about it 'cause you knew some 'pole dan-suhs' . . . 'puh-sonally'."

"Sshh-ut the f-f-fu-front door . . ." Tex removed his hat and scratched the back of his head with his other hand.

"Not only that, but Niki told me to give you a message the next time I saw you."

"She did? What message?"

"She said, and excuse *my* foul mouth, but I'm quoting here, 'Tell that SOB he's screwed, blued, and tat-the-fuck-tooed.'"

Tex groaned, figuring he may as well start looking for a shovel. He was as good as dead as far as that particular voluptuous blond-haired, green-eyed beauty was concerned.

Niki looped her arm through Meagan's as they made their way back to her car. "That was so beautiful, wasn't it? I hadn't been to the ballet since I was a little girl."

"Me either and I loved it. I've seen The Nutcracker, but this was my first time to experience the Moscow Ballet's version."

Meagan unlocked the car and they climbed inside. While waiting for the heater to kick on, she pulled her phone from her purse to take a selfie of the two of them to record the moment. "Your guy did an awesome job with those seats, didn't he? Sixth row—not too shabby."

Niki beamed at her friend. "I know, right? Bo is the absolute best guy, isn't he?"

"I can't argue with that. I mean, I don't know him as well as you do, but he seems very nice."

"He is, Megs. He's generous, and thoughtful, great with kids—you see how he is with Buck, right?"

Meagan nodded. "Yeah, Buck seems to like him."

"And he gets on good with Mitch, too, right? I mean, Mitch hasn't said anything negative towards him, has he?"

Meagan fiddled with her phone and shook her head. "No, not to me."

"What does that mean? Has he told anyone else anything?"

Meagan met Niki's gaze. "How should I know?"

Niki twisted her fingers. "Well, I wondered if he may have said something."

Meagan's left brow arched suspiciously. "No, not that I'm aware of."

"Oh, well good, then. I'm glad. Because Bo is the best boyfriend a girl could ask for. He's so thoughtful."

Meagan's brow lifted as she nodded in agreement. "And he's large."

Niki pulled a pack of gum from her purse, offered Meagan a slice. "He's so handsome, with those McAllister blue eyes of his, like Red's."

"And he's large," Meagan added.

"He's sweet, and smart, and nice—"

"—and he's tall."

Niki glanced over at her friend. "What? Yes, he's every bit as tall as Tex. But he's such a nice guy."

"And he's large . . ."

That last one kicked it for Niki. She turned to face her. "What the hell, Megs?"

Meagan snorted with laughter. "You remember that Popeye movie Mitch made us sit through last weekend—the one where Shelley Duvall plays the character, Olive Oyl?"

Niki gave a half-hearted nod. "Yeah? So?"

"You sound like her when she's trying to convince herself to marry Bluto."

"I do not, and who said anything about marriage? Oh God, you don't think Bo's that serious, do you?" She froze as Meagan snapped a flash picture of her with her phone. "Stop that. What are you doing?"

"Proving my point, girlfriend." She hit a couple of buttons then lifted the phone. "Look at this, would you?"

Niki peeked at the photo, immediately cringing at the horrified look on her face. "Okay, if you show that to anyone else, I will suffocate you in your sleep."

"Pretty bad, huh?"

"It's horrendous, now trash it, please."

"Not exactly the face a girl should be wearing while discussing her boyfriend—aka the 'best guy in the world' should it?"

"He is a great guy, but you shocked me with that 'marriage' statement." She fanned her face with the ballet program, found the car stifling all of a sudden. "I don't want to marry anyone."

"Niki—"

"Not anytime soon, anyway. I've only known him for a month. It is way too early to be thinking about marriage."

"Niki—"

"Besides, I—"

"Nicole."

"What?" Niki faced her friend and waited.

"Can you see yourself in a year from now with Bo McAllister?"

"M-m-aybe." She chewed her bottom lip.

"How about two years, or five years, or married to him for the rest of your life?"

Niki closed her eyes and collapsed in the front seat, as deflated as a balloon in a room full of sparklers. She clapped a hand over her eyes and released a low groan. "No, dammit. No, I can't see myself with Bo. Not a year from now, or two, and sure as hell not for the rest of my life. I'd be . . ." Her voice trailed off.

"You'd be what?" Meagan goaded.

Niki heard her own prolonged sigh, hating herself for it. "Bored—I'd be bat-shit-crazy and bored out of my flipping mind." She pushed out her lower lip in an exaggerated pout. "I never thought I could say this, but he's too—nice." She slapped both hands over her head. "What the hell's wrong with me, Megs? Am I going to be one of those women who only want the guys who'll treat me like crap?"

Meagan gave her a bittersweet smile. "No, hon. I think you're one of those women who can't be with someone she doesn't truly love, no matter how great of a guy he is."

Niki gave a low frustrated groan. "I want my hero, Megs. I want the fairytale—the knight in shining armor who'll come in on his white horse an carry me away."

Meagan's mouth dropped open, as she stared, dumbfounded at her friend. "I never thought I'd see the day when you, in all your audaciousness, would succumb to 'Pretty Woman' syndrome."

"How about my very own Nutcracker Prince? He could come in and rescue me from the Rat king, or in this case, the doldrums."

Meagan's low chuckle surrounded them. "Yeah, that could work too."

"Pitiful, ain't it?"

"Not really. Not if he's out there somewhere, waiting for you. Or even hoping to get back into your good graces?"

Niki met Meagan's smug gaze. "Oh, *hell* no. I am not ditching Bo McAllister for Tex Broussard."

"You know you're crazy about him."

"He dumped me for a pole dancer, sweetie. Not high on the list of criteria for my Nutcracker Prince."

Meagan adjusted the heater and threw the car into drive. "Well, you're probably not high on his list of fairytale princess material yourself, Snookums."

"What the hell does that mean?"

"You jumped into bed with him the first night you met him, Niki."

"Did not." She thought of that pleasurably decadent first time with him, locked up in Red's club—in the ladies room, no less—and again, later, in his truck. "There was no bed involved."

Meagan maneuvered her way into the line of traffic. "Semantics. You had sex with him the first night you met him. That was so irresponsibly slutty. Have you learned nothing from my situation?"

"He wore a condom."

Meagan shook her head, obviously aggravated. "You'd do something like that, and then blame him for not taking you seriously?"

"Are you condoning him sleeping with a pole dancer?"

"I certainly am not. Just as I didn't condone you sleeping—excuse me—having sex with Tex so quickly. I don't need you to remind me there was no sleeping involved."

Niki scowled at her housemate, thinking if she wasn't her very best friend in the world, and telling the truth, she could be really pissed at her right now. "If you don't stop badgering me, I will never tell you any of my girl secrets again."

"I didn't ask you to. It's your own guilt-complex that made you want to tell me—the Sunday morning confessional after a Saturday night sexual encounter at a bar. I'm not your family priest, Nicole." Meagan shook her head, looking every bit the disappointed mother to an unruly daughter.

"Okay, okay . . . *mom*. Jeeze, you need to remember you have one kid, and it ain't me."

Meagan pumped the brakes and came to a stop at the traffic light. "God, Niki—what were you thinking?"

Niki dropped her head back against the headrest. "I know, I know. I wasn't thinking. That's the problem with Tex. Being around him makes me forget myself. All my common sense flies right out the door. I can't have that, Meagan. He'll—he's not good for me."

"You mean he'll hurt you."

"I mean he's not good for me, for my plans. I'll be finished with school in six months or so. I don't have time for that."

"For dating or for heartbreak?"

Nicole gave her friend an irritated glare. "Either or both as far as Matthew Broussard is concerned. That man was put on this earth to break hearts."

Meagan gave her head a slow shake and accelerated through the green light. "I'm not so sure about that."

"Well, I am."

"I think there's more to him than that."

Niki raised her left hand. "I am not talking about this anymore tonight."

"A-a-l-l-righty, then."

She rolled her eyes at her friend's smug comment, thinking Meagan had already reached the advanced level when it came to sounding like a mother.

Several minutes later, Niki knocked on Bo's door to collect Buck from him. Forced to examine both her situation and her self-conscience during the disapprovingly silent drive over, she fully intended to tell Bo he wasn't her type. But not tonight. Tonight she would simply thank him for the tickets and the chance for her and Meagan to enjoy a lovely evening. She chewed on her nail, wondering if she could get through the next few minutes without giving him a kiss, or maybe a simple kiss on the cheek. She knocked once more. Heard raucous shouting inside, before a built-like-a-brick-house figure pulled the door opened and instantaneously took her breath away.

"Well, hello there."

She stared up at him, too stunned to speak for several seconds.

Tex waved a hand in front of her face. "Earth to Nicole. You in there, honey?"

She blinked and inhaled, catching a slightly spicy scent, and knowing, for a fact that nobody did a bottle of men's body wash the justice that Tex did. "Mm—Is Buck here?" *Of course, he's here—where the hell else would he be?*

"If he's not, somebody'd be in big trouble, wouldn't they?"

Sweet Jesus, that voice—deep, with a hint of teasing, sent sex-filled messages straight to her girl parts. "Mm—yeah, I guess so." She pulled herself together by sheer will power. "I need to go. Where is he?" Another round of masculine cheers and jeers coming from the next room caught her attention. "What's going on in there?"

"Boxing match," Tex said. "Pay per view—Bo rented the fight and invited a bunch of us to come over to watch. Didn't you know?"

Another inhalation of him had her wanting to hold her breath, to keep his scent inside her. "Mm, no. Is Buck in there?"

"Naw, he fell asleep on us a while ago and we put him to bed." He stepped aside and placed his huge hand at the small of her back. "Over here," he said, leading her to a small bedroom down the hall.

"Mitch said he played so hard once he got that cast off this morning, he wore himself out." He leaned over the bed, lifted Buck easily across one shoulder, and threw the boy's dinosaur blanket over him. "I'll bring him out for you. Kid's getting heavy."

"I can carry him. I've been lugging him around since he was born."

"I've got him."

"But, I can—"

"Stop being stubborn, Nicole. I've got him."

"I'm not being stubborn."

Tex rolled his eyes. "Yeah, whatever." He turned toward the door.

"Hey." she began, as Buck lifted his head and looked at her.

"Aunt Niki, did you and mom go to those classes tonight?"

Tex placed his hand on the back of Buck's head, pressing him down on his shoulder. "Shhh, Buck, go back to sleep, buddy. You don't know what you're saying."

Buck wasn't having any of it. "Do too. I hewd Mitch tell you that Aunt Niki was going pwactice hew pole-dancing wou-tine."

The air around them disappeared, forming a silent vacuum, crackling with tension. Tex stopped in the middle of the hallway, and turned slowly toward her. If she hadn't witnessed what happened next with her own eyes, Niki never would have believed it. Tex stood frozen, all six-feet-plus of him, as his eyes filled with absolute terror. Fuming, she took a step toward him and he adjusted his position, using Buck as a shield against her wrath.

She narrowed her gaze. "Are you're hiding behind a child?"

"N-n-y-yes."

"Are they teaching that maneuver in the US Marine Corps now?"

He shook his head slowly. "No. But maybe they should? But only for situations like this."

She nodded. "I've got the perfect name for it. They could call it the 'She's Gonna Scratch my Eyes Out' maneuver.' I'm so disappointed in you, Tex."

One hand flew out in front of him, as though to ward off an angry advance. "It wasn't me, it was Mitch. I never said a word to anybody."

Niki ground her teeth so hard, her jaw popped. "Sure you didn't."

"Nicole, wait."

"You are wasting your time," she growled, turning into the living room. Bo saw her and stood.

"Hey, beautiful. Did you two have a good time? Were the seats as good as they said they were?"

Niki slipped her arms around Bo's neck and smiled, hoping like hell Tex was enjoying this particular show. "The seats were awesome, babe. So good, I had to come in here and thank you, personally."

Catcalls and whistles filled the room as she lifted to her toes and planted a long, lusty, tongue-filled kiss on him, ended it by nipping at his lower lip and brushing her nails across his upper thigh. She pulled away, and gave him one last kiss. "You boys have a good time, you hear?" She ran the nails of her right hand tantalizingly slow down the side of Bo's face, seducing him with her smile. "I'll catch *you* later, big boy."

Bo swallowed audibly. "I'll be looking forward to it, beautiful."

Niki gave him one last kiss, and then pivoted slowly on her heels, wearing what she hoped was a smug look. She turned and faltered, unprepared for what greeted her—nothing. Absolutely nothing. She walked to the opened door, and saw Tex putting Buck in his car seat. Niki cursed under her breath, realizing that Tex had missed the entire display, put on entirely for his benefit. A flash-flood of guilt washed over her at the way she'd used Bo. In an attempt to turn a man she wouldn't dare love into a jealous rage, she'd probably given false hope to a man whose only fault was that she couldn't love him.

Without a word, she trudged over to the car and buckled herself into the front passenger seat.

Meagan returned to the driver's seat and shut her car door but lowered the window. In seconds, Tex leaned his forearms on her open window and peered inside.

"He's all buckled up, Mom. You're good to go."

"Thanks for bringing him out here, Tex. He's getting so heavy for either of us to carry."

"No problem Meagan. You be careful going home, you hear?"

Tex looked past Meagan to sear Niki with his gaze. Framed in the car's window, with the glow of the porch light behind him, he looked even more bulked up than he had for Thanksgiving. She gave him one good perusal before forcing herself to face the front.

"G'night ladies."

"Good night, Tex. Hope we see you tomorrow."

"I promised my mom I'd be home tonight. Got family coming in for an early Christmas tomorrow morning. First Christmas since I'm home for good and all. She's gotta make a big deal, you know?"

"Well, sure she does. Good mamas love their baby boys no matter how old they get, or how much trouble they get into."

His deep chuckle resonated throughout the car, tickling Niki's eardrums. "Kinda makes me wish I had that effect on all women."

Niki sent him an accusatory glare—had opened her mouth to give him an acidic comeback when he cut her off.

"Or at least one, anyway." He touched his temple in a two-fingered salute. "Nicole."

Her gaze remained on him until he had walked all the way back to the house and closed the door behind him. Once she realized Meagan had spoken to her, she released the breath she'd been holding and turned to her friend. "What did you say?"

Meagan grinned as she began backing out of the driveway. "I said if you spent as much effort speaking to him as you did trying not to, the two of you would be an item again."

"I don't want to be 'an item' with that man. He can keep however many pole-dancers he has waiting for him back in Beaumont—or the entire state of Texas. I couldn't care less." She turned at the driver's distinct snort.

Meagan put the car in drive and accelerated, grinning at Niki. "You're gonna have to do some rehearsing if you're planning to pass that line off as God's honest truth."

Chapter 6

Missions and the Mundane

"Some people spend their entire lifetime wondering if they made a difference. Marines don't have that problem."
     --President Ronald Reagan

Monday, December 23rd – 14:00 (Afghanistan time)
Team: "Grave 1"
Sergeant Justin Ballantine (Balls, Sarge, TL): Team Leader
Corporal Ben Bonin (Bones): Asst. TL, Point Man, shooter
Lance Corporal Daniel Badgett (Badge): shooter
Lance Corporal Dennis Wade Blighe (D-Dub): Radio Operator (RO)

Ben readjusted his grip on his rifle with one hand and checked out the landscape through his rifle's scope. The wind blew sand against his helmet in a steady and never-ending cadence...*whoosh ...whoosh...whoosh...* that made him want to bellow like a bull.

Buried alive, all of them, in a four-man grave dug by their own hands. They were nearing the end of the latest three-day surveillance gig and had learned enough about the hadji's operations in this area to do some good. By nightfall, they'd be moving out to RTB.

He attempted to stifle a yawn, but couldn't, and got a mouthful of sand for his trouble. He spit and wiped his mouth with the back of his hand, only to get even more grit in his mouth. Sand and grit were a part of everyday life here in Afghanistan under the best circumstances, but for however long it took to complete their missions, concentrated doses of grit surrounded them. They survived with sand in their mouths, sand in the MRE's, sand in every nook and cranny of their bodies. The shit was a pain in the ass, literally, but it could always be worse. Like Balls always said, "Better to be alive and inconvenienced, than too dead to give a flying fuck."

A small movement to the north got his attention and he used the scope to get a better look at it.

Badge spoke from the darkness behind him. "You see something moving out there, Bones?"

Another several seconds and he relaxed his stance. "Nah. Another one of those mangy-ass dogs. Bastard's huge, and ugly as hell." He cocked his head to send a glance Badge's direction. "You know, I outweigh you by a good ten pounds now. Y'all can stop calling me that."

"It's too late, Bones. You're stuck with it. Want me to take over now?"

"Nope, I'm good." Another few seconds had him wanting to hurl—or hold his breath—or hold his breath while he hurled. "Son of a bitch. Was that you?"

"Hell no. That's D-Dub over there. Stinky son of a bitch has been farting in his sleep for a half hour. Why do think I keep asking to take over obs?"

"Gawd. He must've shit his pants, man."

Badge shuffled up next to him. "You could be right. Shove over so I can get some air, bro. It reeks back here." He stuck his face up closer to the opening of their hide site and gasped in the somewhat cleaner air. "That mofo needs an enema or something."

Ben chuckled while keeping his eye on the landscape. "MRE's man—does it to him every time. We need to find him a bottle of that colon-blow stuff before the next mission."

"No shit, man."

D-Dub spoke from the back of the hole. "You two ass-wipes need to shut your mouths over there. We're trying to get some shut-eye."

Sarge, or Justin Ballantine, as the civilian world knew him, spoke up next. "I was sleeping fine until that noxious flatulence of yours burned the hair right out of my nose, D-Dub. I've been in the Corp for six years, man. You are by *far*, the rottenest fucker I have ever had the misfortune to dig-in with. Besides, it's time to take over for these two anyway."

"Sorry Sarge, but I can't keep those MRE's from turning my gut bad. I can manage to hold 'em at bay for the first two days—by the third day, something's gotta give." He shuffled to his knees. "But, you can all rest assured that my noxious farts in no way affect my ability to be the best Marine I can be."

Ben laughed at the comment made from the man he'd met during boot camp at Parris Island over three years ago. He already knew Marines didn't come any better. If they got in a dogfight, he damn sure wanted D-Dub to have his back. "You sure you don't wanta get some more sleep, Sarge? I'm good for another couple hours."

"And miss out on my chance to breathe something besides contaminated air space? Don't do me any favors, Bones."

Ben groaned, knowing he and Badge would have to suffer in silence for the next four hours. Four more hours and they could start breaking down to head back to the base. He did the quick calculations in his head. Around 2 a.m. his time, he'd be able to grab a quick call to his folks to let 'em know he'd made it back all right. Hopefully, the second call to Haley would last a little longer. He *would* make those calls, though. No room for negative thinking in this place—he hadn't travelled halfway around the world to get sent home in a flag-draped casket for his family and girl to cry over. That shit wasn't happening.

Monday, December 23rd - 3:00 pm (Beaumont time)

Haley popped another handful of sunflower seeds in her mouth and checked her phone for the twentieth time in a two-hour period. She'd long ago given up any attempt to read the book resting on her belly. She couldn't concentrate on a thing, knowing Ben was due to return from a mission today. God, the list of things that could go wrong during those few days was endless, as well as unthinkable.

Still, she'd never regret making him sit down to describe his daily life in Afghanistan to her. What he and his team did to prepare for missions, how they got there, the act of 'digging in' with the other three team members. He'd described his 'billets' to her and she suspected he was sharp and resourceful enough to get his team where they needed to go. She had absolutely no doubts about his shooting abilities.

She smiled, remembering the morning he'd taken her duck hunting while he was still on leave. He'd made easy work of it, shooting both his and her limits within an hour. Haley had grown up in a family of duck, goose, and deer hunters, so she was well acquainted with the concept of hunters coming home with nothing bagged because of the occasional miss. They called that a scratch. When his golden retriever had come back with the third Teal that morning, she'd asked Ben if he ever missed. He'd given her that sexy grin of his; the one that made her want to climb the length of him, and shook his head slowly.

"Not with the price of these shells."

"Are you as good with your sniper rifle as you are with a shot gun?"

"Better." His eyes turned hard and steely. "But it's not nearly as much fun."

"I know," she'd said. "I'm sorry for asking."

"Don't be." Ben had leaned forward in the cold, damp, metal enclosure of the duck blind, and got nose to nose with her. "I've got a job to do over there. You can bet your beautiful butt I'll do whatever I damn well have to do to come home to you, Haley." He had kissed her then, not for the first time during the two-week period they'd been nearly inseparable. For some reason it had been the most memorable for her. That kiss had completely erased any doubt she'd had as to whether his feelings for her were sincere.

She closed her eyes and released a low groan, thinking that God had created her Marine's lips for the sole purpose of kissing. Correction—for the sole purpose of kissing *her*. If the good Lord was willing, she'd have the chance to give him as many kisses as she wanted.

She picked up her phone to check the time. Two minutes later than the last time she'd checked. She held up the phone with both hands and shook it. "Call, dammit, call."

Haley rolled over on her belly, rested her head on her forearm. Worry, fear, frustration—she didn't know which feeling wore her down the most. "God, please let him be okay. Please let him make it back to the patrol base alive and in one piece. And please, please, *please* let him call."

The phone vibrated in her hand an instant before Keith Urban started crooning their song. The timing startled her so badly she lost her grip and the phone slid to the floor. She scrambled to pick it up. Swiping the screen, she yelled into the phone. "I'm here, Ben."

"Can you hear me, Haley?"

"Yes, yes—I can hear you. Are you okay?"

"I'm fine, babe. I made it back to the PB without incident. How are you?"

She bit her lip, trying to hold back the tears of relief. "Fine, now that I know you're safe. Can you talk long?"

"No, and the reception may not hold up. There's a storm brewing out there—a cold front is moving in. Glad we came in when we did."

"Me too. Is it very cold over there?"

"Cold and wet, and it's about to get worse, but I don't want to talk about the weather here. What are you wearing, beautiful?"

She smiled at the teasing lilt in his tone. "Oh, I dressed sexy for the occasion—jeans and a sweater. How about you?"

His deep chuckle filtered through her phone. "The same damn thing I've been wearing for three days, with the addition of a couple of pounds of sand and grit."

"Were you able to get in a few good MRE's this time around? I don't want you losing so much weight they start calling you Bones again."

He snorted. "Babe, there's no such thing as a good MRE. They all taste the same. And I'm afraid I'm stuck with Bones. Once these grunts get stuck on something, it's nearly impossible to change their minds."

"I guess so, but I hate what you had to go through to have them start calling you that." She knew he'd dropped over thirty pounds in only two months during his previous deployment. Hauling well over a hundred pounds of gear and supplies in the brutal heat of Afghanistan's summer months had been a sure fire way to drop a lot of weight in a little bit of time. The thought sickened her.

His silent pause held the weight of a thousand words. "Damn, I miss you, Haley."

She swallowed the sob building in her throat at his words, determined to be strong for him. "I miss you so much, Ben." She cleared her throat and tried to think of something to lighten the mood. Her crying over the phone would only make it more difficult for him.

He lightened the mood for her. "Did you get your rose this morning?"

"Yes, and it's every bit as beautiful as all the others. I'm getting quite a collection."

"Cool, what color?"

"Deep red, almost purple. Thank you so much."

"You're welcome, and you're worth it. So, I know it's still the 23rd there, but it's already Christmas Eve over here. Are you anxious for Santa to pass?"

Haley grabbed the snapshot she'd printed out of him, a close-up, and passed her hand lovingly over the face. If only he was here with her instead of 8,000 miles away. "The only thing I'd like for Christmas is you under my tree, and Santa can't bring me that. Is the E-reader still working, or did the sand get to it?"

"No, it's fine. Works great over here. It was very thoughtful of you—"

She heard some muffled words and her heart began the familiar routine of panicked pounding. She knew what that meant. "Ben?"

"Yeah babe, I gotta go now."

Her heart's pounding doubled in intensity and speed. She readied herself to lose the sound of his voice. "Can you call me on Christmas Day?"

"I'll try like hell to, beautiful. You have a good day, okay?"

"I will, and you too. Thanks for calling me—and for the rose—and . . . well, for calling." Damn, she hated ending these calls. "I miss you so much, Benjamin." She hated the hitch in her voice, hated making it any worse on him than it was. "I wish you were here so I could show you."

"Hearing you say that makes me feel better, babe. I miss you too. Gotta go."

"Talk to you soon, and I'll see you later." She'd vowed early on in the relationship never to tell her Marine goodbye.

"Roger that."

She heard the click of the sat phone cutting off, hugged her phone close for a moment, as though she was hugging him. Haley fell back against her mattress and allowed herself a few minutes of tears. Tears of relief, mixed with longing and loneliness. It still astounded her that she could feel so much for a man she'd met three months ago.

Finished with her tears for the moment, she sat up and dried her eyes, determined to be stronger. If Ben could handle the day-to-day dangers of being in Afghanistan, and being away from his family for seven months, it shouldn't be this difficult for her.

Another five months and he'd be back in Hawaii. No more deployments and no more worrying about him. By this time, next year, he'd be out of the Marines.

She stood and headed toward the door, whispering the one prayer she repeated so often she didn't have to think about it.

"Keep him safe, God. Please, keep him safe."

December 24th, 9:30 am (Beaumont, TX)

Haley exited her bedroom and halted, lifting her nose in appreciation of the smells bombarding her. Her stomach growled at the tantalizing aromas of turkey roasting in the oven, along with a multitude of other savory foods cooking on her mother's stove-top.

"G'morning, Mom." She gave her mother a hug and reached for the same juice glass she'd been drinking from for fifteen years. "Is it okay if I check on Dakota before helping you in here?"

Angie Broussard reached for a mixing bowl in the cabinet. "Sure, sweetie. I think your dad fed her already, but you go on ahead."

Haley downed a glass of juice, cringing at the cold against her sensitive teeth, and then grabbed a biscuit from the baking sheet. She seated herself on the bench to slip on her boots, and looked up when someone knocked at the side door. She approached the door, sliding the last couple of steps in her socks. Ginger Chaisson, from the local florist shop, stood in the doorway holding a large bouquet of flowers. Familiar with her by now, Haley opened the full-view glass door to let her step inside.

The delivery woman beamed up at her. "Got another delivery for you, Haley. Two days in a row—that boy must be some kind of crazy about you."

"Oh my gosh, they're gorgeous." Haley gushed over the beautifully adorned Christmas themed arrangement. The bright red basket contained a dozen roses, mixed with greenery and sparkly red and gold fillers, giving it a festive appearance. "Thanks so much for taking the trouble to deliver this, Ms. Ginger."

"Oh honey, we fight over who gets to bring these to you every week. We were almost as excited as you are to get this new order." She leaned in closer. "Because that means he's still out there, alive and well. Tell your young man we said to have a Merry Christmas, will you?"

"I'll do that, and thanks again—so very much. Merry Christmas."

"Merry Christmas to you, Haley, and hopefully, I'll see you next week." Ginger waved and headed off toward her delivery van.

Haley took a few moments to admire her roses then got back to the business of seeing to Dakota.

A half hour later, she'd put a large pot of potatoes to boil, when she got a text that elicited a loud squeal of excitement.

"SKYPE IN 10 MINS."

"Oh my God, he's going to Skype me. They must have driven back to FOB Delhi." She took two steps toward her bedroom, and then stopped to stare at her mother, sending her a look of desperate pleading. "Mom— I don't know how long he'll be able to talk."

Her mother waved her off with a sweep of her hand. "Go, there's nothing left to do that I can't finish myself."

Haley ran to her room, thankful that she'd washed her hair and bothered with a little eye make-up this morning. She started her laptop, set it up on her desk, and signed in to her Skype account. Then she arranged the flowers so they'd be visible to Ben. She applied a little lip gloss, gave her hair a quick touch-up, and then heard the familiar pop of the Skype program. She sat in her desk chair and gasped as his handsome face appeared on-screen, looking every bit as thrilled as she was.

"Hey baby."

He smiled and took a deep breath. "Merry Christmas, beautiful. How's my girl today?"

Her cheeks hurt from the ear to ear smile plastered across her face. Did he really have to ask? She gave her head a slight shake. "I can't believe I'm seeing you. I was expecting a phone call maybe, but not this." She sighed, trying to focus through the tears in her eyes. "I miss you so much, Ben, and Merry Christmas to you, too."

He focused on something beside her. "How do you like your roses?"

She wiped at her tears. "They're beautiful, and these are so fragrant. I wish you could smell them." She held up the basket, turning it so he could see it better.

"Excellent—they did a good job for you, then."

"Yes, they did," she said, blinking back tears.

"Hey, now. What's wrong?" He reached his hand out toward the screen, almost as though he was trying to touch her.

"I've been dying to see you."

"If you can make the drive to Lake Erin at some point tomorrow, you can see me again. I'm going to open gifts with my family during another Skype session and I'd really like you to be there. I already mentioned it to mom and she said they'd be thrilled to have you and your family if they'd like to come along." He leaned in a little closer. "And uh, don't tell her I told you, but my mom has a little something for you over there."

"She didn't have to do that, but if it means getting to see that handsome face of yours two days in a row, you bet your ass I'll be there. Only if you're sure your mom won't mind sharing the Skype call with me. I'll be alone, though. My parents have plans for tomorrow. What time should I be there?"

"I told her 16:00 hours your time."

"That's 4:00 p.m. right? That means it'll be . . .." She stopped to do a quick, ten-digit calculation. "It'll be 2:30 in the morning over there."

"You're getting the hang of converting the time-zone difference."

She held up both hands. "Only if I'm allowed to use my fingers." She waited for his laughter to die down. "Seriously, Ben, as much as we love *seeing* you, I don't think any of us want you to lose so much sleep, especially if you have to go out on another mission any time soon."

"They're letting us rest up for the holidays, Haley. Don't worry about me. So, how's Miss Red Dakota doing? You got any races coming up?"

"She's getting lazy. I haven't competed in a month. But I have one next weekend in Lafayette." She sent him a pout. "I wish you could be there."

"Imagine I'm in the stands watching you, and post the video to Facebook so I can see it."

"I'll be sure to do that. So, do y'all do anything special over there for Christmas?"

"By the time I got here, my box of goodies from you and mom was waiting here for me. That, alone, made it Christmas. Oh, and we got a batch of Christmas cards and pictures and stuff from a bunch of kids at the school where my mom teaches. Those cards and drawings were really entertaining. Some of them were very creative."

Haley looked up at the sound of knocking on her bedroom door. She laughed as her mom, dad, and brother entered, each of them decked out in a red and white Santa hat. "Ah, Ben, I think Santa's elves are here for a visit."

Haley's mom waved at the screen. "Hi Benjamin, we wanted to wish you a Merry Christmas."

Ben laughed and nodded. "Thank you, Ms. Angie. Merry Christmas to you, too."

Tex stepped up, leaning toward Haley's laptop screen. "Hey man, I been where you are, so I know how bad it sucks being over there for Christmas. We wanted you to know we're all over here wishing you the best and praying for your safe return." He gave him a salute. "Semper Fi, Corporal Bonin."

Ben saluted him back. "Semper Fi, Sergeant Broussard—and thanks. It means a lot to see a fine, upstanding, retired Marine such as you, wearing *that* hat just to give me a laugh."

Tex guffawed with laughter. "Hey, glad I could help. Now, we know you don't really want to see us, so we'll let you get back to little sister, here."

"Thanks everybody, you made my day."

Haley waited until her family had left the room before turning to Ben's image. "Aw, that was sweet of them."

"It sure was, but where's your Santa hat?"

She reached across her desk for a similar hat, and slipped it on her head. "Ta da!" She struck a pose as Ben's smile lit up the screen. "You like?"

He nodded. "You're going to have to wear that for me the next time you see me. That's kinda hot."

"I guess that would depend on what I'm wearing with it."

"Or not wearing with it," he added quickly.

She laughed as he tried to stifle one of several yawns she'd witnessed since the beginning of their session. "You're tired, aren't you, Benjamin? Why don't you go get some sleep since I'm going to see you again tomorrow?"

"I will, besides I think Sanchez is over there chomping at the bit to get at this thing. You're sure you'll be at mom's tomorrow?"

"I'll be there, Ben."

He nodded. "Good, now say it for me, babe."

She beamed at him, repeating the mantra they'd come up with. "A year is nothing compared to forever."

"That's my girl. Take care of yourself."

"*You* take care of yourself. I'll see you later." She placed her hand flat on the screen and he followed suit, the outline of his large hand overlapping hers.

"Roger that."

He gave her one last smile before she heard that dreaded pop, like a bubble bursting.

And like that, he was gone.

Once her face disappeared from the monitor, he pushed away from the makeshift desk. "It's all yours, Sanchez."

"Sorry Bones, but the wife's in the hospital having our second kid."

"Hey, congrats, man. That's great."

"No it ain't. She ain't due for two fucking weeks and I was supposed to be in for this one. This is the second time I'm gonna miss the birth of my kid. So the doc said we can Skype the delivery. That's why I've gotta have this spot, man. I can't have some douche behind me getting a free peep show of my wife's privates."

"No, I guess not."

Sanchez sat at the computer and shook his head. "I mean, I'm thankful for this opportunity, you know? But I can't believe I'm stuck in this shit hole instead of home, holding my wife's hand while she gives birth to my kid. This shit ain't right. It just ain't right."

"Good luck, man. I hope everything goes well." Ben walked away, not knowing what else to say to the guy.

One thing he knew for damn sure—that wouldn't happen to him. By the time he'd be ready to have a kid, he'd long be out of the Corps. He walked away, revisiting the plans he'd made. He had his future all mapped out—like laying out a GPS course for a mission. He'd move into the house his mom and step-dad rented for his two younger siblings, both attending college in Lake Coburn. It was plenty big enough for all three of them.

Two years later he'd have his Associate's Degree in electronic instrumentation. Yeah—get a good job—make some decent money. Previously, his plans had only included himself, and how he would stay single long enough to build up a sizable savings account before making any major purchases.

Now he found himself thinking in different terminology—*we* instead of me . . . *us* instead of I . . . and *our* rather than my.

Was it too soon to think that way about a woman? He pictured Haley, her brown eyes sparkling with excitement and unadulterated joy, as well as a few unshed tears. She was genuine—he'd known that within minutes of introducing himself to her at Red's club in Lake Coburn three months earlier.

He remembered her scent, her satiny smooth skin, the feel of her in his arms as they danced that night. How much deeper his feelings had grown for his little horsewoman by the end of their time together. Hell, when it came to quality time, he figured they'd crammed about as much of that into his time off as they possibly could. They'd camped around a bon fire with family and friends, gone teal hunting one morning, spent a great afternoon watching her do her thing at a barrel race competition, had some time with her family, and even more with his.

If they didn't know everything there was to know about each other by now, it wasn't for lack of trying. From long talks while lounging lazily on her grandparents' creaky old porch swing, to phone conversations long past the time her Paw Paw had chased him off—he'd learned so many things about her.

Her favorite flowers were roses; she loved chocolate hazelnut spread, especially with strawberries, and cookie dough ice cream. She tolerated buttered popcorn, which happened to be her family's nickname for her, but had an absolute addiction to sunflower seeds. Her two nervous habits were chewing her nails and popping her wrists and she was ticklish as all hell. Snakes scared the absolute piss out of her, but spiders or bugs didn't—probably because she spent so much time in dusty old tack rooms, and it freaked her out if her arms or legs were constrained in any way.

Her idea of fun was a friendly game of washers, and one round—never two—of a drinking game called Ring of Fire. He knew she got grouchy with too little sleep, but her kind of grouchy was something he could live with.

Haley's parents had raised her as he'd been raised; to act responsibly, work hard, and treat others with respect. She adored her parents, grandparents, and her older brother.

Of all her little idiosyncrasies, the one he loved the most was her soft heartedness. She couldn't watch an SPCA commercial without crying, and wanted to take every stray pet home with her. The thought of anyone abusing an old person, a child, or an animal turned her livid.

What you saw with Haley was what you got—a kind-hearted person with a good head on her shoulders. There wasn't a single sign of a high maintenance, materialistic, drama-queen in that tight little package of drop-dead gorgeousness.

And damn if all he could think about was spending every waking moment with her. She was the first, the *only* woman, he'd ever come close to feeling this way about.

Ben made his way to Sniper platoon's tent, and dropped down on his bunk. He supposed it was too soon to know for sure, but at this rate, the odds of him feeling this way about anyone else hovered somewhere between slim and absolute zero.

Slim and zero? Hell yeah—those were the kind of odds he could live with.

He closed his eyes and pictured the beautifully appreciative smile she'd graced him with over the flowers during their Skype session. He couldn't wait to surprise her with her real Christmas gift tomorrow. He'd had this planned since the day he'd last held her in his arms.

He couldn't wait to see the look on her face.

Haley knew if she gave herself time to think about the brief Skype session with Ben, she would be a sobbing mass of uselessness for the rest of the day. Instead, she poured herself into helping her mom with the Christmas Eve meal preparations.

Matt's innocent query as to whether she was okay got him a hand in his face for his trouble. Hand signal for *I can't talk about it*. Her brother had given her a sad smile and a brief hug as show of support.

The arrival of an aunt, an uncle and half-dozen cousins brought further distraction. The bustle and noise kept her too busy to think about Ben . . . almost. She couldn't help but imagine him being on the other side of the earth celebrating Christmas with his Marine brothers instead of blood relatives. Every so often, she'd look up and catch Matt's gaze on her. He'd give her a wink and an understanding half-nod, as if to say everything would be all right.

If only she could be sure of that.

They squeezed in around the dining table for her father's variation of the standard blessing of the meal, adding special thanks for his son's safe return. As he finished, the sound of Matt clearing his voice across the table drew her attention.

"Thanks for that, Pop. I'd like to add a request for God to watch over all the military personnel around the world. Many of them are deployed and spending this day with their other family rather than blood relatives. I called them family as well, because even though they aren't blood, they are all brothers." He punctuated the last words with a slight lift of his brow in his sister's direction.

The sound of chairs scuffling against the hardwood floors resounded throughout the room as people began seating themselves. Haley eased her way to her big brother's side and gave him an appreciative hug.

"What's that for?" he asked."For making me feel better about Ben being over there."

"It's true, you know. He's with his brothers, like when Mitch and I were there."

"Bros before Hos?" She sent him a wink and he burst into laughter.

"Not exactly the point I wanted to make."

She sighed and closed her eyes, picturing Benjamin as he'd appeared during the Skype session, his face drawn and looking underfed and exhausted. "I know he's not eating enough. He's a little thinner than he was a couple of months ago."

"They aren't starving him, sis. It's his choice as to how much food he wants to bring on missions. The problem is, those Marines have an ungodly amount of stuff they have to haul around in their packs. They tend to ration during missions—and unfortunately, that means dropping some weight."

Haley's clenched jaw was like a neon arrow flashing her distress. Matt laid his arm heavily across her shoulders. "Don't you worry about your Marine, Haley girl. Ben will eat like a horse and lift weights to bulk up as soon as he gets to Dwyer or wherever they send him towards the end of his deployment—even more so, when he's back at Kaneohe Bay."

Still, she couldn't help but feel guilty at the over-abundance of food spread out on their table and crowding every surface in the kitchen. "Oh God, Matt. I hope you're right."

Chapter 7

Merry Christmas from the Middle East

Ben woke at 02:10, five minutes before the alarm on his watch had a chance to alert him. He disarmed it and rose from his bunk to hit the head and wipe the sleep from his eyes. He made his way to the MWR center, an acronym for Morale, Welfare, and Recreation services. As with all things, Marines had butchered that to and even quicker pronunciation of M-dub. He entered the shack with the bag of Christmas gifts his family had mailed to him, happy to have the place to himself.

Wasting no time, he logged into Skype at 3:55 p.m. Lake Erin time. Within seconds, he had connected to his desk top computer back at home in Lake Erin. He stared into the faces of his younger siblings, Kristy and Zeke. Hushed whispers of "There he is," and "Shhh—" issued from somewhere off to the side. His mom and step-dad's faces popped into the view-frame as a loud and somewhat synchronized chorus of "Merry Christmas!" erupted from the speakers.

"Merry Christmas, everybody!" He tried not to look too disappointed, thinking maybe Haley couldn't make it for some reason, until his mother's comment halted his train of thought.

"Are you eating enough, Benjamin? Haley's right, you have dropped some weight."

"Have you spoken to her?" God only knew how he managed to keep his voice from cracking.

"Sure I have."

Ben thought his heart would jump out of his chest when his mother reached out to someone. "Come over here, little lady. He's trying to put on a good act, but we know who he *really* wants to see here."

Haley's sweet face filled the screen looking apologetic. "Sorry, I went to the bathroom. You came online early."

He grinned. "That's because you need to pee when you get nervous." Laughter resonated from the speakers as Haley blushed and covered her face.

"Aw, Ben, you embarrassed her."

His sister's chiding didn't affect him nearly as much as the disappearance of that beautiful face. He deepened his voice and got a little nearer to the screen. "Merry Christmas, Haley."

She lowered her hands and fidgeted, pushing onward through her mild embarrassment. "Merry Christmas, Ben." She raised her finger. "But you *were* early."

He couldn't help but chuckle at her defiance. "Yeah, I couldn't wait another minute to see y'all." She rewarded him with a brilliant smile. "So, which gift should I open first?" He reached down to lift the bag of gifts, all brightly wrapped.

Haley stood by, watching Ben's reactions as he opened several gifts from his family members. They opened their gifts also, making sure he was a part of the festivities. She didn't need to be the center of his attention during the call. The rare treat of seeing his face for two Skype sessions in a row, especially when he'd normally be stuck at a remote PB or worse, out on a mission with his team, was gift enough.

Once the gifts were opened, Ben cleared his throat loudly. His furrowed brow and serious tone conveyed some unspoken message to the four other members of his family, who held their collective breath.

Ben's voice contained a hint of mystery as he spoke. "Haley. It's time for your gift now."

"But I already got that beautiful bouquet of flowers yesterday. And seeing you today is all the gift I need."

He sent her a smile that would charm the feathers right off a bluebird as he leaned forward in his chair, pinning her with his gaze. "I'll decide what enough is." Masculine grunts from the two other men in the room accompanied his comment.

"Oh really? Not if I get up and walk out of here, you won't." She crossed her arms, giving her chin a defiant lift. Two feminine coughs and a whispered "You go, girl—train 'em in the early stages," from his mom, accompanied a quiet snort of laughter from Kristy.

"Haley . . . stay," he warned, in a low voice.

She leaned toward the monitor, cocked her head slightly, and quirked her left brow.

His tone softened as a smile played at one corner of his mouth. "Please."

As though she could deny him anything when the mere sound of his voice made her insides melt. "Okay."

Her Marine's mouth twitched with amusement, a sure sign that he knew he already had complete control of the situation. But that was Ben . . . confident in his abilities. It didn't surprise her that he found it so easy to tease and flirt from the other side of the world, even in the presence of his family members.

"Open the desk drawer," he said, pointing to the area in front of her. "The top one on the right."

She rolled back his desk chair so she could pull open the drawer. "Okay." She kept her eyes on the screen, not wanting to miss a second of seeing the face that, even sleep deprived, made her want to melt.

"Now reach to the back of the right corner."

She slipped her arm into the drawer and reached back, pulling out a box about 4 inches square on all sides, and with a little weight to it.

"Go ahead and open it."

Haley slid her nail under the tape and pulled off the red glossy paper. She took a deep breath and lifted the lid, revealing a square box made of what appeared to be pewter. She flipped it out of the box to examine it. "Oh, how pretty." she gasped. The black onyx hinged lid bore a fleur de lis design, also pewter, and studded with crystals.

She ran her hands over the dazzling surface, admiring its craftsmanship. "I love this, Ben. It's beautiful." She held it to her chest and smiled into the monitor.

His eyes hinted at laughter. "You gonna that thing?"

Her heart thundered in her chest as she held the box out and gently lifted the lid. Another box lay nestled inside a bed of red silk, this one encased in black velvet. She lifted the box, glancing up at his mother, who stood by with one hand on her chest, her eyes lit with anticipation.

Haley took another deep breath and lifted the lid. Diamond stud earrings sparkled from a bed of black velvet. "Oh my God." Her breath rushed out of her. "I can't believe this. They're beautiful."

His voice, low but commanding, reached her. "Put them on for me."

She freed the solitaire studs from the box, slipped off her own tiny drop earrings, and tried them on. Kristy placed a stand mirror on the desk and Haley examined her reflection for only a second before returning her gaze to Ben. "I love them, but you didn't have to do all this, Ben."

"Ask him what carat they are and if they're real," Kristy hissed from behind her.

Haley shook her head without breaking eye contact with Ben. "I don't care what carat they are, or even if they're real. I love them."

"Yes, they're real, and a half carat . . . combined."

"Way to go, big brother." Kristy held her fist up to the monitor until Ben returned her virtual fist bump.

Haley touched her ear lobes. "You really didn't have to spend that kind of money on me. All I got you was an e-reader." She waved her hands in front of her eyes to stave off the threatening tears.

"You are totally worth it, babe." He nodded, giving her another sexy as hell smile—only one of many that turned her insides to mush. "You look good in diamonds. I'll have to remember that."

"Just don't think I need diamonds to care about you."

"I know you don't, but I wanted to do something special for you. It was worth it to see that smile." He pulled his gaze from Haley to catch his mother's eye. "Mom?"

Monica leaned toward the monitor, kissed her hand and placed it on the center of the screen. "I hear you, Ben—and I love you—we all do. Merry Christmas, Son." Once the other family members did the same, she began herding them out. "Come on, everybody. Let's give these two a few minutes of privacy."

"Oh, but this is your visit. I got to see him yesterday." Haley turned, torn between wanting to be 'alone' with Ben and not wanting to step on anyone's toes.

Monica gave her a wink from the door. "It's fine, Haley. Take your time. You get in a good visit with your Marine while you can."

Haley wiped a tear of gratitude from the corner of her eye. "Thanks, Ms. Monica." She faced Ben, and heard the door shut quietly behind her. "Your mom's so cool."

"Yeah, she understands."

"You don't have any more surprises up those desert cammie sleeves of yours, do you?"

He laughed quietly. "No. I'm done for the day."

She wiped at her brow. "Good. I don't think I could take much more of this."

He leaned forward. "Well, when I get home to you, you're gonna have to learn. There's plenty more where that came from."

"I mean it, Ben. I don't need diamonds from you. You don't have to buy me things." The smile he flashed tugged at her heart.

"I'm not talking about things, Haley. I mean making you happy in other ways. Making sure you know how much I appreciate you."

"I want you to come home to me." She left the rest unspoken—healthy, hurt, or crippled. She wouldn't care, as long as he came home to her. "Home, so I can touch you— hold you."

A low groan escaped from him as he leaned toward the monitor, his fingers locked, laced tightly together. "Believe me, I want it too. This time, next year, I'll be home for good." His face stretched in a huge grin as he flexed the fingers of one hand. "But in less than five months, I'll see you in Hawaii."

She sighed. "Oh, God. I can't wait. I still can't believe you're paying for my trip."

"I can't wait to see it through your eyes. Kaneohe Bay is such a beautiful place. The entire island is beautiful."

Her gaze never left his face as he spoke in a mesmerizing tone, he described white beaches with crystal clear water, waterfalls surrounded by tropical plants and exotic flowers, and secluded lagoons. She listened quietly as he told her about all the things they would do together once she was there. All she could think about was feeling his arms around her again.

"Ben."

He stopped speaking for a moment and focused on her. "Yes?"

"I want you to take very, very good care of yourself over there, do you hear me?" Try as she might, she couldn't keep her voice from quavering. "You be careful."

"Always, babe. Always."

"I mean it, Benjamin. I want you . . ." Her voice trailed off, as she tried to come up with the right words.

His eyes sparkled with mischief. "You want me? Damn, May can't get here soon enough."

She sucked in her breath, and then panicked as the screen flashed briefly. "What was that?"

"Ah hell, we're getting some satellite signal interference." He waited for the signal to stabilize before he spoke up again. "Now, you were saying how bad you wanted me."

There it was again, that sexy little grin that made her want to jump through the monitor. Holy hell, he didn't know the half of it. She plodded forward, trying to stay on subject. "I was saying that I want you to know—to really know—that I'm here for you, Ben. I am now, and I will be until you come home, and long afterward if you still want me. I don't want you to waste one second doubting that I won't be. Do you understand what I'm saying?"

Ben ran both hands through his short hair, and then locked them behind his head. He paused there before bringing his arms forward. He rested his forearms on the table surface and gave her a slow nod.

"I understand what you're saying, Haley. I believe I've known since that first evening we met, or I wouldn't have spent one more day with you, much less the remainder of my leave." He smiled again. "I won't let you down."

By this time, she was a hot mess of confusion, torn between wanting to blubber like a baby, and trying to stay strong for him. "I j-just w . . ." She had to swallow the lump in her throat to continue. "I want you to come home to me, Ben."

"I will. Now come on, you know the drill. Say it for me, will you?"

She spoke in a watery voice. "A year is nothing compared to forever."

Ben's mouth tightened. "Are you kidding me? Again, and say it like you believe it this time."

"I do believe, but this one year sure is a bitch."

"In combat boots, I know, but it's nothing you can't take. Say it for me again."

She sat up straight and took a deep breath. "A year is *nothing* compared to forever."

"Excellent." The screen image flickered several times. "Babe?" He raised one hand.

"Ben? Can you hear me?" She raised hers also, panicked as it faded out for a full second before it came back. "Ben?"

"Haley. . ."

"I'll see you later, Marine." She spoke in a firm voice, praying he heard her before she lost him for good. The image flickered off again, and then came back; long enough to see him smiling back at her as he gave her his standard sign-off.

"Roger that, Babe." Haley thought she saw him wink before the image faded out, flashed on for a nanosecond, disappeared—and stayed off.

She cursed under her breath, waited a full minute with no result before pushing the chair back. She gathered her gift and its wrappings, stopped to pick up discarded paper from the earlier round of gift opening, and stuffed it in the white plastic garbage bag someone had left in the room. A tap at the door had her meeting Monica's gaze.

"Don't bother with all that, Haley. I'll catch it later. He had to sign off?"

Haley bit her lower lip, and shook her head. "We lost the signal."

Monica's smile faded. "I'm sorry. It kind of sucks when that happens, huh?"

She stuffed the last of the paper into the bag and handed it over to her. "Yeah, it does."

The other woman gave her an understanding pat on the shoulder. "Did you at least get to say your goodbyes?"

"We got to do our thing." She traced the jeweled fleur de lis on the decorative box. "This is really beautiful. Did he get you to pick this out for me?"

Monica laughed. "Absolutely not. He bought that and had it wrapped and in the drawer before he left to go back."

Haley's jaw dropped. "Seriously? He did all this while he was home?" She gave her head a slow shake. "When did he find the time?"

"I think it was his last morning home, when you spent the night here and he let you sleep late."

"I can't believe he did something so sweet and unbelievably romantic."

"Well, it's obvious he's crazy about you. For my son to go through this much planning in advance, you have surpassed the gold level and gone straight to platinum."

"Thank you for sharing him with me today. I can imagine how difficult it is for you all to walk out of this room when his face is still up on that monitor."

Monica pulled her close for a one armed hug. "Honey, we're thrilled he has someone. I figure the more reasons he has to want to come home, the more careful he'll be over there."

Haley took a shaky breath and released it, wanting nothing more than to curl up in a ball and cry. "I hope you're right." She gazed into the woman's kind eyes. "You have to be."

Chapter 8

New Year's Eve in the Manner of Marines
— Deployed and Otherwise

"For to Marines, love of liberty is not an empty phrase, rather it's displayed by blood, sweat, and tears for the fallen."
   --General James 'Mad Dog' Mattis

December 31st – Afghanistan 21:58 hours
Journal of LCPL Benjamin Bonin: 3rd Marines, 3rd Battalion, Weapons Company

Here it is, Haley, New Year's Eve. In two hours a new year starts, our first new year as a couple. I know I'll speak to you tomorrow morning sometime, assuming I can get through to you. I also know you wanted me to keep a journal while I was here, so I've decided to start tonight. Here, in this shit hole, today is no different than yesterday for all of us out here. Same shit, different day, a hell of a lot more depressing, knowing our friends and families are about to slam a few down and make some noise.

God, I hope you're careful over there, babe. Don't get me wrong, I want you to have fun, but damn, it kills me when you go out. Not because I don't trust you, but because of the few dip shits over there who don't give a rat's ass about women unless it's to use and abuse them. Like that prick whose nose I broke the night I met you. What should have been a simple dance, turned into something twisted because one guy couldn't hold his liquor without turning into a first class asshole. It kills me that I can't be there to protect you. I know that you're with your brother sometimes when you go out. I know Tex would probably cause more damage than a broken nose if anyone tried to hurt his baby sister. But I also know you're out with your girlfriends tonight. So, until I hear your voice or see that beautiful face again, it'll bug the shit out of me.

I'm gonna shut it down for tonight being that I've got a little surprise in store for a few friends of my own over here.

See you next year, babe.

P.S. I know you said I should write this journal like it's for my eyes only, not yours. Although I have toned down the profanity some, it's definitely not gonna be squeaky clean. Sorry babe, but it helps me to vent.

Ben closed the journal Haley had sent him along with the Kindle for Christmas. No sooner had he shoved it in his bag, than his first 'guest' arrived, carrying his canteen, as per Ben's instructions.

Badge sat cross-legged on the floor of the huge tent. "What's up with the canteen, man? We gonna toast to the new year with H20?"

Ben pointed to the canteen. "If you have water in that thing, drink it. Trust me, you'll need to hydrate." He pulled out a jumbo-sized bottle of mouthwash, the clear kind, and cracked it open.

"What the hell, man? You trying to tell me something?"

Ben shook his head and grinned. "A buddy of ours sent this all the way from Hawaii and the one thing I do know is that it ain't mouthwash."

Badge's face stretched in a huge grin. "Teej sent you that? What'd he have to say?"

Ben pulled a notecard with a hand written message inside and held it up to read it. "He says, *Happy New Year to the best damn bunch of Jarheads I've ever had the pleasure of serving alongside. Kinda wish I was with you guys . . . then again, kinda not.*" He held up a snapshot of the man in question, sitting in a wheelchair, with a gorgeous redhead sitting on his lap.

Badge let loose a low whistle. "Day-uhm. Those long legs of hers almost make up for the one he lost. You think she's legit?"

Ben shrugged as he reached for Badge's now empty canteen and poured a share of the alcohol in it. "You know T.J. as well as I do. We probably won't know unless we hear wedding bells. Hold off on that until everybody else is here."

Within a few minutes, D-dub, Max, and Blake had all shown up with their canteens in tow. They passed around the photo and message from T.J., all commenting on his good fortune with the redhead as Ben filled their canteens with the man's generous donation of "mouthwash". The five of them lifted their canteens in unison as Ben lead with a short, but sincere, "To Teej. Thanks for giving us a taste of something other than the same old shit." One more rousing round of Ooh Rah's, and they drank to the Marine brother who'd lost his leg to sniper fire during their previous deployment.

"Oh man, that's good stuff."

"Shit's smooth, ain't it?"

"I almost forgot what alcohol tastes like."

"Let me see the brand of that mouthwash again? I'm gonna hafta buy stock in that shit." D-dub's comment drew snorts of laughter from the other four.

They toasted to fellow Marines, to the new upcoming year, or anything else for that matter, for the sake of toasting. Once they'd finished off the last of their alcohol, D-dub stared mournfully at his canteen. "Well, hell. It was good while it lasted. Thanks for sharing with us, Bones."

Blake nodded in agreement. "Yep. I gotta admit, if somebody sent that to me, I'd be tempted to keep it to myself."

Another round of thanks and agreements had Ben shaking his head. "That's 'cause you jerk-offs are a bunch of alcoholic mofos, and you're Yankees. Now see, you could all learn something from me." He placed his hand on his chest. "I'm a man from the great southern state of Louisiana, brought up by good people with Cajun backgrounds, and taught good old Cajun hospitality." He leaned over to retrieve something from his duffle. "The Cajun way is to give thanks for good fortune, and to share it with others, whenever possible." He lifted a second large mouthwash bottle. "And that's how we laissez les bon temps rouler in Louisiana."

The next hour had them trading stories from their own escapades with drinking, fighting, women, and family, in general.

Max took another drink from his canteen and wiped his mouth with the back of his hand. "Man, the last night before I joined the Corps, I was doing this same thing. We got together at my best friend, Bobby's house. Next thing we knew, my buddy, Joe gets up to go to the head and he stops at the hallway—I mean freezes. Then he says, real quiet-like. 'Bobby, you don't have a pet skunk by any chance, do ya?' Bobby says, 'Dude, what the fuck are you talking about?' Joe lifts up his arm and points down the hallway. 'Don't freak out, guys, he says, but there's one right there.' He starts backin' up real slow to the door, motions us to follow him."

"What'd you do, man?" Blake asked.

"I got the hell outta there. We all did, as calmly as we could. I'd been sprayed by a skunk once in my lifetime, and I wasn't about to let it happen again. We left the front door open and sat in my quad cab waiting for that son of a bitch to leave. It would walk up to the front door, stick its head out every now and then, and then turn around and go back inside. Finally, around two in the morning, it waddled on out and went on its way."

Ben took a pull from his canteen and recapped it. "That'll put a hell of a damper on a going away party. You ever find out how it got inside?"

"One of the guys had gone out to smoke and left the back door unlatched. It was a brick home on a slab. Wasn't difficult for the damn thing to come in or out." He shook his head. "I was ten years old the one time I got sprayed. I was spending the week with my grandparents in southern Missouri. I went hunting in the woods in back of their house, and my paw paw's old dog scared one up." He grimaced from the memory. "My poor grandma bought every damn can of tomato juice in town and I had to bathe in that shit. She burned my clothes and my brand new

Nike's, too. She said it'd be easier than trying to get the stink out."

"That sucks, man."

"I know, right? I couldn't have been wearing my old, cheap shoes." He shook his head. "Fucking skunk."

"I never got sprayed, but my little brother did when he was about six," Blake offered. "Mom bathed him in tomato juice, too."

Ben squinted at Blake. "Was that the brother you told me about, the one with the UTI when he went to the doc?"

Blake chuckled. "It sure was."

Ben busted out laughing. "Man, you gotta tell 'em that story."

"Tell us, man," Badge urged.

"Well, my little brother, Richie, was ten years old, but Richie was a tall kid, so he could have passed for eleven or twelve. He tells my mom he's got a problem—down there." Blake pointed to his crotch area. "He's all embarrassed, doesn't want mom to go in with him, and our dad's on a business trip. So mom asks me, I'm 17 at the time, if I'd go in the examination room with Richie to see the doctor.

Now I lived in a small town, and the doc has been practicing forever, right? The old dude must have been close to eighty at the time. He examines Richie and he asks him if he ever masturbated. Richie nods, says 'Sure I do.'"

A round of snorts accompanied Blake's story and he held up one hand to continue.

"Doc asks, "Does it burn when you ejaculate?" Richie gives me this look, and I can see it in his face—clearly the kid doesn't know the meaning of the word."

Another round of low chuckles filtered through the guys listening to the story as Blake continued.

"Now, I'm already shocked as all shit that my little brother is jerking off at ten—especially since I didn't start until I was a mature man of twelve. I tell him, 'You know, when it squirts out.' Richie nods yeah and tells the doc, "Oh, yeah man. It burns like fire." So, the doc asks him how many times a day he masturbated, with ejaculation, on average. Richie mulls this over for a few seconds and says all matter of fact like, 'About six times a day.'"

Badge choked on the last pull from his canteen.

"Wh—what?" Max stammered.

Blake nodded. "I'm telling you man. The doc almost passed the fuck out."

D-dub stared at him in shock. "Dude, you're shittin' me."

Blake raised both hands. "Hang on. It took a few minutes to straighten it all out, but it turned out Richie got the words masturbate confused with urinate." Their corner of the tent exploded with laughter.

Max finally caught his breath enough to face Blake. "Did the old doctor have a heart attack?"

"No, but he retired a week later. Said he didn't think he could survive anymore surprises like that one. And believe me, everybody in town knew what happened by the next day."

"Poor kid, so much for doctor-patient confidentiality," Max muttered.

Blake shook his head. "Doc never said a word. I, on the other hand, told everybody I knew. That shit was too damn funny not to share."

As their laughter finally dissipated, the sounds of someone singing *Auld Lang Syne* drifted over to them from somewhere outside of their tent. Realizing they'd laughed and drank their way to the New Year, the five of them raised their canteens.

Ben chose a simple toast. "To the New Year, my brothers. May we all end it the same way we started, alive and with our limbs and privates in one piece, along with sharp minds, and our sanity intact."

"Well, except for D-dub," Badge added. "Because we all know it's too late for that bat-shit crazy mo-fo." His comment triggered one last round of chuckles, along with one 'fuck-you very much' before they tipped their canteens to finish off the last of the celebratory eighty-proof 'mouthwash'. They stood and shook hands among each other before heading back to either the head or their own bunks.

"New Year's eve sucks without fireworks, man."

Ben shook his head, grinning at D-dub's grumbled complaint as his buddy walked away. Blake's reply sobered him immediately.

Damn, D-dub, we're on the opposite side of the world from everyone we love. And the one thing you miss is fireworks?"

Badge called out to them. "Step outside our perimeter and set off a few rounds."

"Yeah, bro. You'll get your fireworks," Max added.

Ben sat with his back against his pack and pulled up the pictures of Haley on his phone, wishing for a single minute with her, knowing it wouldn't be enough.

Less than four months. How had a girl he'd only known for that short a time period crept into his heart as she had? He didn't believe in telling anyone he loved them unless he was totally committed. Family members, sure— hell, you gotta love your family, but a woman? Nah—he'd vowed early on he wouldn't be like other guys he'd known. They'd tell chicks they loved them to get a piece of ass, then dump 'em and move on to the next one. Not his style.

Coming from divorced parents, who'd both found loving relationships later and remarried, he knew that commitment to one person wasn't meant to be taken lightly. He'd always known that once he found someone he wanted to be with, he'd be with her until death, whoever's came first.

He flipped through photos of Haley with her horse, Dakota, and her red terrier dog, Paisley, with him, with her parents, with Tex, with his siblings, barrel racing, frowning, smiling, and laughing.

Did he love her already? He thought so. Could he tell her yet? No way. Thinking something wasn't good enough to bring love into the equation. He had to be sure. He had to know she'd never look at another man, and that he'd never look at another woman. Once he married, he didn't want divorce mixed in with the equation.

"Happy New Year, Haley. I hope you're still around this time next year so I can say it face to face." He turned off his phone to save the battery and stuffed it in his bag, before stretching out to catch some shut-eye. He couldn't turn off the images of her appearing behind his lids, flipping from one to another like a high definition slide show.

She'd come to him in Hawaii on May 5th. May 5th was less than five months away. "Oh God," he groaned. *God, please let the next few months fly by.* He ached to see her, to hold her in his arms. They would have an entire week together—and five and a half months later, he would be home for good.

What's a year? A year was nothing compared to forever. He made Haley repeat it to him at the end of every conversation, whether it was in a phone call, Skype, or text message. To his relief, it always seemed to make her stronger. That strength made it a little easier for him to end those calls.

He winced at a particular memory of Haley crying in his arms. God help him if she ever fell apart during a phone call or a Skype session as she did near the end of his visit home. He would never let her know how tough that was for him to witness, to feel her body shaking, wracked with sobs as she lay crying on his chest, completely inconsolable.

He prayed now for God to keep giving her strength. To show him what to do so he could help her pull from that reserve of strength. He wanted it for her, but it was also selfish on his part. Because here, on nights like this, away from all the comforts of home, the only thing he wanted more than to be home, was to be home with Haley.

Tex knocked several times before he heard a muffled call to enter. He hesitated slightly, hoping he hadn't interrupted something personal. His fears proved unfounded as Mitch finally pulled the door open. The sight of his old buddy wearing an apron that said "Warning: The FDA recommends you wait until *after* the meal to insult the cook" had him smothering his laughter.

"Hey, brother. Should I be watching for an interview in the Ex-Marine edition of Good Housekeeping, or something? You look like a souped-up version of Betty fucking Crocker—on steroids."

Mitch raised his hand, along with an eyebrow as a word of warning. "Nix the f-bombs bro. The kid's here." Then he extended his hand. "Ooh Rah, brother. Meagan insisted—didn't want me to get barbeque sauce on her 'favorite shirt'."

"I hope you aren't finished yet. Cause you know your pit skills don't hold a fu—flipping candle to mine." Tex took the time to wipe his boots on the rug at the front door before walking inside.

"I don't know, man. I've been getting some practice."

"Pfft—I'll be the judge of that."

Meagan exited the kitchen wiping her hands on a dishtowel. "I thought I detected the distinct aroma of pure Texas BS in the air." She lifted her nose and pulled in a deep breath.

He performed a suave, three-fingered adjustment to the brim of his Stetson and grinned. "Hey now, don't mess with Texas, sweetheart."

She beamed up at him. "How are you, good-looking? You ready to ring in the New Year with us?"

Tex wrapped his arms around her for a big hug, ending it by lifting her off her feet. "Yes I am, and you know you adore the smell of Texas BS."

Meagan laughed as her feet touched the floor again. "Well, sure. Otherwise, I'd have called it a stench, rather than aroma."

He rested both hands on her shoulders. "When you gonna give up on teaching this guy some class and move on back to God's country with me?" He gave her an obvious wink as Mitch put his arms around her waist from behind.

She clasped her hands around Mitchell's and cocked her head to speak to him. "Don't worry babe, you and I both know better, don't we?"

Mitch kissed the side of Meagan's neck as he returned the wink from Tex. "Uh huh. That's sour grapes talking because he threw out his last chance at love to let a stripper take a spin around his pole."

"Hey, I got a hell of a lap dance out of it once the doors closed." He leaned in closer to finish. "And it didn't cost me a dime."

Meagan shook her head and headed back toward the kitchen. "You are such a pig, and oh, so predictable."

Tex pointed at her. "And you're judgmental. Strippers have to make a living too, you know. Some of those girls are stripping to pay for college."

She turned, her fists resting on her hips. "I'm well aware of that. I don't blame the stripper. I blame you for keeping my best friend waiting to hear from you while you enjoyed your lap-dance, free or otherwise." She turned her back on him but grumbled the entire trip back into the kitchen area. "Then had the nerve to come back here, acting all shocked when she didn't attack you like a starving woman would a chicken fried steak."

Tex followed Mitch into the kitchen. He leaned his massive bulk against the door, crossing one boot over the other. "Okay, Megs, now that we all know I'm the scum of the earth, tell me one thing. In your honest opinion, is there anything I can do to steal her out from under Bo McAllister's nose?"

Meagan looked up from stirring the meat mixture for the rice dressing. Her shoulders drooped suddenly as she released a long sigh. "Honestly, Tex? From what I get from her so far—another man, maybe. But you? I don't think so."

Tex did some shuffling in his size 14 Luchesse boots. "I guess I knew that all along." He removed his hat to rake his fingers through his hair. "Guess it's time to move on, then."

"Yeah, I'm sorry, Tex, but we uh, kinda figured that out already." Mitch and Meagan shared a look loaded with suspicious vibes.

Tex narrowed his gaze at her. "What the hell does that mean?"

"We set you up with someone for tonight." She spoke quickly, as though she didn't want to lose her nerve.

He glared first at Meagan, then Mitch. "I don't do blind dates. Bro, you *know* that."

Mitch nodded. "I know that, and it's not a date. I told you we were having some people over for an early supper before we go to the club tonight. She's one of the people."

"And these other people you got coming to this shindig—they're all couples, I suppose."

"It's all people you've met before—Sarah, my sister, and her husband, Tanner, Annie and Drake LeBlanc, and . . . Drake's secretary, Aubrey Abshire, who happens to be a very *nice* lady."

"Nice?" Tex was about ready to knock that smug look right off of Mitchell's face. "You better come up with something besides nice, or my ass is outta here."

Mitch shrugged. "I mean, she could stand to lose a few pounds, or a hundred, and if she ever gets that huge, hairy wart removed from her nose, I'm sure it'll do a lot to improve her profile. Of course the triple chin . . ."

Tex straightened and shook his head before jamming his hat back on and heading toward the door without another word.

Meagan muttered a low curse aimed at her fiancé. "Honestly, Mitch, are you trying to chase him away? Aubrey's gorgeous, Tex." She grabbed her phone from the cabinet. "Hang on and I'll show you a picture of her."

"I want to see a full-body shot, too, not one of those 'selfie' pictures women take. I heard they doctor those things up then plaster 'em all over Facepage, or whatever the fu—hell they call it."

"No, no—this was taken at a birthday party we all attended. Look, there's Aubrey." Meagan pointed to a red head standing to one side in a group shot.

Tex stared at the figure on the screen, noting that, although she wasn't model thin, thank God, she was shapely, which was fine with him. Even as a younger man, Tex had preferred his women with a little extra meat on their bones. Squeezing something soft and pliant was a hell of a lot more of a turn on than trying to hold a brittle bag of skin and bones. Some of those freaking runway models were downright scary looking, in his opinion. "I can't see her face from here." He watched as Megs touched the screen with two fingers to zoom in before turning the phone his direction. He took it from her to study the face of the woman with long reddish, curly locks and big green eyes, staring back at him. "Nice. What's the story with her? Why is someone who looks like that single?"

Mitch rummaged through a drawer and pulled out a long handled basting brush. "Her husband dumped her for another woman, and honestly? The only thing I can figure is that she wouldn't lower her standards enough to make him happy. The dude seems to like his women a little on the trashy side."

"And she's definitely not trashy; I can vouch for her," Meagan added, hurriedly.

Tex studied them both before giving a slow nod. "Okay, but if her laugh sounds like a jackass braying, or she farts in her sleep or something—I'm going to kick your ass, bro." He pointed a long finger at Mitch.

Mitch raised his hands. "It wasn't my idea, it was Meagan's."

Meagan gave a slight cough. "Wow. Thanks for having my back, babe."

Mitch turned to her. "Did I, or did I not tell you this man didn't like to be set up?"

"You did."

"And I told you he'd be pissed, didn't I?"

"Yes, you did."

"And I told you there was a possibility he'd want to kick my ass, didn't I?" He continued at her nod. "Yet you insisted on inviting Aubrey without consulting him first, did you not?"

"Excuse me, but I do not need to get permission to invite someone into my own home." She walked right up to Tex and stood there, with arms crossed and one hip cocked. "So, what, are you going to kick *my* ass now?"

Tex had to admire her sauciness. He couldn't help but think that living with a roommate who possessed an abundance of the trait for so long, it was bound to rub off on her. God knows, nobody did saucy better than Nicole. Waves of regret washed over him—devastating, tsunami sized waves that, according to Megs, appeared too damn late to be of any assistance. Pushing aside the thought, he placed his large palm on Meagan's head and gave her a gentle push, keeping his hand in place.

"Hey!" She started swinging playfully at Tex, her arms nowhere near long enough to reach him.

"Relax short-stuff. No real man ever hits a woman, especially with her crazy-ass fiancé standing watch like some kind of rabid, pit-bull bodyguard. Something tells me if anyone ever laid a hand on you, including me, size wouldn't matter one damn bit."

Meagan stopped swinging and threw a wink in Tex's direction before turning to Mitch. "You see, babe? I *told* you size doesn't matter."

Tex bellowed with laughter as Mitchell's jaw dropped open in shock. "You know that's a load of crap, right?"

Tex only laughed harder.

Mitch turned to Meagan. "Okay, tell him you were joking."

Meagan grinned at Tex before giving Mitch a brief nod. "Go ahead, Marine. Throw me under the bus again like you did a minute ago." She walked out of the room, bumping fist with Tex on the way out. "Don't mess with Texas, baby."

Tex wiped tears of laughter from his eyes as he finally caught his breath enough to speak. "She burned you, man. She burned you good."

Before Mitch could come up with an adequate comeback, Buck came bounding into the room with all the energy of an unleashed puppy.

"Uncle Tex! It's going to be a whole new yeaw, tomowwo."

Tex lifted the four year old, resting him on his hip. "Hey man, look at you. You're growing like the weeds in my grandma's back pasture."

Buck gave him an exaggerated nod. "Mama says she's going to hafta buy me new pants soon, cause all mine aw going to look like high-wataw pants."

"That's a fact. I can see those pants rising up your leg right now." Tex grabbed the hem of the boy's pants leg and gave it a gentle tug.

"Yep, being on crutches didn't put a stall in his growth spurt, that's for sure. Next thing you know, he'll be as tall as me." Mitch ruffled Buck's hair then tickled his neck, setting the child off into a fit of giggling.

Tex spoke in an overloud whisper. "That ain't saying too much buddy. How about you set your sights on growing as tall as your Uncle Tex, instead?"

Mitch laughed. "I think he lacks that particular gene of freakishly tall height in his chemical makeup."

Tex reached out to lay a heavy hand on Mitchell's shoulder. "It's all right bro. We can't all be descendants of Goliath or the prodigy of Gods."

"Yeah, some of us can actually walk through a door without ducking—"

"And don't forget about getting your picture on that box of 'magically delicious' cereal, short stuff."

"Oh, that is low, bro."

Tex grinned. "Almost as low as your eye level."

Meagan walked between them with an armload of towels on her way to the laundry room. "Are you boys still arguing over size?"

"I'm six foot tall. That is not short."

"That's a half a foot less than me."

"Six inch difference—big deal."

Meagan closed the laundry room door and stopped in front of her fiancé, hands on hips and biting her lower lip. Mitch crossed his arms and looked down his nose at her. "Don't even think about it, Megs."

"What's it worth to you?"

He leaned over and whispered something in her ear. Tex couldn't hear it, but whatever he said had her blushing to her hair follicles.

"No difference. No difference at all." She giggled then let out a screech as Mitch sent her on her way with a firm slap to her behind.

Buck chortled gleefully. "Mitch spanked mama's butt."

Meagan turned with a gasp. "Christopher Buckley! That is not something to say." She glared at Mitch, who at least had the good sense to assume a hangdog expression.

Tex's chest rumbled with laughter as he set Buck down. He watched the boy run to his mama, pleading with her to go outside, then reduced his voice to a low murmur. "Speaking of genetics and DNA, anything new going on with him? Like, maybe more ghostly appearances of the dead paternal Marine in his bedroom?"

Mitch shook his head. "Not since the accident on Halloween night."

Tex watched his friend's face pale slightly. No doubt, he was revisiting the terror of seeing Buck thrown fifteen feet by a speeding car during trick or treat.

"Buck is still adamant about what happened. He says Chris told him he'd always be with him, even if he couldn't actually see him anymore."

"Strange happenings, man, the kid seeing his dad in that #8 Texans jersey, and holding a conversation with him." Tex gave an involuntary shiver.

"And Chris telling him that he couldn't pronounce his R's either when he was his age." Mitch straightened his spine suddenly. "It's funny you should bring up DNA, though . . ." His voice trailed off as Meagan re-entered the room, apparently having heard the last of the conversation.

"We have bigger fish than that to fry now. Did Mitch tell you we got a letter from an attorney representing Chris's parents?"

Tex couldn't help but envy the references to the two of them as 'we' in her comments, even though her tone foretold of impending complications. "A lawyer?"

Her mouth twisted in a sardonic grin. "I know, right? They've spent years ignoring him, refusing to even consider he could be their grandson. Now they want to obtain evidence as to whether or not he is, in fact, their blood."

Tex frowned. "That's kind of a ballsy move, and not in a good way, either." He didn't miss the unmistakable clench of Mitchell's jaw as he moved closer to his girl, a sure sign of his protective instinct kicking in. "A word of advice? Don't make a move without first retaining an attorney of your own."

"I don't want to bring lawyers into this, Tex. They're Buck's grandparents, and I know Chris would want them to be a part of his life." Meagan glanced from Mitch, to Tex, then back up to Mitch. "Maybe this will be the thing to open up the line of communication between me and my parents as well." She lifted her face for a kiss from her man. "It'll be fine, you'll see." A grunt from Mitch accompanied her exit from the room.

Tex picked up two aprons from the counter, comparing them, and chose the more masculine of the two. He lengthened the adjustable neck strap and slipped it over his neck before tying it around his waist. "She's entirely too forgiving. That sounds like trouble to me." He followed Mitch out the back door to check on the pit. The sweet aroma of smoking meat infused with pecan wood clung heavily in the cold, crisp air.

"Don't I know it. I've begged her to let me help in retaining someone. She refuses. She's adamant that this is what Chris would want for his son—to know his grandparents—but I can't trust anyone who can turn their backs on their own kids as easily as they did. It reeks of a need to control everything and everyone around them."

"I agree with you. I'm sure Chris wants his parents to know and accept his son as their flesh and blood, but sure as hell not to take total control of his life. Considering her past experience with them, it seems to be the norm for those people."

"Roger that, but I can't make her see the danger in this situation. Ever since we got that letter, red flags have been popping up in my mind." Mitch laid a fist on Tex's shoulder. "Maybe you can help me persuade her before you leave to go home?"

Tex gave him a determined nod. "You know I'll do anything I can to help."

By 6:00 p.m., all of the guests had arrived. Tex got to see, with his own eyes, that those phone shots of Aubrey hadn't done her justice. By 7:00, everyone had stuffed themselves with delicious southern barbeque, along with all the traditional fixings.

Serious vibes between Drake Leblanc, Mitch, and Meagan, caught Tex's attention. He turned from his beautiful not-a-date to listen in on the conversation pertaining to the legal documentation their hostess had received. It hadn't taken long for Drake to insist she not move a muscle without retaining an attorney, specifically him.

"I know this guy and his firm's reputation, Meagan. They don't mind playing dirty to get what they want. His only concern is winning the case for his clients in order to earn his high-end fee, no matter how dishonest or immoral their wishes are."

Tex turned to the woman he'd had no trouble attaching himself to. Several minutes of conversation had revealed both intelligence and a keen sense of humor in Aubrey. The girl was a beautiful package of voluptuousness, with a little bit of plump in all the right places. Just what the doctor ordered to get over Nicole. He took a moment to question her quietly. "What's your opinion of all this?"

Aubrey sipped from her wine glass and nodded. "I think he's absolutely correct. Meagan should be careful with this. I mean, think about it. They could have sent her a sincere correspondence from two people who wanted to get to know their grandson. Something that says they're sorry for past judgments that lost them their only son. That isn't a personal letter from concerned grandparents, it's a legal threat. Thinly veiled for now, I think, but a threat, none the less."

Tex turned back to his friends. "Meagan, let Drake represent you, hon. It's better to be safe and prepared, than not and get shot in the back."

Several different responses, all in agreement, came from the room's occupants. Annie McAllister LeBlanc, Drake's wife of nearly two years, placed her arm around

Meagan's shoulder. "Don't you worry, Megs. My hubby is the best at what he does, and that will be to protect Buck. Please, I don't think any of us in this room will be able to sleep if you don't let him handle this."

Meagan let her head fall back, issuing a long sigh. "Okay, even though I'm not convinced we need protecting from the Martins, though. I've known them all my life."

"As you have your parents, but that didn't stop the four of them from turning against you and Chris when you needed them most, did it?" Mitchell's words, though Tex knew they hadn't been intended to hurt her, seemed to hit home as she winced at their obvious truth.

"I know. I know you're right, Mitch." She looked around the room at her concerned guests. "You're all right, and yes, Drake. I'd love it if you'd represent us. I still can't help feeling sad about this. Why couldn't they have picked up the phone and called? Or better yet, come to see us? I would have welcomed them."

Mitch drew her in close to him with one arm. "I know, babe. I think that's why the rest of us are all so pessimistic about their intentions. They chose this path over something much simpler. That translates to control."

Tex's stomach churned with an uneasy feeling that foretold of trouble for his two good friends. He watched as Mitch pulled Meagan closer, as though trying to shield her from all things harmful. Tex's gaze clashed with his Marine brother's, and they exchanged nods. Mitchell's look of steely-eyed determination said it all.

God help anyone who tried to hurt Meagan or Buck.

The group of eight entered the club around 8:30 and headed for the roped off section at the corner of Red's club, reserved for family and VIP guests of Red.

Tex pulled out a chair for Aubrey and seated her. "What are you drinking tonight, pretty lady?" She seemed to mull it over before answering.

"I'll have a Margarita—on the rocks and no salt, please."

"Very good, I'll be back with that—" He paused to glance over to the line of customers waiting at the bar, "—as soon as I can. I hope you're not too thirsty, this could take a while."

She scanned the line and gasped. "Sheesh, look at that line. Make it a beer. Domestic. Surprise me."

He pushed his way to the crowded bar and joined the line of animated customers. Trying to tune out the hum of conversations around him, he scanned the patrons seated along the length of the bar. The sight of the tall, auburn-haired man seated three chairs down had him doing a double take. Bo McAllister stepped aside, revealing his date, the voluptuous blonde wearing some kind of body clinging, shimmering, contraption of a dress that screamed *"Look at Me!"* in any and every language on the planet.

"Son of a bitch."

There was no possible way she could have heard his murmured curse, but in the second it took for their gazes to clash, he knew it was her first sighting of him, too. He nearly stepped forward when her lips formed his name, but then Bo leaned over to block his view of her as she spoke to him. The man turned and waved at him, then took Niki's hand to lead her over.

"How you doing, Tex?" Bo gave him a hearty handshake. "We'd decided to wait at the bar until you guys made it here. Are the rest at the table already?"

He nodded. "I'm good, McAllister. Yeah! Yeah, they're over there." As Bo turned to see where he'd pointed, Tex took the opportunity to sear Niki with his gaze. "Good to see you, Nicole."

"Tex."

Bo turned back to them. "I know the others, but who's the redhead? Is that your date?"

If Niki had bothered to watch him instead of giving herself a case of whiplash to stare at the table, she would have noticed his wince at Bo's words. Even though it was the simple-truth, why did he feel as though it was an accusation, or a sign of his guilt?

Before the words 'set-up' or any other excuse left his mouth, Niki swiveled around to face him.

"Funny, she doesn't look like a pole dancer."

"How the hell would you know a pole dancer when you see one?" He leaned closer. "Or maybe you shop at the same stores? You're looking very . . . available, by the way." He shrugged. "I'm assuming that's the look you were going for."

She raised one brow. "Assume away, Mr. Broussard." She turned on her spiked heels, her short blond tresses disappearing in the crowd as she made her way to their table.

Tex met Bo's gaze in the lingering tension of her departure. "Sorry, bro. She's got a perpetual case of the hates-my-guts beyond repair."

"I know. But you can't be all that surprised, right? I mean, that's Niki we're talking about. There isn't a man on earth that girl will take shit from."

"Yeah, but I thought we could at least be friends without all the sarcasm and insults." He raised both hands, palms outward. "That's all I want, man, I swear."

Bo grabbed the two drinks he'd ordered from the bar. "Want in one hand, man . . ."

"Crap in the other," Tex finished for him as they both chuckled.

By the time he got the drinks, Tex was about to jump out of his skin. Niki had been over there with his 'date' for too long already. No telling what kind of bullshit she'd filled Aubrey's head with. He headed back to their table, groaning inwardly at the sight of Nicole and the redhead deep in animated conversation. Tex approached, setting a drink carefully next to her. "Here you go, pretty lady. Margarita, on the rocks, and no salt, as you requested. You look too damn good tonight to settle for a domestic beer."

"Aw, thank you, Tex." She took the drink and sipped from the straw, rolling her eyes. "Oh that's a good one."

"So, Aubrey—" He settled into the chair next to her, eyeing Nicole, who'd chosen to sit directly across from her. "Have you been introduced to Nicole and Bo, yet?"

"I have; a delightful couple, if I do say so."

Tex grunted. "Yes, indeed—delightful and informative, no doubt." *Not to mention judgmental as hell.*

Aubrey's head pivoted his direction. "Informative?"

Tex kept his silence as Niki jumped in with her own explanation. "I think he means gossipy, which is a jump to an incorrect conclusion on his part. I mean, that he'd think I'd find him interesting enough to even want to gossip about him."

Aubrey's gaze travelled from Niki, to Tex, and then on to Bo who sat next to his date. "Is there something going on here that I need to know about?"

Tex answered with a flat out "No."

Niki threw back the last of her drink and placed the empty glass on the tray before picking up the fresh one. "Absolutely not." She tossed the narrow straw onto the tray and took a sip. "Unless you enjoy a good story."

Tex turned to Aubrey and grinned, shrugging one shoulder. "It's all right by me. I've got nothing to hide."

To his absolute delight, Aubrey gave him a brilliant smile before shaking her head at Niki. "The only thing I'm interested in tonight is having a little fun. So, how about it, cowboy? I was told you had some moves on the dance floor." She nodded toward the band. "That sounds like a Texas two-step to me."

He shoved his chair back, all too willing to get out of the current situation. He held his hand out to her in what he hoped she'd see as a gallant gesture. "I'd be proud if you'd do me the honor."

"Gladly." She accepted his hand and rose, letting him lead her to the throng of dancers. Within seconds, the two of them were spinning and dancing in a counter clockwise circle around the dance floor, at too quick a pace to carry on a proper conversation. When that song ended and switched to a country ballad, he pulled her close to continue their dance, as well as the conversation.

"You're an exceptionally good dancer, especially if you can manage to keep my big old size 14's from crushing those pretty little feet of yours." He grinned as she threw her head back, laughing.

"I wear a size 10 shoe, Tex. That only qualifies as a little foot for a dinosaur—a woman, not so much."

He glanced down at a pair of russet colored, leather boots, nicely embellished with buckles and at least a three-inch heel. "They look fine to me." And he meant that, too. There was something he found so sexy about a tall woman with enough self-confidence to wear heels. "You're what, a couple inches shy of 6', so you'd look kind of strange balancing on a pair of size 5's."

"With these DD's?"

Tex grunted as she indicated her considerably prominent breasts, another turn-on for a man of his particular tastes.

"I'm so top heavy I'd never be able to stand up straight, much less walk without toppling over. I'd be planting these puppies in the dirt every time I turned around."

He laughed as she shook her head, her beautiful smile revealing an unabashed sincerity he was beginning to find more and more refreshing.

"My big feet come with the territory," she said, wincing. "Out of four siblings, I'm the shortest one in my family. My dad and three older brothers are all between 6'5" and 6'7", and they still call me munchkin, believe it or not."

"What about your mother?" A shadow passed over her eyes, making him regret the question.

"She was about 5'8" when she passed away a couple of years ago."

"Oh, I'm sorry, Aubrey. If you don't mind me asking, did the red hair come from her or your father?"

"My mom, definitely. She was a Murphy, and it's one of the most common surnames in Ireland. Although it's ridiculous to think all Irish are freckled and redheads, she definitely fit that particular stereotype." Aubrey lifted a lock of her hair and let it fall. "Lucky me, huh? All this red hair and the fair skin tone to go along with it. If I spend more than thirty minutes in the sun without heavy duty UV ray protection, there isn't much difference between my skin color and boiled crawfish."

"I never had that problem. I mean, my hair is blond, but I always tan extremely easy. Is it the same for all redheads?"

"I can't speak for all of them out there, but for me and my mom it definitely was. She developed melanoma, a spot on the back of her arm she'd neglected." Aubrey lifted one shoulder in a half-hearted shrug. "A year later she was gone."

"I'm sorry to hear that." He lowered his face to catch her gaze. "I'm hoping you use the necessary protection when you do go in the sun. I'm sure you know the drill: hats, sunblock with a high SPF, and reapply often. . ."

She gave him another beautiful smile. "Most certainly, and in conjunction with yearly trips to my dermatologist so he can keep an eye on any suspicious looking spots. You know your preventative measures, Tex."

"My little sister, Haley, also has fair skin, so our mom stays on her butt about it."

"And how about Marines stationed in Afghanistan for ten or twenty years? Were you in the mountainous area or the desert region?"

"The desert region most of that time, and sure, I stay on her butt too. I wear hats when I work outside, but I'm afraid my skin is beyond help. It's damn near turned to leather."

She surprised him then, by lifting her hand to his face. "Not at all, Tex. It looks good, despite what you and the U.S. Marines have put it through."

He tipped his hat at her. "Why thank you, ma'am."

She shook her head, her low chuckle carrying to him. "I probably shouldn't point this out, but I bet you have women falling all over themselves to get at you. Six and a half feet of solid muscle with blond hair, blue eyes, and those *dimples* for crying out loud—which totally stacks the deck against all women kind—and dripping with southern boy charm."

"Ah, but the question of the hour is does it have you falling all over yourself?"

"Nah, I'm immune to stuff like this. I'm here because my bosses wife wouldn't take no for an answer. I think Annie was afraid I'd sit at home and cry myself to sleep."

Tex narrowed his gaze on his dance partner. "Maybe I'm being a little presumptuous, but you don't seem the type to cry over spilled milk."

Her eyes widened as one brow arched in amusement. "What makes you think that?"

"You seem too confident. It shows in the way you carry yourself."

"I've had my moments, but my ex has pulled far too much crap for either of us not to suspect this was coming." Her brow wrinkled in concentration. "We had no business getting married as quickly as we did. You can't possibly learn what you need to know about a person to marry them in three months. I must have been suffering from a hellacious case of temporary insanity."

Tex pressed a gentle squeeze to her hand. "I can't say I haven't been *there*. I think it runs in my family. That, along with the propensity for being a perpetual smart ass."

Aubrey gave him a somewhat lady-like snort. "Your condition may be perpetual, but not nearly as devastating as my severe lack of judgment. Mine caused me to fall into a financial hole I'm still trying to claw my way out of. That SOB racked up my credit card, and then emptied our savings account before running off with his 'soul-mate'. The idiot said I should be grateful, because he gave me the house. Of course, it came with an $1,100 monthly mortgage, which I could only have paid if I never ate again and cut off all the utilities."

"Equity?"

"Next to zero, but no matter; I should be grateful. Oy, what a guy, huh?"

"Humph, what a jackass. No wonder you aren't crying. The milk in that carton probably soured ages ago. I hope you got some of that savings back."

Aubrey chuckled low in her throat, a sexy sound that soothed his Niki-bruised ego.

"Some—what he hadn't already blown in Acapulco with the hussy of the month. I used it to pay off my credit card debt." Her eyes sparkled with amusement. "And then there's the nifty little alimony payment to help cover that mortgage." She gave him a wink. "Men too stupid to cover their tracks shouldn't commit adultery."

"Ah, revenge is a dish best served cold."

"Yep, and it didn't hurt that my boss is a damn good lawyer."

"So, you're able to manage, financially, I mean?" He grinned at her nod. "Good for you. Sounds like you're on the road to recovery."

"It's not paved in gold, but at least it's paved and the potholes are minimal." She looked past him and jutted her chin forward. "What's up with you and blondie—Niki, is it? You two have a history?"

He cleared his throat and tugged at his collar. Her burst of laughter had him sending her a sheepish grin. "Is it that obvious?"

"Oh yeah. Whatever you did, you did it good—or bad—whichever the case may be. She's still irate with you."

Tex stole a look in Niki and Bo's direction. "Ya think?"

"Uh huh—so what'd you do, big man? Stand her up? Dump her because she got too 'clingy'? What was it?"

"Well, we never actually had a date. I mean I did *see* her a couple of times, but it was nothing planned." He gave her a non-committal shrug. "And instead of driving down from Beaumont the next weekend like I told her I might do, I kinda didn't. And she kinda got wind of the reason I didn't—and, well, it kinda blew up in my face."

Aubrey's gaze lingered on him long enough for an acute discomfort to set in, a quirk playing at the edges of her mouth.

"She may, uh—assume you're an exotic dancer."

Aubrey's brow furrowed. "Exotic dancer? Are we talking strip clubs and poles and things like that?" She burst into laughter as Tex answered with a smug grin. "Oh my Lord, would she be so way off base with that assumption. I don't have nearly the core strength or muscular control it takes to be a pole dancer."

"See, that's what I said." Tex shook his head at her bemused expression. "Not that you don't, but that pole dancers possess that kind of strength. Once I had the opportunity to check that out, I couldn't pass it up. You understand that, right?"

She nodded, trying to smother her laughter. "I know this is the part where I should at least try to look affronted and say all guys are pigs. The truth is if I was a guy, I'd probably have to check it out, too." Her brow rose in question. "Even if only to prove the theory wrong."

Tex grinned big and bold. "I might be erring on the side of TMI here, but that theory is right on the money."

Her eyes lit up. "Awesome. I know someone who teaches the classes here in Lake Coburn. It's mechanics, you know? How to use leverage, three points of your body touching the pole at all times, stuff like that. I may have to look into it. I heard it's a great way to get into shape, and loads of fun, too."

He stood back for a moment to cast an appraising look at her curvaceous-ness and shook his head. "It may be a good way for you to stay in shape, but take it from a man who appreciates a woman with curves. You are fine as you are, honey."

Her grin spread from ear to ear. "Keep talking, Tex. You are so good for my seriously damaged self-esteem. It's a real shame it won't get you into these pants."

His guffaw carried over the music. "Fair enough, but I don't need to get into your pants to know that I like you, Aubrey. How about we both agree to have fun for now?"

Her eyes narrowed suspiciously. "I don't have a problem with that, as long as your idea of 'fun' isn't a hand full of meaningless sex-capades. I'm not that type of girl, you know."

"I never thought you were, and I would love to see you again. As for sex, I'd be a fool to turn it down if you offered, but that call is totally up to you. I'd still like to see you, with or without it." Her brilliant smile was proof enough that he'd found the right words.

"Oh, yeah. So extremely good for my self-esteem." She cast a glance towards the end of their table where Niki and Bo sat, deep in conversation. "But even so, I may have some fun with this if it's all right with you."

Tex chuckled and gave her a nod. "Knock your socks off, sweetheart." He finished the dance by dipping her and giving her a friendly hug afterwards before leading her into a Cajun style jitterbug that had them both out of breath by the time it ended.

"I've got to rest my dogs," she pleaded, before heading back to their table. "Ooh, that was *fun*." She lowered herself daintily in the chair he pulled out for her. "I wonder if I could work some of those dance moves into my performance at the club?"

Tex chuckled at the sly wink she passed him, quick to notice the easily perceptible stiffening of Niki's posture. In seconds, she'd grabbed Bo's arm and pulled him to the dance floor—not without first spearing Tex with her needle sharp glare.

"What the hell was that?" Annie LeBlanc stood over them both, staring toward Niki and Bo. "She looks as though she found a basket full of last year's hard-boiled Easter eggs."

Tex cleared his throat, passing his thumb and forefinger over his mustache and goatee. "I have no idea what you're talking about."

Annie crossed her arms over her chest and grinned. "Liar."

Aubrey's laughter cut through the air. "He is, but it's only to protect my reputation. The truth is I was having a little fun at Niki's expense. I'm sure I'll burn in hell for it."

"For what? Come on, dish."

"It seems Nicole is mistaken about my occupation. Somehow, she's got this idea that I'm an exotic dancer."

"As in a stripper? Are we talking professional stage stripping, like burlesque?"

"I believe it's the kind of dancing that involves a pole." She glanced at Tex, whose face heated with a good mixture of embarrassment and amusement as both women laughed until they were wiping tears from their eyes.

"Go on—give it your best shot," Tex insisted. "I deserve it."

Aubrey pulled a tissue from her purse to dab at her eyes, and then gave his shoulder a comforting pat. "Oh, sweetie, I think you've suffered enough."

Tex shook his head, thinking Nicole's might be of a different opinion.

Three hours passed quickly in such good company. Determined not to hurt Aubrey's feelings, Tex made a conscious effort to avoid any and all contact with Niki. Minutes before the New Year, everyone in the bar donned the shiny paper hats or grabbed the noisemakers they'd been given to join in the celebration. The countdown began and still, Tex tried not to glance in Nicole's direction. As the bar patrons brought in the year with confetti, horns, and rousing cheers, Tex exchanged a brief, though robust kiss with his 'date' and wrapped her in his arms for a hug. His gaze fell upon Niki and Bo, caught up in a celebratory kiss. During their after-hug, Niki's gaze collided with Tex's. All in the name of good will, he managed to send her a smile and a slight nod. Her response was to lean back and plant another kiss soundly on Bo McAllister's mouth.

He turned away from the display, sensing it was purely for his benefit.

No matter what Aubrey said, Tex had a slightly different opinion. As far as Nicole Reeves was concerned, he had years of suffering left to endure.

Chapter 9

Failed Mission, Losses of Love and Life

Ben slipped into the M-dub and dropped heavily onto a seat in front of a computer. Stifling a yawn, he signed in and connected, anxious for a visual of his girl. Within moments, he saw the face that filled his dreams—when he wasn't too exhausted to dream. He found her, sitting on her bed, looking antsy as hell. He could tell the instant her eyes focused on him that his appearance shocked her. Her gasp accompanied a furrowed brow, lined with worry.

"Oh Jesus." Her hand flew to her mouth for a moment, until she managed to recover. "Ben—hey. I'm sorry, but is there a food shortage or something?"

He sent her his best smile. "Aw, come on, babe. It's not that bad. It's not the US Marine's fault that I find MRE's about as appetizing as bat guano."

"Appetizing or not, you need to eat—something—for Christ's sake. Benjamin . . ."

He clamped his jaw at the tell-tale tremble of her chin. "I'm fine, Haley, really. I've been busy, that's all. How're your folks and Tex doing? Oh and how'd that last race go with Dakota? Where was that—in Lafayette, I think?" He'd learned early on that the best strategy for a weepy Haley was to change the subject and keep her talking. Never had he regretted the clean shave rule at Delhi quite as much as today. A full beard, or even a scruffy one, would have done wonders to hide the fact that he'd dropped another couple of pounds since their previous Skype session. He released his breath in relief as she began to answer his questions, knowing she did so for him.

"Mom and dad are fine, and so is Tex. They say hello, by the way. Tex is dating a paralegal or legal secretary now—something like that."

"He's not with Meagan's roommate anymore?"

"No, he blew it with Niki."

"I thought you said they were perfect for each other?"

"They were, but I somehow underestimated my brother's propensity for making bad decisions when it comes to women."

Ben reached out, touched the monitor, wishing he could hold her for a minute, but forced himself to smile and listen to her talk about her brother's escapades with women. Not that he cared, but the sound of her voice soothed him, as long as she wasn't fighting back tears or lost in a full blown cry session. Damn, he was crazy about this girl.

"Dakota and I placed first at the Lafayette event. It was worth about four hundred bucks, so that's good."

"That's awesome, babe. When's the next one?"

"There's one up in Vernon Parish next week, but I don't think I'll be able to make it." Her screen wobbled as her red terrier jumped up on her bed. "Paisley, no."

He laughed as Haley moved her dog off to the side, fussing at it to get out of the way. "She wanted to say hi."

Ben waved. "Hi Paisley, now get the hell off the keyboard before you cut us off." He crossed his arms and sat back, studying her. She'd worn her hair loose, and down around her shoulders. He knew that was for his benefit, otherwise, she'd have it pulled back in a ponytail. Boy, did he appreciate it. He couldn't help but smile when she caught the ends of one long, reddish brown lock and twirled it around her finger. The simple act caused his heart to ache with longing.

She stopped and sat up quickly. "What's wrong?" she asked, somehow alert to his shift in mood.

"Not a thing, but man I wish it was me twirling your hair like that. God, I can't wait to see you in Hawaii."

She released a groan. "Me either. Tell me about it again, Ben."

He leaned close to the monitor. "What do want to hear about, babe? The perfect Hawaiian weather, the beautiful white beaches, pristine waterfalls—or what I'm gonna do to you once I get you all to myself?" Her lips parted and one brow rose provocatively, drastically raising the tempo of his already thudding heart.

"Let's see . . ." She pursed those lips he could imagine wanting to kiss even when he was old and gray. "I can always Google the weather conditions on Oahu. I guess I am a little curious as to what you *think* you'll do to me when you get your hands on me over there. You'll need my permission, you know."

His chest rumbled with his reply before he even spoke the words. "Oh, I'll have your permission."

She coughed delicately. "You're sounding mighty sure of yourself, Corporal Bonin."

"I am. I'm sure of a lot of things, like how you won't be able to keep your hands off of me." His grin and wink made her burst into that throaty laughter that had him wanting to reach through that monitor and pull her back to his side.

She pointed a finger at the center of the screen. "Well, I'm not into skeletons, Benjamin, so you'd best start putting away some food. I want to see you with some meat on your bones. Speaking of which, you should be getting another package of goodies soon. I mailed them right after our last phone call. Chock a block full of Ramen noodles and oatmeal, your two favorite things. And I still can't believe you mix those two foods together to eat." She shuddered visibly. "Yuck."

"Don't change the subject, Haley."

"Did I?"

"We jumped from what I'm going to do to you in Kaneohe Bay, to food. I eat enough. You know we sometimes trim the excess off the packs to make it easier to travel the terrain. By the time you see me in May, there'll be more than enough of me to latch onto." He slapped his chest playfully. "There's a hell of a lot more going on under this gear than meets the eye. Trust me, babe."

She nodded, her eyes softening a bit. "I do, Benjamin. With all my heart."

Ben sobered for a moment before leaning in close, and placed both hands on either side of the monitor. Haley braced herself, predicting some heart-wrenching statement that would make her even more crazy about him than she already was.

"Listen to me, Haley."

She leaned forward. "I'm listening."

"I wouldn't be thinking about all the things I want to do with you over here, if I didn't care about you; if I didn't already suspect that you wanted the same thing. This isn't a game, to either of us. I know that about you, as well as myself."

Haley swallowed hard at his admission. *I know you want me, but do you love me, Ben? Do you go to sleep praying not to wake up if God takes me because you don't want to live in a world that doesn't include me? Because that's what I do—every night—that's what I do.* She lassoed all the possible comments, herding them to a silent corner of her conscience.

"No, it's definitely not a game." No way would she pour her feelings out to him during a Skype session, with no telling how many Marines, among others, listening in on their conversation. She studied him, his brown military issued skull-cap pulled down over his ears for warmth. Ben's breath turned to white puffs due to condensation from the cold. It irritated her to think he had no place he could go to warm up. "No heat in there?"

He shrugged. "I suppose they're running low on fuel for the generators again, and wood too for the heaters. It's no big deal."

"I can't help but worry about you over there." Ben adjusted the cap and tugged at the jacket that covered the multiple layers of undergarments he needed to keep warm during the cool Afghan winters. "What's the temperature over there?"

Ben cocked his head to one side, giving her a smug grin. "Really? We're talking about the weather now?"

She smiled, wishing she could kiss that smugness right off of his face. "Yes we are. Have you seen any snow yet?"

"Actually, there were a few flakes floating around as I walked over here." He turned in his chair as though to check something out. "Yep, it looks like we'll have a little on the ground by morning." He swiveled back around to face her. "It's probably around thirty degrees out there, but I'm warm enough. Can we get back to business, now?"

"Sure, tell me what the temperature will be like in Kaneohe Bay when I go in May."

Ben threw both hands in the air and laughed. "I give up. The girl is bound and determined to change the subject on me."

She beamed at him as Paisley crawled back onto her lap for a rub down. "I tell you what, Ben, Whatever you have 'planned' for me, I'm sure I'll love it." She leaned forward to let her next words hit their mark. "Every. Single. Second."

He swallowed hard, his Adam's apple bobbing before issuing a long, low groan. "Aw, man."

"What's wrong?"

"I'm thinking I'd give anything to be that dog right about now, that's all."

Haley glanced down at Paisley, four paws in the air, enjoying the belly rub from her mistress. She lifted her gaze to meet Ben's intense stare. "I'll pencil you in for a belly rub, babe, I promise."

"Don't think I'll let you forget that, either."

"I won't forget." She leaned in close and gave him a seductive wink. "As a matter of fact, I'll rub down anything you want me to."

"Anything?"

She nodded. "Anything."

He issued another low groan before letting his head fall with a loud thump onto the table.

"Suck it up, Marine," she said. "It's less than a year now, and—"

He popped his head up to finish for her. "And what's a year compared to forever?"

She smiled. "It's nothing, Ben. One year is absolutely nothing compared to forever."

Ben and the rest of his four-man team crossed the canal at its narrowest point, taking turns trudging through the waist deep water. A mile or so later, they did the combat boot version of tip-toeing south, past a Taliban village in the dead of the night. For a change, the wind was on their side, allowing them to travel without setting off the usual cacophony of barking dogs—the Taliban's version of ADT home security. Damn local dogs—those sons of bitches were a real pain in the U.S. military's ass. Another 200 meters got them where they were expected to pull off the mission. It was an ideal position, surveillance wise, but a dangerous choke point if anything compromised their location. Unless they could pull a Jesus and walk on water, the mile wide Helmand River at their back was a no-go as an escape route. With each man carrying 125-175 pounds of supplies, the deep canal in front of them was also un-crossable.

Ben and his TL dug into the canal's berm, creating a hide site big enough for the two of them, while the other two found suitable vegetation for coverage behind them. By sunrise, they had settled in, completely hidden from the enemy, and overlooking a muddy field. The second team set up 500 meters straight ahead of them, while the known Taliban village of Krum sat 600 meters to the left of Ben's team.

He stifled a yawn and grabbed his binos to check out the area. Several farmers passed them on the way to work in their fields, and Ben made a silent bet with himself on how long it would take to get some Taliban activity. Instead, a movement at the end of the berm caught his eye, causing a severe roiling in the pit of his stomach. "Hey, Sarge. We got a kid and his dog heading this way."

"Oh, man, are you serious?" He picked up his own binos to confirm. "Well, sure e-fucking-nough. Here he comes. Nothing to do but wait until he gets close enough to see us. If he doesn't catch sight of us, that mangy ass dog of his will," he growled. "All we can do is haul ass back to the crossing point before he gets a chance to run home and tell his Taliban daddy. We'll have to make it there before he and his buddies, or they'll sure as shit cut us off."

They waited until the kid was practically inside their dig-out before Balls jumped up. He pointed an MK in the kid's face, and the poor thing looked as though he was about to shit his pants. The snarling dog bared his teeth and the rifle shifted directions, right at the animal's head. The kid, obviously afraid for his companion's life, pulled the dog back by its scruff and turned pleading eyes toward the Marine.

"Go ahead." Balls flicked the barrel of his firearm in the direction of the village. "Go back and tell your pop we're here." Everyone knew the kid didn't understand a word of English, but it wouldn't stop him from doing exactly that. The kid turned and ran back the direction he'd come from. His dog gave them a few half-assed snarls, and then followed suit.

"Shit. Call main, Badge. Tell 'em we're RTB. Let's move out."

"Roger that, Sarge."

Ben shoved his spotting scope, binos, logbook, and thermals into his go-bag. He and Balls jumped off the berm to meet the others. They got their rucksacks on as Badge and D-Dub held security, and then did the same as the other two packed up the radio and their own gear.

Ben took the lead, setting the pace for the others. Under normal circumstances, he could run a mile with 175 pounds strapped to him with no problem. Add the complications of muddy fields and sleep deprivation, and it raised the difficulty bar by several points. His mud-caked boots fought for solid ground as he kept his rifle pointed at the village and compounds they'd snuck quietly by the previous night. Ben kept a constant check on his flanks, and prayed the berm wasn't hiding a group of hadjis preparing to attack. Adrenaline pumping through his body, he ran blind for a full mile without being able to see if the Taliban fighters would be there to intercept them at any second.

Dead tired and dragging their asses, the four of them arrived at the crossing, amazed they hadn't heard the sound of men on motorcycles by then. They took a knee to check out the situation. The crossing was simply a canal that went from knee deep to waist high, with a cut out for the berm. The opposite bank contained lots of shrubs and vegetation—plenty of places for the hadjis to hide. The other three set up observation, watching for any movement on the far bank, as Ben waded through the water, extremely open to attack. Once he made it to the other side, he kept a close watch while the others crossed over.

Significantly less vulnerable but still in danger, they took a knee to wait for the second team to link up at their position. Thankfully, it happened quickly and Ben led the two teams at a full out run all the way back to the PB in broad daylight, and with a failed mission under their belts—two of the most unwelcome situations for any sniper unit.

No sooner had the eight men crossed into friendly lines than Main called in. The FOB's Aerostat blimp had picked up images of their abandoned hide site being overrun by nine hadjis armed with AK's. Armed with that information, Ben dragged ass to his spot at the PB, exhausted and thirsty. He downed the bottles of water they had waiting for him and peeled off his gear, too damned wiped out to think of anything—not even how easily shit could have hit the fan. He dropped onto his cot and fell asleep within seconds.

"Bones, I gotta talk to you, man."

Ben's eyelids fluttered open at the sound of urgency in D-dub's voice. "What?" He sat up quickly, throwing his legs over his bed.

"She dumped me, Bones."

His forehead pulled down in a frown. "Who?"

"Samantha, my girl—she dumped me."

"Shit man. I'm sorry about that." He craned his neck to look up at his buddy. "You okay?"

"Hell no, I'm not okay. She told me she'd wait for me and now she's not." He shrugged. "I mean, I ain't gonna slit my wrist open or anything like that. But this sucks, you know?"

Ben gazed up at his buddy, truly sick at heart for him. God knows how he'd feel if Haley threw him aside. He'd be a basket case. "How'd she tell you?"

"Over the fucking sat phone."

"I mean, how'd she actually say the words? Was she a bitch about it?" God help her if she was. He hoped like hell she hadn't flaunted a new man under the poor bastard's nose.

"No. She was crying when she said it. In fact, it didn't sound like she even wanted to do it." He scratched at his head. "Something sounds off, man."

"Well, shit, bro. I don't know what to tell you. Sit on it for a while and try talking to her again later?"

"If she even answers my calls, man. She told me it'd be best not to call her back."

Ben rested a hand on his buddy's shoulder. "She could change her mind, D. Maybe she needs time to think about things. You don't know what's going on over there."

D-dub stood abruptly. "That's what bugs me. I *don't* know what the hell's going on over there." He shook his head, opened his mouth as though to speak, and closed it. Without another word, he spun around and walked away, leaving Ben to watch his retreat.

Ben fell back in his cot, determined to get a little more shut-eye. Unfortunately, D-dub's predicament refused to vacate the confines of his mind. What would he do if Haley told him not to bother calling back? What kind of shape would he be in if she decided not to wait for him?

Like shit warmed over.

He couldn't help but wonder if this situation would influence D-dub's performance during missions. Hell, something like that could upset the entire team. Any single thing one man did out there, had an effect on the rest of the team. Was it even worth taking the risk of having a girl back home if there was the slightest possibility she would dump you?

Ben closed his eyes, pulled up the mental image of Haley, all soft innocence and smiling one minute, and sexy as hell the next.

Was she worth taking the risk?

He smiled, remembering the feel of his hands on her tight little body, the look on her gorgeous face, down to the freckles on her sun-kissed nose. Then he thought of the sparkle in her eyes every time she graced him with one of her beautiful smiles.

Hell yeah, she was worth the risk . . . but only sometimes.

Like every damned second of every damned day.

The last failed attempt behind them, Ben's team planned a follow-up mission, this time completing it successfully. They hoofed it back to the patrol base in a miserable light drizzle that only added to the piss-poor travel conditions of the already soggy soil. During the trip back, the skies darkened, rolling with thunder and the promise of a full blown storm. They RTB'd about an hour before sunrise, thankfully before the heavens opened to release the deluge it had threatened for hours. For a place that got virtually no precipitation, it seemed to be getting its yearly allotment of rainfall in a single week.

No sooner had they reported in, they received the news of another fallen brother. No one on his team had known the Marine, personally, but that didn't matter. Out there, the loss of a Marine brother hit everyone hard. Without fail, everyone's first concern was "Who did he leave behind?" This particular Marine departed this world, leaving a wife with no husband, and a two-year-old son with no daddy. That tragedy, along with the miserable weather, made for a darkened mood among the sniper platoon.

Ben hit his corner of the hesco wall and dropped his gear. He sat for a good ten minutes, exhausted to his core, wanting nothing more than to hear a voice from home. As though God had answered his prayers personally, D-Dub appeared, his face a mask of somberness, despite the good news he delivered.

"Hey man. Thought you'd want to know, the SAT phone's free if you want to call your girl."

Ben stood quickly. "Thanks man, I appreciate it. Did you call Samantha yet to see if she'd changed her mind?"

"I did, bro. Some dick answered the phone. Guess I got the answer I was looking for."

Ben paused long enough to cast a concerned eye over his brother. "Damn, D, that sucks. I'm sorry about that. You all right?"

D-Dub shrugged and passed a hand through his hair. "Screw her, man. There are plenty of women out there who'll appreciate what I do. I don't need shit like that in my life."

"You got that right." He placed a hand on D-Dub's shoulder anyway, feeling blessed for having Haley.

"Besides, it's quicker this way, you know what I mean?"

"I guess so. I'm sorry man," he mumbled, as his friend preceded him out of the tent. "I'm gonna go make that call, now. But you be sure and let me know if you need to talk or something, okay?" He slapped his buddy on the back and went in search of the phone, praying he'd have a clear enough signal to get through.

Two minutes later, he heard the familiar ringing of a stateside phone, and despite the cold, he sat there sweating over whether she would pick up or not. Finally, a frantic voice picked up.

"Ben?"

"It's me, Haley."

"Oh my God, it's good to hear your voice. I heard the phone ringing when I was showering, and I had this feeling it was you."

"I interrupted your shower?"

"Yes, and I'm dripping all over the tile. I'm freezing my butt off, as a matter of fact."

"Want me to call ba—"

"Don't you *dare* hang up this phone. I've been dying for some word from you. I wasn't expecting it tonight. Is something wrong?"

He turned to motion at another Marine who'd also arrived to use the phone. "Not with me. I'm fine, but it's been a crappy day. I wanted to make sure you knew I was all right. Can you call my folks for me?"

"I surely will do that. God, you don't know how much I miss you."

"I think I do, babe. I can't talk long, Haley. But, I wanted to tell you how much I appreciate you being there for me."

"Ben, what else is going on?"

"A couple of things. We uh, we lost someone yesterday."

"Oh no. Somebody you knew?"

"No, not from my team or anything, but damn, he had a wife and kid, Haley." Her breath escaped in a half sob. He should have known the news would make her cry, as soft-hearted as she was.

"Oh God, I'll keep his family in my prayers." She sniffed before continuing. "What else, Benjamin?"

"What?"

"You said a couple of things happened. What else?"

"Oh, yeah—uh, D-Dub's girl dumped him. She found someone else."

"Oh. I'm so sorry for him, but you know I won't do that to you, right? You don't have to check up on me, even if I'm thrilled by your unexpected calls."

"I know that. I just needed to hear your voice." He paused for several seconds. "Haley?"

"Yeah, Ben?"

He thought he heard her teeth chattering. "Ah, shit, you're standing there soaking wet and freezing. I need to let you go." *Yeah, like before I make a fool out of myself.*

"Ben, you sound a little—I don't know—off kilter. Are you sure there's nothing else wrong?"

The thought of her standing there, freezing her cute little ass off to get another minute of conversation with him, made him feel fucking awesome. "So, are you completely naked? Or half-ass wrapped in a thin little towel?" Her laughter rang out, lifting his spirits further.

"Not naked, and yes, I am only half-ass wrapped. But at least it's a big, thick towel." She clucked her tongue at him. "You are so bad."

"I can be as bad as you want me to be." He grinned at her nervous laughter, knowing she'd be embarrassed as hell if she knew what his mental image of her was doing to him. "God, Haley—I love y—your laugh." He coughed, realizing what he'd almost let slip. If her lack of reply was any indication, she realized it, too. Haley finally broke the uncomfortable stretch of *what-the-hell-do-I-say-now?*

"Ben?"

"I need to go now. There are guys here waiting for the phone."

"I know."

"Will you say it for me?" He didn't have to wonder if she knew what he was talking about. She'd be smiling as she gave him her reply.

"What's one year? It's nothing compared to forever."

"Roger that, babe. Talk to you later."

January 31st – Afghanistan 06:52 hours

I almost fucked up—I almost let those words slip out. The ones I swore I wouldn't tell her unless it was to her face. It may sound chicken shit to some, but I can't, I won't say them the first time over the phone. She deserves better than that. A hell of a lot better than that. I gotta tighten up when I talk to her. Can't be a big puss when I talk to her over the phone. Lesson learned—Do NOT call Haley unless I have my shit together. I know she felt it, heard it in my voice— she knew I was holding back. I hope like hell I didn't hurt her feelings. If I did, I'll make it up to her. I know she wants me to tell her. I know she wants me to say the words first. I know she's stopping herself from saying it because she's afraid if she does, I'll be gone. That's not the case, but how the hell would she know that? She wouldn't. Even if she said them to me over the phone, or in a text, or an email, or during a Skype session, I still wouldn't say them back. Not that way—not until I can show her, face to fucking face, how much those words mean to me. And man...do I plan to show her. Valentine's Day won't mean shit to me over here, but I plan on making it mean something to her back home. Please God, let Haley hang in there. I promise I'll make it up to her if she does.

Chapter 10

Throw Me Something, Mister!

Haley sat on top of her bed with her open laptop, willing the Skype screen to activate, bringing the image, the voice of Ben to her. She pressed a hand to her stomach, wishing away the butterflies she always got while waiting for any contact from the love of her life. No, she hadn't told him yet, but surely, he had to know. Every night she prayed he could sense her love from all the way on the other side of the world, could feel it surround and protect him over there. She chewed her thumbnail in nervous anticipation. Any minute now.

The familiar swishing sound interrupted the thought. Her gaze practically burned a hole into the middle of the screen until Ben's face finally appeared. He beamed at her, obviously having received the box she and his mother had sent. Mardi Gras beads draped around his neck, hanging from his ears and off of his sunglasses.

"Happy Mardi Gras, Haley."

"Hey, Benjamin. I see you got the box of goodies. Did you play pretty and share with the other guys?"

"I shared the beads, mom's platoon cookies, and most of the hard candy. But you know I don't share my Snicker Doodles. Thanks babe."

"You're very welcome. You seem to be in a good mood. What's going on?"

He leaned in closer to give her a wink. "You'll see soon enough."

Haley leaned back against her headboard and adjusted the laptop. "Are we going to play this game again? You know I can't stand the suspense, so why the hell do you tell me these things?"

His laughter sounded over her speakers. "Because I *know* you can't stand the suspense." He leaned forward again, giving her an adorable grin. "I only do it to give you something to look forward to, of course. Is it working?"

She sighed. "I look forward to so many things where you're concerned, it's not even funny."

He sobered abruptly, sent her a look so full of promise she shivered. "The same goes for me. Some days, it's all I can do not to think about it."

"Think about what, in particular?" She knew what the answer would be, but wanted to hear him say it again.

"Kaneohe Bay—being with you in Hawaii. In your bikini, or wrapped with one of those scarf things the girls wear over there—"

"Sarongs . . ."

"Yeah, those. I can picture you, a tropical flower tucked in your hair, with one of those sarongs tied around your hips, knotted on one side." He held up a finger. "But I can still see your belly button, you know? And it's so fu— flipping sexy, I want to dip my tongue in it." Her low growl had him grinning. "You want me to stop now?"

She gave her head a brief shake, determined not to let his self-satisfied expression do her in. "Nope. If you can take it, I can too."

"Oh—good. Then I'll tell you how I can already feel what it'll be like to wrap my hands around your waist and pull you close—to dip my mouth into the crook of your neck. I'll have to pull back all of that glorious hair of yours to do it, though. So, I'll pull it back with one hand and hold you close with the other—and then I'll kiss that spot that drives you crazy. You know, that spot?"

"You mean my ticklish spot?"

He laughed huskily. "All your spots are ticklish. I have never known anyone as ticklish as you are." He cut off her near comeback. "But that's okay. It's a sign your body will be responsive in so many other ways."

Her breath released in a rush. "Okay, you really need to stop that now."

"So I guess you can't take it."

She barely kept from rolling her eyes at him. "I guess you're right. You win again."

"It's not a matter of winning and losing, babe. It's a matter of getting you so worked up you won't be able to think of anyone but me."

"I already can't think of anyone but you. You—talking to me that way—saying those things to me—it makes it . . ." She stopped, uncertain how to finish.

"It makes you anticipate what I'm going to do to you . . ."

"Uh huh . . ." she said, breathlessly.

"And anticipation makes pleasure more intense."

She frowned. "Says who?"

He sent her his signature sexy grin. "Some chick whose book you downloaded on my Kindle."

"Are you telling me I gave you the information you're using to torture me?"

"Don't think of it as torture, babe. Think of it as . . ." he stopped, seemed to consider his next words. "Think of it as preparing yourself for a world of pleasure." He leaned forward again. "Think you can do that?"

She fanned her face. "I think I'm having some kind of thermal reaction moment."

He lifted both hands in victory. "Then my work here is done."

Her hand dropped helplessly onto the bed. "Now see. That's just mean."

"Not mean. Determined—when I get you alone, you'll beg me to do all sorts of things to you."

She cocked her head to the side, deciding she could give as well as she got. "How do you know you won't be the one doing all the begging, Benjamin?"

"Because if I can't make you want me as much as I want you, not a damn thing's gonna happen in there, or anywhere else, for that matter. I'm not about to pressure you into doing anything you don't want to do. That's not how you deserve to be treated."

"How do I—aw, Paisley." She screeched as her dog chose that moment to jump on the bed and try to curl up on her lap. She scooted out of the bed and carried her laptop to her desk, never losing sight of Ben. She settled herself in the desk chair and adjusted her screen. "Now, what were we talking about?"

"You were about to ask how you deserved to be treated," he said, grinning at her. "And my answer would be—with respect."

Haley covered her mouth with one hand and blinked several times to clear the fog of tears from her eyes. "You warned me how competitive you were, but this is insane. Will you ever let me win?"

He leaned forward, so he was close to the monitor and looked straight into her eyes. "Babe, when I finally get you all to myself, I'll make sure you win in every way possible—as often as you want—and in as many ways as you want. That's a guarantee."

Haley fanned the heat from her face, knowing her blood pressure was probably through the roof.

"You okay over there?" he asked, wearing his typical 'one-up' shit-eating grin.

"I'll live. I keep wondering, if you can make me feel this way with your words . . ." She didn't have the nerve to finish her thought. As usual, Ben had no problem finishing it for her.

"I can hardly wait to make you feel in so many other ways . . ."

Ben walked back to sniper platoon's tent, more confident than ever in his relationship with Haley. If she had any doubts about the lengths he was willing to go to make her happy, after Valentine's Day, those doubts would be long gone. He'd put that particular plan in motion weeks ago, without her knowledge, of course. He loved surprising Haley. Maybe it was because nobody had ever been able to surprise him—not even as a kid. He'd always had the ability to read people, and for the most part, knew they tended to give themselves away.

He got a tremendous amount of satisfaction from making this particular girl's eyes light up with pleasure every single time he did something unexpected. He'd seen it on dozens of occasions back home. From something as simple as handing her a single pansy from his mother's fall flower garden to giving her dog, Paisley, a bath for the heck of it. She appreciated any small effort he made to make her smile. That, in turn, made him want to do anything in his power to keep a smile on Haley's face.

She'd made the mistake of telling him her brother, Tex, had made plans to attend the Lake Coburn Mardi Gras parade with his girlfriend and friends. He promptly made her promise to go along, insisting it was the largest in the area, second only to New Orleans. He'd even encouraged her to participate with his siblings in what would be her very first Courir de Mardi Gras. It was the Cajun tradition of the 'Chicken Run'—an all-day ride on horseback, culminating in a huge meal of gumbo and potato salad, along with a Cajun dance for the participants.

"And I'll want to see proof, so you'd better have plenty of pictures and videos with *you* in them," he'd warned. Every plan he made for Haley was to keep her from sitting at home, miserable and missing him.

Was he worried she'd have a little too much fun with some other guy? Nope. Nor did he worry she'd stand him up in May. Neither did he worry that once she left him in Kaneohe Bay, she'd go home and forget all about him. He didn't have room in his life for doubts.

He reached the tent and maneuvered to his own bunk without making a sound. He laid there, his hands clasped behind his neck as he thought of life post Corps, with his girl in it.

He was damned-sure willing to put every egg he had into one basket, and that basket was Haley.

"Throw me something mister!" Haley reached up and caught a handful of brightly colored beads. "Thank you!" she shouted and waved back at one of dozens of passing floats. She lifted Tex's cowboy hat, and looped them around his already bead-decked neck before replacing the hat.

"There you go, big brother."

"You doing all right up there, sis?" Tex tapped the boot resting against his chest.

"I'm fine, but if you're tired of carrying me around on your shoulders, you can let me down," she insisted.

"Nah. You don't weigh a damn thing, girl."

"*That* must be nice," Aubrey commented from beside Tex. "Nobody's been able to say that about me since I was a little bitty baby."

Haley shouted over the crowd noise. "At least you're tall enough to see the floats without having to sit on somebody's shoulders. I'd love to be your size."

Aubrey danced in place, shaking her head to the tune from a passing Cajun band situated on a float. "Well, I've got to admit; my size comes in handy for carnival season. If anybody tries to steal my beads, I bump them outta my way and scoop 'em right up." She slapped one hip for emphasis.

His sister laughed at the sweet lady he considered a 'friend'. As wonderful as Aubrey was, he had to admit, eventually, that she didn't come close to replacing Niki.

"Coming down, sis." Tex lowered Haley gently to the ground and straightened, adjusting the sizeable collection of beads around his neck. "I think this parade's going to wrap up in about thirty minutes or so. How do you two ladies feel about going someplace for a bite to eat? I had a late lunch and no supper. I'm about starved."

"Sure. You want steaks, seafood, Mexican, Asian, fast food? I can name a dozen good restaurants on this street alone."

Haley's head popped up. "My vote is for Mexican."

Tex turned to Aubrey. "You got a problem with eating Mexican tonight?"

She shook her head. "Nope, and Casa Manana is down the street." She nudged Haley with her elbow. "Best margaritas in town, as long as your brother's driving, right?"

"You got that right."

Fifteen minutes later, Tex had somehow maneuvered his truck on the side streets to park behind the building. The three of them piled into the restaurant, thankfully, before everyone else in town had the same idea. It was crowded, but not to capacity. Even though, they seated themselves at the bar to wait for their table. Within minutes of that, Haley was sucking up a margarita, while Aubrey sipped at a glass of chardonnay. Tex threw back a bottle of beer to quench his thirst, and then asked for a tall glass of cola before following their waitress into the main dining room.

The three of them had already ordered from the menu when their hostess sat another couple at the table next to them. Tex reached for his drink, his arm freezing mid-air as Niki's gaze locked onto his. Instead of seating herself in the chair Bo had pulled out for her, she turned to the hostess and whispered something.

The hostess shook her head. "I'm sorry, Miss, but we don't have any available tables by a window."

Bo examined the table, obviously confused by her request. "What's wrong with this table, Niki? We were damned lucky to get it, considering the parade crowd about to swarm this place."

Niki looped her purse strap over her shoulder. "You know, I don't think I feel like Mexican tonight. Let's go back to that steakhouse you talked about. You deserve to have a steak."

Clearly exasperated, Bo scanned their surroundings, his gaze encompassing his neighbors seated a few feet over. He grunted and turned to the hostess. "This table is fine, ma'am. Don't worry about moving us." He pulled a chair out for Niki. "Sit. You insisted on Casa, you're damned well getting Casa." Looking sheepish, Niki sat and began to fidget with her purse.

Bo took two steps over to greet the three people at the next table. He reached for Tex's outstretched hand first. "Good to see you again, Tex . . . ladies."

"You too, Bo. Are y'all coming from the parade as well?"

"Yep, but we were parked all the way on the other end, at the starting point. I thought it would be easier to leave and avoid the heaviest traffic downtown." His gaze followed Niki's trek to the women's restroom. "We by-passed several perfectly good restaurants and my favorite steakhouse all because somebody *had* to have Casa."

Tex lifted his shoulders. "Sorry man, the ladies picked it. I just do the driving."

Bo raised his hands. "I hear you, man." He acknowledged his sister first. "Haley, did you catch enough beads to last you all year?"

She nodded. "I have bags full." She lifted one she wore from her neck. "But this one is my favorite." The necklace boasted giant green, purple, and gold two or three inch diameter balls. "I'm going to bring it to Ben when I meet him in Hawaii in May."

Bo leaned over to examine it. "That's a nice one, all right. They don't throw many that size, so you were lucky to catch it."

Tex snorted at the comment. "That damn thing almost knocked me out. Hell, I may still end up with a black eye from where it slapped me."

"You should have negotiated for hazard pay."

"I would have, if I'd known it was coming."

Bo turned to Aubrey. "Where are your beads? Don't tell me little bit here, grabbed them all."

She waved her hand. "I donated all mine to the Haley Broussard cause. This was her very first Lake Coburn Mardi Gras parade."

Bo's face registered surprise. "And how'd you like it?"

Haley sent him an enthusiastic nod. "I loved it. It's bigger than the one we usually go to in Port Arthur. This one has some really gorgeous floats."

"It's supposed to be second only to New Orleans in this state."

"That's why Ben wanted me to come to this one. I also participated in my first 'Chicken Run' today. That was so much fun. And our dad was happy about it, because he said it brings us back to our Cajun roots. He remembers going with his Paw Paw Broussard when he was a little boy."

"Ah—the Courir de Mardi Gras. Where'd you run?"

Haley's eyes sparkled with excitement. "It was a small one in Lake Erin, Ben's hometown. I went with his younger brother and sister. Next year, when he's home, he's going to take me to some place called Fred's."

Bo burst into laughter. "Fred's in Mamou, Louisiana—the reputation far exceeds its physical attributes, but that place is steeped in Cajun tradition. You have to go at least once in your lifetime."

"What is it, exactly?" Tex asked.

"It's a bar that's been around forever," Bo said.

Aubrey laughed. "My dad used to say it dated back to prehistoric man, but I think it opened in the mid nineteen-forties."

Bo's gaze seemed to linger on Aubrey. "I take it you've been?" he asked her.

Tex didn't feel the slightest bit of jealousy as Bo zoned in on his "date", further proof that there was nothing but friendship between Aubrey and himself. In his opinion, Aubrey was a much better fit for Bo McAllister than Nicole ever would be.

"Three or four Lundi Gras celebrations and several Saturday morning broadcasts, in my younger days," Aubrey admitted. "I haven't been in about five years, though. Is Taunt Sue still running the place?"

"As far as I know she is. It's been awhile for me, too. To tell you the truth, I'm not sure I can handle my alcohol at 8 o'clock in the morning anymore."

Tex issued a low whistle. "Eight a.m.? Lundi Gras? I don't know what y'all are talking about. And who the hell is Taunt Sue?"

Aubrey burst into laughter. "Sorry, Tex—you fit in so well around us that I sometimes forget you aren't from here. The original owner of the bar, Fred, died decades ago, but his ex-wife, Miss Sue, runs the place now. Everyone calls her Taunt Sue—"

"Tante—t-a-n-t-e—is French for the word, aunt," Bo explained. "You see, Fred's used to be a regular bar with regular hours and they've had a Saturday morning radio show since the early sixties."

Aubrey picked up the explanation again. "But now, they only open on Saturday mornings for the live radio broadcast. 8 a.m. to noon or so—you have to get there early to get a spot because it's standing room only for a solid four hours."

"Except for Lundi Gras, or Fat Monday, which is the Monday before Mardi Gras," Bo added. "And let me tell you—that is a hell of a party."

By that time, Niki had returned to the table, and sat patiently looking over the menu. The waitress appeared, forcing her to speak, since Bo hadn't seemed to notice her return.

"I hate to break up the chit chat, Bo, but are you ready to order?"

He turned to Niki, looking a little surprised—and if Tex had to guess at Bo's mindset, he'd say somewhat disappointed to leave his present company. But, being the gentleman he was obviously raised to be, he returned to his date.

Tex managed to keep his attention fully on the ladies at his table throughout the meal. If the truth be told, it wouldn't have done much good to do otherwise, being that Niki had seated herself with her back to his table—purposely, no doubt. Even though, his mind strayed to occasional thoughts of her—her laughter, her scent, the feel of her in his arms, the little noises she made when she was about to . . . *Oh hell* . . . he threw his napkin on the table and leaned back in his chair.

"Are you finally done?"

He nodded, widening his eyes at Aubrey's question. "I'm stuffed. But that was damn good grub, even for a Mexican restaurant in Cajun country."

Aubrey nodded at his plate. "You did it justice, my friend. Two baskets of tortilla chips, about four bowls of salsa, the biggest dinner they offer here, and not a bit left." She shook her head. "It must be nice to be able to eat like that and still not have an ounce of fat on you."

He shrugged. "I work with horses all day. A person tends to burn off a lot of calories trying to control thirteen hundred plus pounds of animal. And some of 'em don't make it easy, believe me."

"Do you have a favorite?" she asked, as the waitress delivered the check for their table.

"Well, sure. My own horse is my favorite. But Captain Perry can be a stubborn SOB."

Haley's snort punctuated her follow-up. "That horse is a freak. He's what, Matty—16 and a half hands high? God, he's huge."

Aubrey grinned at Tex. "Well, your brother would look silly with his legs dragging the ground on any normal sized horse, right?"

Tex sent her an adamant nod. "Damn straight—a big guy needs a big horse." He turned to send his little sister an indulgent smile. "I'm sorry mom and dad ran out of the growth gene before you came along, Popcorn."

"Not half as sorry as I am, dammit."

Aubrey reached out to pat her hand. "Your Marine doesn't seem to mind. All those roses, diamond studs, and an all-expense paid round-trip ticket to Hawaii? You must have something he likes."

Tex grunted in disapproval. "Hm—sounds more like she's got something he wants."

Haley sent her brother a wicked glare. "And he might get it, too."

Tex shifted in his chair. "Now, see, I didn't need to hear that."

"Then you should keep your hypocritical comments to yourself," she countered.

He pointed a finger at her. "If you don't behave yourself, I may buy a ticket and fly with you to act as your chaperone. I'll make damn sure you two never get a minute alone. I'm sure mom and dad wouldn't mind a bit." Haley started that side-to-side head bob women loved to execute while making a point.

"I'm twenty-one years old, big brother. I don't need you preaching to me."

"I don't care how old you are—you will always be my baby sister."

She raised her hand. "I'm not listening to a second of the old double-standard BS you're spouting. Not when you go through women like water through a rusty bucket." She stopped suddenly, her eyes wide with horror, and covered her mouth. "Oh, Aubrey. I'm so sorry. I didn't meant that you . . . that y'all . . . that you're just . . ." She sighed, dropping her shoulders in shame. "I'll shut up, now."

Thankfully, Aubrey didn't seem offended. "I might take offense if I was one of the many women your brother will *go through*." She shot a glance in his direction. "He hasn't yet, and I think it's safe to say he never will." She laughed, as Tex pulled an imaginary dagger from his heart. "Oh stop it. You know as well as I do, we're both only here to have a little fun." She reached over to pat his hand. "As much as it pains me to say this, you remind me too much of my own brothers." She cringed a little then shook her head and laughed. "But I adore hanging out and showing the two of you around."

Tex nodded. "And we appreciate it, too. Hell, you may want to look into a career change. You're about the best looking tour guide I've ever seen."

"Aw, thanks—*Matty*." She laughed at the face Tex made. "I think it's adorable how Haley calls you that."

Tex placed the tab amount plus an extra twenty in the folder and handed it to the waitress, telling her to keep the change. "When Haley was a little ol' fart, she could not pronounce my name. Mom always called me Matthew, but when she tried, it sounded like a sneeze. Mat-choo." He grinned at his sister. "So mom taught her to say Matty." He stood and stretched, arching his back. "I've got some business to attend to for a minute, ladies, and then I'll be ready to go."

Niki touched-up her make-up in the bathroom mirror for the third time. She checked her phone again, finally deciding enough time had gone by. Surely, Tex and his entourage had left by now. She couldn't stand one more minute of listening to their animated conversation, especially when she and Bo had barely spoken a word to each other. She knew he was pissed at her, and she couldn't blame him. In her own defense, the sight of Tex had taken her by surprise. As had the fact that Tex was with that woman again. While Bo considered her request for another table as childish and rude, she knew it had merely been her self-defense mechanism kicking into overdrive. She'd had to settle for seating herself with her back facing them. Still—every laugh, every word spoken by that sexy baritone, had launched an out and out attack on her nervous system.

Why did all the sexiest guys have to be jerks?

She exited the ladies room and stepped into the corridor leading back to the eating area. As soon as she rounded the corner, she came face to chest with a huge wall of sexiness in a blue chambray shirt.

"Excuse me, miss. Did I hurt yo . . ." The apology froze in mid-air as Tex realized who he'd come close to plowing over.

She nearly lost her breath at his close proximity. She inhaled, disturbed by her sudden light-headedness, and wondered if the man showered in testosterone. Unfortunately, their gazes had already locked and she had no other alternative but to stand her ground. Lurid images of him with a pole dancer flashed through her mind like an X-rated movie—and all while she waited at home for a call that never came.

"Yes. You did." Mortified by her trembling voice, as well as an unexpected and overwhelming urge to cry, she side-stepped the giant of a man.

"Nicole . . ." Tex reached for her.

Niki had been ready for it, twisting easily out of his reach. She took the longest route she could find back to the table, blinking quickly to clear the fog of tears hampering her sight. By the time she made it to Bo, she'd recovered completely.

Looping her purse strap over her shoulder, she smiled at Bo. "I'm ready when you are, sweetie." She aimed a quick glance at the other table and gave Haley a half-hearted wave before heading toward the exit.

By the time Bo started his truck, Niki's teeth chattered from her nervous tension, and her head pounded with the beginnings of a migraine.

Thank you Tex.

Her misery complete, as far as she was concerned, this night couldn't end soon enough.

Chapter 11

Valentine's Day Indulgence

Haley groaned with pleasure as the massage chair worked its magic on her. She released a long, languid sigh as the nail technician wrapped her second foot in a hot towel and placed it gently on the footrest.

"Have you chosen your color yet?"

"This one." She lifted the card resting in her lap and tapped the pale rose color.

"Ah . . . good choice."

"How are you doing over there, Haley?"

She turned to address Ben's mom. "I'm great. This feels so good, Ms. Monica. How about you?"

"Like a million bucks. Pedicures are the best, aren't they? I'm feeling very pampered right now."

Haley nodded. "You and me, both. I've had pedicures before but never the full spa treatment." She settled her head back on the chair rest and released a long, low sigh. "I could sleep here all day long."

Monica gave a low chuckle. "The people here at Scarborough's know what they're doing, that's for darn sure."

"Mmmm. So does your son. I never expected him to do something like this. He continues to surprise me in so many ways."

"He's a good kid."

"He's an amazing man. You obviously raised him to respect women."

"I tried. You're welcome, by the way."

Haley laughed as she faced Monica again. "Thank you, ma'am."

"Ben always was a good boy—extremely considerate—didn't give me too much trouble. I mean, there was the normal stuff like a little too much partying during high school. I'm a mom. Mom's worry, so I stayed on his butt about that. Of course, he was an athlete, so his coaches urged him to take good care of himself, as well. That helped."

"You taught him responsibility."

Monica laughed. "I may have started the ball rolling— taught them all to pitch in around the house. They all had chores to do before they could go out and spend time with their friends. I guess we've got to give the Marines the real credit." She sighed. "They made him a man, but he'll always be my little boy." She turned to Haley and smiled. "You'll see when you have kids one day." She paused before continuing. "You do want to have kids one day, right? Because I'm not ashamed to admit I'm dying to be a grandmother." Her hand flew out. "Not right now, of course, but I know there are women these days who, for some reason or the other, don't want to bring children into this world."

"Oh, I'm not one of them. I want kids someday. My mom is like you, though. She's chomping at the bit for grandchildren. Every time one of her friends pulls out one of those grandparents' brag books, my mom complains. She says the Marines robbed her of at least fifteen years of doting."

"She can't blame all of that on the military. Plenty of career Marines have families while they serve. Maybe your brother didn't want to drag a family through the military lifestyle. All of that moving around gets kind of rough."

Haley's smile faded. "It's a little more than that, Ms. Monica. Towards the end of that two week period we hadn't heard from Ben, I was miserable. On edge, terrified and snapping at everyone. Matty told me that was why he'd decided early on not to settle down until he was out of the military. He said he'd seen too many people die over there. Good people, Marines and otherwise, with wives, husbands, children, families waiting for them at home, families who would never see their loved ones again—or not alive, anyway."

She paused and took a deep breath. "So, yeah. He made a choice, but you're right. He did it for all the right reasons." She turned toward Monica, saw her brush away a tear. "My mom says she can finally sleep at night now that he's home for good."

Monica's face crumbled as she slapped one hand over her eyes. "Oh God . . . I can't wait for that."

Haley blinked back tears and smiled. "Me either. I fall asleep praying for him every night." She took the hand that Ben's mother extended from the massage chair next to hers.

"You're the first, Haley. You know that, right?"

"The first?"

"The first girl he's really cared about enough to count. The first since he's been in the Marines, for sure. I'm glad he's got somebody else who cares about him as much as I do."

"I'm crazy about him, Ms. Monica. I really am."

"You're in love with my son, aren't you?"

"Yes, ma'am, I am. And I want him home for good, safe and sound."

The older woman's face sobered suddenly. "What if he comes home safe, but not quite so sound, Haley? Would you still want him then?"

Haley gave her hand a gentle squeeze. "As long as he comes back with the same heart, I'll want him. As long as he wants me around, I'll be here."

Monica dabbed at the corner of her eyes and gave her a brisk nod. "That's all I needed to know."

Haley dug into her salad at the Italian restaurant Monica chose for lunch. Ben's Valentine's Day gift, a four hour spa package, hadn't ended until 2 p.m. and by then both women were famished.

"I love the salads here—black olives, red onions, and croutons—yum." Monica popped an olive in her mouth and carefully fished a pickled pepper from her bowl with fingertips that boasted a fresh French manicure.

Haley examined the digits closely. "Your nails are pretty. Mine are always so short."

"It doesn't seem practical to have long nails when you work with horses."

She took another bite of salad and closed her eyes, still relaxed from the Swedish massage. "Mm—it's so good. My stomach growled during my entire massage. By the time she finished I was way past being embarrassed about it."

Monica used her fork as a pointer. "That's because of your fast metabolism. I'd trade my nails for that any old day."

"It's fine as long as I've got the opportunity to eat when I get hungry. But when I get in a situation like today, it can get a little rough." She turned at the sound of a familiar voice to the left of her, saw Bo McAllister and Niki being shown in to the dining area. "Hey, there's my brother's ex, Niki Reeves and her new boyfriend. The last time they showed up at the same restaurant as me, it didn't go so well."

The waitress appeared with the entrees and Monica pushed the salad bowl away to make room for their plates. Once they'd settled on who ordered what, Monica picked up the conversation again. "So, why didn't it go well?"

"I was with Matty and *his* new "friend". It got a little uncomfortable."

Monica stole a quick glance at the couple. "I think she knows you're here."

Haley looked up, saw Niki waving at her and waved back. "I really liked her for my brother. I keep hoping they'll end up together."

Laughter from the other table drew Niki's attention, another gentle reminder that she owed Haley an apology. After all, it wasn't his younger sister's fault Tex was a jerk. The couple of times she'd met her, Haley had been nothing but sweet—perfect sister-in-law material. Niki smiled at the ludicrous thought.

When she stopped to analyze the situation, she barely knew Tex—although she had *known* him in the biblical sense. She cringed inwardly at how easily she'd given herself to him. God, she'd been such an idiot. Meagan was right about sending him all the wrong signals. No, he hadn't been her first, but somehow she'd hoped, even then, that he'd be her last.

They'd had such a connection, both mentally and physically. She remembered the pleasure he'd given her, and the way he'd responded to her touch . . . her face heated at the thought. Even now, one sight of him had her longing to rip his shirt off, run her hands over that big, broad chest. Boy howdy, had they ever connected.

She fanned her face, knowing she had to let it go. Besides, she had someone of her own. She smiled as her date approached the table—Bo McAllister—smart, sweet, sexy, funny, and handsome. She knew he was a hard worker with good values, as well as a great family—all good things.

So why—why didn't the sight of him turn her insides to melted butter? Why didn't she get that same urge to tear his clothes off of his fabulous body . . . the body that did absolutely . . . *nothing* . . . for her?

He sat across from her and picked up a menu. "Have you decided what you're hungry for?"

Not you, obviously. Stop it, Niki. He's a great guy. She sent him a too-bright smile. "I'm leaning toward the grilled shrimp. How about you?"

"That sounds good, actually. I'm not all that hungry." He adjusted his collar, did a little fidgeting before clearing his throat.

"Are you okay?"

"Uh huh, I'm fine." He grabbed his glass of water and took a gulp. He cleared his throat one more time as he tapped his fingers nervously on the table. "I—uh—I think we should talk. That is, I mean—I have something to ask you."

Niki's glass froze half the distance to her lips. *What? No, no, no—not this. Not now. Not ever, with him.*

He paused to pull his buzzing phone from an inside pocket of his jacket, pushed a button and set it on the table.

Her stomach flipped as Bo stole a glance toward the floor. *What the hell was he about to do?* She stiffened as he slipped out of his chair—nearly screamed as he got down on one knee.

"Stop!" The word burst from her mouth much, much louder than she intended before she could stop herself.

Bo looked up, his face a mask of confusion. "What's wrong?"

"Just don't. Don't do whatever it is you're about to do," she hissed, casting self-conscious glances around the dining room.

He reached for something under the table then straightened. "I dropped my card when I pulled my phone out of my pocket. I'd forgotten to put it back in my wallet." His platinum card landed on the table with a light slap. Bo took his time replacing the card in his wallet. He slipped the billfold into the back pocket of his jeans. He leaned against his chair, releasing a long, low sigh. "For the record, I'd have to date a woman longer than four months before I proposed. But, I guess that answers my question."

Heat infused her face, burned her ears. She raised her hands to her cheeks, totally mortified at her misjudgment. "Oh Bo. I am so sorry. It's . . . I don't . . ." She let the comment die, clueless as how to dig herself out of the embarrassing situation she'd caused. "What question was that, exactly?"

"Do you see the two of us having any kind of future together?"

Her heart pounded in her chest as she struggled for an answer that wouldn't hurt his feelings.

"It's not there, is it?" He leaned back in his chair and used his finger to point back and forth between them. "I mean between the two of us. There should be more than this, right?"

She released the breath she'd been holding and bit her lower lip. Finally, she nodded. "I've never been in a serious relationship before, Bo, but in my honest opinion—yes. I think there should be more." She raised one hand, palm up, and indicated the man before her. "I mean, look at you. You're the perfect guy." She gave her head a slow shake. "I have no idea why you don't do it for me."

"I like you a lot, Niki. You're fun as hell to be around—when you're not making a spectacle of yourself in a public restaurant, I mean."

His wink drew a snort of laughter from her. "I'm sorry."

He waved off the apology. "It's okay. Honestly, we can't force ourselves to feel something that's not there. Either of us."

She nodded. "So, what do we do now?"

He picked up his menu. "We order, because I'm starving."

"Okay, but I can pay for my own meal."

He seemed appalled at the suggestion. "Absolutely not. I can buy a friend lunch when I want to. We are still friends, aren't we?"

Niki smiled at the man before her, once again wishing she could feel something more for him. "You're a good man, Bo. There's someone for you out there. And now, you're free to look."

"Yeah—about that." He made a face and sucked in a breath through his teeth. "I've kind of been talking to someone. We're friends but, I'm fairly certain we'd both like it to be more. I wanted to be the one to tell you."

"Oh. Well, I appreciate you telling me."

"Thing is, there's a little history between you two. Please don't take this out on her."

She stared him down. "Who?" His further reluctance to mention a name gave her the clue she needed. "Oh, you've *got* to be kidding me. Can't that woman find a guy I haven't dated?"

He shrugged. "Aubrey and I ran into each other at the mall theater the other day. I mean, literally. We were both waiting to see that action flick you didn't want to see with me. I walked right into her and destroyed her bag of popcorn. I thought it was only fair to share my bucket with her."

Niki frowned. "Of course you did."

Bo issued a low chuckle. "We got to talking. It turns out we have lots of the same interests, and well . . ."

"She does it for you. I get it, Bo."

"Yeah. She kinda does." He rubbed his chin and got a faraway look in his eyes. "I mean, she *really* does."

"Uh, excuse me, but I'm still right here, you know."

"Sorry, but it's the truth. To tell you the truth, I figured you'd be thrilled. Now, Tex is free." She opened her mouth to protest, but he raised his hand to stop her. "I know you're carrying a torch for the guy. And—" He ducked his head and nodded, "—I'm thinking maybe you should give it another shot."

"But, Bo, he—"

"The guy was a Marine for twenty years, Niki."

"That doesn't excuse him from bad behavior."

"Were the two of you dating exclusively?"

She rolled one corner of the cloth napkin between her fingers. "No."

He lifted his hands. "Can you tell me you've never had a moment of bad judgment? Done something you regretted?"

Niki squeezed her eyes shut, remembering several instances of 'bad judgment' with Tex. Hell, if she was being honest with herself, her entire life from the age of 16 to 22 had been full of bad judgment material. Would she take them back, or at least change the circumstances if she could? Sure she would. Like it or not, Meagan had hit that nail right on the head a few months ago. She had acted "irresponsibly slutty" and did blame him for not taking her seriously. Something else she said pricked at her memory—something about not being high on his list of fairytale princess material.

She opened her eyes, caught Bo staring at her and wearing a big grin.

"I've done lots of things I regret."

"Well, there you go. Give the guy another chance."

"I'll think about it." She picked up her menu again. "But just for giving me grief, I'm ordering the most expensive item on here. I hope you have plenty of room on that platinum card of yours."

He nodded. "Get after it, Niki."

It turned out that 'thinking about it' and actually getting the nerve to approach Tex again were two different animals. Especially since Bo's good advice coincided with cramming for final exams in her accounting studies at the university.   An entire month had passed before Niki swallowed her pride enough to consider reaching out to Tex. It took another week to go through with it. Regardless, here she was, her stomach queasy with butterflies, listening to the phone ring. Finally, the voice she'd heard in her dreams answered, his voice ubiquitous with concern."

"Nicole? Is something wrong?"

She placed her hand on her thudding chest, sure he could hear it. "No. Why would you ask that?"

"Thank God. I figured if you were calling, someone must have died."

At least he kept my number in his phone.

"So, what's going on?"

"I—uh—wanted to see how you're doing, and see if . . ." She placed her hand over her stomach. This eating crow thing wasn't for sissies. "To see if you wanted to go to a movie or something. Not a chick flick, either. Maybe that new sci-fi action movie that's out?" Several silent moments passed. "Tex?"

"Are you asking me out on a date, Nicole?"

She cringed at the sound of teasing in his voice, as if this wasn't humiliating enough. "We-ell, I guess I am."

"Oh man, I can't believe this. Your timing—is *so* fuc—I mean—extremely bad."

"Look, it's no big deal. I thought maybe we could hang out—but if you're dating someone else already—"

"It's not that," he cut in quickly. "I'm on a ranch in Blanco."

"Where is Blanco?"

"South central Texas. About fifty miles north of San Antonio."

"Oh. When will you be back on this end?" His pause made her curiosity turn to concern.

"I won't be. Not anytime soon, anyway."

A chill ran through her at his words. She dropped heavily to the bed to keep from her knees from buckling. "You moved—for good?"

"Well—I'm here learning the ropes to a small cattle ranch, and trying to get a loan to buy the place."

"I hadn't—" Her voice caught and she had to dig deep to continue. "I hadn't heard that." Had Meagan known about this? If so, why the hell hadn't she told her? "That's great, Tex." She attempted to sound sincere. "Does it look promising?"

"Yep. He's agreed to sell me seventy-five head of his breeding stock. He's in his mid-seventies and says it's been good to him, but he's getting too old for all the stress and labor of ranching. Even small ranches, like this one, are hard work."

"I'm sure they are."

Yet another silence filled the airwaves, this one heavier than ever—laden with regret and emotional turmoil. Too damn late. She'd waited too long to call him. One more bad decision she'd have to live with for the rest of her life. Niki rested her forehead in one hand and fought back tears. She considered putting herself out of this misery by ending the call. If he bothered to call back, she could say they'd been disconnected. If not—well that'd be a sure sign from him that he didn't want to be bothered with her anymore, wouldn't it? She lifted her head to stare at her phone, placed her thumb on the end call button, and hesitated a moment.

"Nicole, are you there?"

Niki took a deep breath, raised the phone to her ear again. "Yes." The single word was all she could manage.

"I'm kind of at a loss, here."

"Uh, yeah—me too, Tex."

"I don't know what to say, hon."

She took a deep breath and released it slowly. "You have a good life, Tex. If you're ever on this end for a visit, give me a call, okay? Maybe we can have a cup of coffee or something. See ya, around."

"Nicole?"

She blinked back tears just long enough to find the disconnect button and hit it. Discarding the phone on the bed beside her, she turned on her side. There, in her room, curled up into a fetal position, she took advantage of the rare opportunity to cry herself to sleep.

Tex stared at the phone. Talk about your moments of shock and awe. The very last person he'd expected to hear from was Nicole Reeves, and sure as hell not to ask him on a date. She'd forgiven him, but why?

He glanced over at the miles of fenceline he still had to check for gaps and fence posts going bad. More importantly, why the hell call now? Now—that he was ass deep in responsibility and commitment to a completely different life in a completely different state? If she'd called earlier, before he'd found this place. Dammit all, he couldn't walk away from this now. This was what he'd worked so hard for—saved his pay—made good investments. He wanted this—his own ranch—his own brand hanging above that ornamental gate. Not a necessity for these modern times, but it was the one thing he'd always wanted to see.

He checked the next post, shook it with all his strength and found it to be sound, the wire good and tight, and went on to the next.

He deserved this, didn't he? Twenty years as a Marine, sacrificing his time, his safety, making choices he knew were necessary, following commands that some would consider hard-hearted, though any soldier would deem necessary to bring his own men home, alive or otherwise. Screw anyone who judged the U.S. Military unjustly and found them guilty. Let 'em walk a mile in his boots—for any one of the dozen deployments he'd experienced.

The last couple of years had been considerably pacified, compared to the deployments in the first seventeen years. Man, the shit he'd seen during some of those earlier years. Afghanistan had been the worst for him, personally. The way those hadji bastards used their children and women. Horror stories came to mind—stories he'd tried to erase. *Don't think about it—put it away.* Maybe one day he'd share his stories, but not today.

People here had no idea what some of those assholes were like.

He shook another post, found it sturdy enough, but the wire slack. He set to work on making it tighter.

American women had no idea how bad it was for the female population over there. Afghanistan was bad, but Somalia—oh God, Somalia. That place had a special place of horror in his mind. He'd never forget coming across the young Somali girl of sixteen, near death and freshly disfigured by the hands of her own father, all because she'd been raped by three men from a neighboring village. Her tears, as she'd described how her father had accused *her* of adultery, had been difficult to watch. Her words, difficult to hear as their translator repeated the story to him. He'd never forget his ice cold fury at coming face to face with the father. The man had charged into the hut where their medic had been treating his daughter, shouted out his indignation at their interference by attempting to help her.

Tex tacked the wire into place, checking its tension and gave his head a mental shake. He'd killed men before that incident, during missions and skirmishes. He could say he enjoyed it—knew it was necessary to survive out there.

But that particular man—if you could call him a man—he could have killed easily, without the slightest pause to his conscience. He'd lost control of himself as his hateful speech had been translated. He'd literally picked him up by his neck, pinned him against the wall of the hut, stopped only by the girl's plea to spare him. She'd insisted that her mother and siblings would starve to death if her father died. Even through her pain and suffering, she'd been the better person. Letting that one man live, weighed heavier on his conscience than any of the men whose lives he'd taken.

That bastard hadn't deserved to share the same air space as that poor girl. How could a father treat his daughter so cruelly? How could anyone who calls himself a man treat a woman in such a way? That asshole, and so many others like him, wanted their women two ways: ignorant and afraid. Resentment and deep seated hatred for all things American and its evil western ways ran high within those with twisted minds. Not everyone believed as that man did, of course, but too damn many of them did.

It got him to thinking about Nicole, and how difficult it must have been for her to make that call, especially considering the pole dancer incident. He pulled a blue bandana from the pocket of his jeans and stopped to wipe his brow. Why had he stood her up the way he had? No, they hadn't actually had a date planned, but he'd said he would call and he hadn't. He'd played the game, enjoyed the spoils, and hadn't taken her seriously. Why? Had he become so desensitized by the things he'd witnessed the last twenty years, he couldn't see how badly he'd hurt her feelings?

Tex stuffed the cloth back in his pocket, and walked to the next post. Another shake proved the post was solid enough, but again, the wire tension needed some adjustments. With a good grip on the pliers, he attacked the wire, and found himself thinking of Nicole again.

"Shit!" He threw down the pliers with a long series of Marine-worthy curses, and removed his glove to examine his pinched finger, the future site of a nasty blood blister, no doubt. "Suck it up, asshole. That's what you get for thinking about a woman when there's work to be done."

Pulling on the glove, he got back to work, determined to put her out of his mind and tend to the duties at hand.

That worked for about ten minutes.

Until it didn't anymore.

Chapter 12

Easter Surprise

Angie Broussard's voice called out to anyone within earshot. "Somebody get the door, please—I've got my hands full here."

"I got it, mom." Haley sprinted down the hall in her socks, sliding to a stop in front of the door. She pulled it open, and squealed at the enormous, beautifully wrapped Easter basket being held out to her. "Is that for me?"

Shurl Antoine nodded, her big, white-toothed grin standing out from her smooth cocoa complexion. "Girl, you know it is. I wish I had a man somewhere, anywhere in this world, who was crazy enough about me to send me stuff like this." She handed over the basket and pointed at the huge chocolate bunnies wrapped inside. "Mm, mm, mm—girl, I'd be big as a house, and that's a fact."

"Since when does the flower shop deliver baskets of candy?"

Shurl began explaining the situation with a flourish of hands. "My friend, Ms. Ginger's daughter came in and got that place all technologically updated. She's got a website and everything, now. You can go online and order darn near whatever you want. We'll buy it, wrap it up nice and pretty, and deliver it. That's about all I do over there. I love it."

Haley gasped at the treasure trove of goodies. "Oh man. Look at all that chocolate and—oh yeah, it's from Benjamin, all right. My baby knows I love my Skittles and sunflower seeds."

Ricky Broussard walked up behind her. "How do you know I didn't send that? I know you like Skittles and sunflower seeds too."

Haley turned to face her father. "Did you?"

"Of course not. I'd have bought you something practical, like a new pair of rubber boots to muck the horse crap out of Dakota's stall—which needs it, by the way." He took the time to examine the contents of the basket. "You plan on sharing with your old man? I see some peanut butter eggs in there."

Shurl threw her head back, filling the living room with her laughter. "You a trip, Mr. Ricky. Have fun checking out all those goodies. I got a hot date with my two little nephews to dye some eggs. Y'all have a blessed Easter."

"You too, Shurl, and thanks." Haley called out to the girl she'd known since grade school. She set the basket on the breakfast counter and reached for her phone. "I've got to take some pics for Ben." A few camera shots posted to his Facebook page later, she removed the ribbon and cellophane wrap, discovering everything from marshmallow bunnies, to licorice jelly beans tucked inside the sturdy rattan basket. "Here dad, these are for you." She threw him the bag of licorice candy. "And mom, I believe these are for you." She held out of box of cordial chocolate cherries.

Her mother hugged the box close. "Oh, how sweet of that young man—he remembered these are my favorites?"

"He must have, because he knows I can't stand them or licorice." She grabbed her sunflower seeds and Skittles out of the basket. "These, I don't share with anyone, but the rest is up for grabs."

"Well, that was thoughtful as hell of him," her father said, clearly touched by Ben's consideration. He smiled, his eyes twinkling with mischief. "I'm pretty sure those peanut butter cups were meant for me, too."

Haley reached for the bag of candy and tossed it to him. "Here you go, dad. There's plenty enough for everyone. Too bad big brother's not around to help us eat all this." The sight of her mother's eyes suddenly filling with tears had her immediately regretting the comment.

"Don't remind me. I still can't believe we had to give him up to the military for twenty years, only to have him move three hundred miles from our home and working too hard to come home for holidays."

Ricky lightly rested his hands on his wife's shoulders. "Now, hon. You know Matt's always wanted a ranch."

"And I wouldn't deny him that. But does it have to be a four and a half hour drive from us? We've spent too many holidays without him. I want my family together." Overcome with emotion, she spun on her heel and returned to the kitchen.

Haley sucked in her breath and faced her father. "I shouldn't have said that, daddy. I didn't mean to upset her."

"You saying it didn't send your brother away. We'll come to terms with his decision, eventually." He sighed and ran one hand through his silvered hair. "I need to go feed."

"You want me to do it?"

He shook his head, reaching for his boots by the door. "Nah, the girls might get jealous if I show up with another woman." He grinned at his daughter, his eyes revealing a hint of laughter as he slipped on his boots and headed to the back yard.

Haley stopped long enough in the kitchen to give her mom a hug. "I'm sorry, mom."

"Oh honey, it's not your fault. Matt's made his choice, and even if I respect it, I don't have to like it."

Haley went to her bedroom and closed the door. She pulled out her smart phone and hit a button. The phone rang several times before Tex picked up.

"What's up, squirt?"

Haley walked to her bedroom window to watch her dad. "What are you doing, big brother?"

"Mending fences."

She smiled at his answer. "Is that figuratively, or literally?"

His low chuckle traveled through her phone's speaker. "No, I'm really checking for posts to replace in the back pasture. How about you?"

"I'm watching dad throw feed to his 'ladies' through my bedroom window." She adored seeing her father take his afternoon stroll through the chicken yard, surrounded by at least a dozen hens.

"The man is a veritable chick magnet."

She laughed at his comment. "You got that right."

"So, did you call to bullshit or is something wrong?"

"I want you to do something, Matty. I want you to come home for Easter tomorrow."

A long sigh accompanied his reply. "Man, I've got a shitload to do on the ranch, sis."

"When was the last time you spent Easter here? As a matter of fact, how many holidays have you spent at home in the last twenty years?"

"Well mom and dad were gone for Thanksgiving but we'd celebrated early. And I was there for Christmas. Other than that, not a whole hell of a lot, I'd guess."

"Mom wants you home. This move to Blanco has them both really upset, even though dad totally supports your decision."

"They didn't act like they were upset when I told them about it."

"Because they know you've sacrificed a lot to get what you wanted. What you need to remember is that they sacrificed too. Years of worrying about you, wanting you home, and missing you for holidays—it was rough on them. And now you're moving yourself four and a half hours away—"

"I made it in three and a half."

"Yeah? Well, not everyone drives like a wild man. They feel robbed. Can't you understand that?" His pause told her he was mulling it over.

"I'll work late to finish up around here and leave early tomorrow morning. I'll be there no later than ten o'clock. But don't tell them, I want it to be a surprise."

"Make it nine, and come dressed for church."

"Church?"

"Yep, it'll mean so much to mom. You could meet us there and really surprise them."

"Are we talking St. Anthony's Cathedral downtown, or that new one closer to Orange? Because I could make it quicker to the cathedral and be waiting for y'all, that'd get the waterworks over with before we go inside."

Haley's heart fluttered with excitement for her parents. "I can talk her into the Cathedral."

"You know, you might want to warn the priest ahead of time so he can pick up a second collection for the building fund. St. Anthony's will probably go up in flames as soon as I set foot inside, heathen that I am."

She turned away from the window and dropped onto her bed. "Dad always says if it weren't for heathens, priests and preachers in this world would get mighty lonely up there trying to convert rows of empty pews." Her brother grunted in agreement.

"Okay, it's a deal, but you can't tell a soul about this."

"Thanks, Matty. I love you. Leave early enough so you don't kill yourself on the drive over."

"I will. Love you too, Popcorn."

Haley lay on her bed, excited at the prospect of seeing the smiles on her parents' faces tomorrow. She covered her eyes with one hand, wishing she'd have as much reason to smile as they would.

She groaned, and rolled over on her belly, aching for the sight of Ben. God, it had been so long since she'd seen his face. And the calls had been few and far between lately. She grabbed her phone, checked Facebook for any messages she might have missed, just in case he'd been able to get to a computer. It was the Easter season, what better time to wish for a miracle?

Nothing. *Damn.*

Once she'd made sure her phone volume was set to the highest level, Haley tucked it close to her. She turned onto her side, hoping to sleep away one more afternoon with no word from Benjamin. Sleep—it was her only solace from the heartache and loneliness of missing Ben.

Chapter 13

Missed Opportunities

Nicole stifled a yawn as she checked her GPS again. She'd been driving since 5:00 a.m. and sorely needed a cup of coffee. The fact that she'd told no one her plans both frightened her and gave her a feeling of empowerment. Once she'd made the decision to do this around nine o'clock the previous night, it had turned into one of those life-changing moments of affirmation—a real *I can do this* moment.

I'm in complete control of my own life, of my own future, and I'm willing to step out of my comfort zone to achieve what I want.

So she'd risen at 4:00 a.m., thrown a few things into a bag, and put herself together as much as the early hour had afforded. She'd left a note for Meagan, explaining only that she'd be gone all day, would call her once she reached her destination, and had wished them a Happy Easter. She knew Meagan and Buck would be spending the day with Mitchell at his sister's place. She'd been invited, of course, but had simply told her friend she would pass this time around.

It was bad enough to risk a broken heart over this, but her pride wouldn't allow her to tell another living soul about this trip, just in case it didn't turn out as she hoped.

Where the hell was her GPS sending her? Was this address so far out in the boonies it was off the grid? After thirty minutes of dirt road driving on unmarked routes she finally arrived at a sprawling ranch-style home. To her relief, the mailbox next to the driveway indicated the physical address she'd entered in her navigator App.

She turned in, parked, and exited her car, cautiously listening for the growl of a dog—or a coyote, or possibly even a bear.

I can understand him wanting his space, but this place is in the middle of nowhere.

His truck wasn't in the drive, but she supposed it could be parked in the garage. Casting careful glances in all directions, she approached the door. Several sessions of knocking with no answer, had her wondering how stupid she'd been to do this. What the hell was she thinking by driving all the way to Blanco, Texas without making sure he'd be there?

She crossed her arms and shook her head in frustration. "Oo-kaay—you can add this to your Stupid-Is-As-Stupid-Does list. Not your best moment, Nic—"

"Can I help you?"

Nicole jumped at the voice, spinning around to see an older gentleman, maybe in his mid-seventies, approaching from the back of the house. He was tall and slim, brandishing a bright smile, and a head full of silver hair.

She rushed her explanation. "Oh, I'm sorry. I knocked for quite a while."

He pointed to the back yard. "The wife and I are sitting out here, enjoying our coffee. What can I do for you?"

"I'm looking for Matthew Broussard. This is the address I have for him."

"Matthew? You don't mean Tex, do you?"

"Yes sir, Tex. Is he here?"

"Tex stays at the cabin down by the lake. It's about a five minute drive from here." He cast a woeful glance at her 2006 Accord. "You won't make it in that thing. That road is pretty chewed up. You'd need a 4-wheel drive to get in there."

"Oh. Well, I was hoping to surprise him, but maybe it would be best to call him." She pulled out her phone.

"Is she looking for Tex?"

A plump woman with snow white hair and a pretty face approached, dressed in what Nicole had always considered 'Sunday best'.

"Yes ma'am, I am, but your husband says I won't be able to make it to his cabin in my car."

"It wouldn't do you any good, not even if you were driving one of those fancy Hummers. Tex isn't there. He won't be back until late tonight or tomorrow."

Nicole raised her hands in the air, and let them fall to her sides. Her head drooped forward in utter defeat. "Of course he isn't."

So stupid.

She took a deep breath and released it slowly before facing the couple again.

"I guess I came for nothing, then. I'm sorry to have wasted your time."

"No trouble at all, Miss. Who should we say came calling on him?" the gentleman asked.

"Um . . . actually, it's better if he doesn't even know I came by. Would you mind terribly not telling him?"

The woman's brow furrowed. "Are you sure? You're the only visitor he's had since he's been here. I think he'd be glad to know someone came by to see him."

She gave the woman a brisk nod. "Oh, I'm sure. It's the one humiliation I can spare myself in this situation, trust me."

The older couple exchanged curious looks and the old gentleman shrugged as his wife continued. "Well, if you're sure . . ."

"Yes ma'am. I'm sure. Please, don't tell him." She backed slowly away, raising her hand. "You two enjoy your Easter Sunday."

The woman's face lit up. "You also, dear."

Niki thanked them for their time and waved as she drove out the same way she came in.

She stopped in the city of Blanco for a bathroom break and breakfast at a fast food restaurant. She wolfed down a bacon, egg, and cheese biscuit, and then climbed back in her car. She sipped on the remainder of her large coffee in a more relaxed frame of mind. Niki took her time going home, far more capable of appreciating the scenic landscape of the area. Regardless of his reasons, Tex had chosen a lovely area of Texas to set up ranching. The rolling hills, roadside pastures full of wildflowers—she found it all aesthetically appealing. All in all, it was a lovely place to live.

Too bad she couldn't shake the uneasy feeling that Tex had chosen its remote location for one reason only; to get as far away from her as he possibly could.

Tex pulled up at his cabin in time to see the digital dash clock flip to 6:30 p.m. It had been taxing to drive to Beaumont and back in one day. Especially when he had so much damn work left to do around here. No arguing with that. But the look on his mother's face as he'd stepped out of the shadows to surprise her at the church—that had been priceless. He'd taken Haley aside post-service and thanked her for making it happen. With one call, his baby sister had reminded him what was truly important.

She'd know that now, wouldn't she—as miserable and lonely as she was for Corporal Bonin. Poor kid hadn't heard from him in nearly three weeks. He could see how it ate at her—the sadness in her eyes, the strain, the stress of constantly checking her phone for a missed call or some word from him. Not once had he seen her without that phone, either clutched tightly in her hand, or inches away. He knew she'd expected to hear from Ben on Easter Sunday. But for the people over there, the days, the weeks, and months blended into one other.

There were no weekends off and no holidays for deployed Marines, only a brief period of recuperation between missions. If Ben was lucky, it'd be long enough to catch up on the sleep he'd lost, and to rehydrate his body. Maybe enough time to come down mentally from one mission before hyping himself up for another. More days of the same old shit, mixed with sand and grit. He remembered well the diligence paid to keeping his eyes focused on the horizon, for any little thing that looked out of place, like reflective surfaces, or dust trails—anything indicating covert or unfriendly activity. Avoiding the ever present IED's and land mines placed by hadjis filled with hatred for any military personnel, but with a special hatred for U.S. Marines.

Dear God, if Haley only knew some of what went on over there, she'd lose her flipping mind over it.

He entered the small cabin he'd called home for nearly two months. Falling into the chair next to the door, he struggled to pull off his dress boots, and vowed to have a decent bootjack in the place by tomorrow.

Add that to the long list of to-do's for this ranch.

He yawned, amazed at how sitting behind the wheel for four straight hours could exhaust him physically. Days of sun-up to sun-down labor only invigorated him. He equaled it to being in the Corps—long boring days of waiting for something to happen versus the adrenaline high of being in the thick of things.

Tex closed his eyes, let his head fall back on the seat, and cleared his mind, or tried to, anyway. Soon enough, it filled with thoughts of Nicole. At one point during the day, he'd been on the verge of calling her, thinking he could drop by for a long overdue heart to heart. If nothing else, a heart-felt apology on his part for taking advantage of her. A quick conversation with Meagan had told him she'd left town for the day. It hadn't surprised him. Missed opportunities seemed to be standard operating procedure when it came to Nicole.

He fought the urge to let the lethargy consume his body as well as his mind, and forced himself from the chair. He slipped his feet into well-worn work boots at the door and headed outside. With a few minutes of dusk to spare, he headed to the feed shed and shelter he'd built for his horse. Captain Perry's whinny carried to him as soon as he stepped outside.

"Hey boy, did you miss me?" He reached out for the horse whose two snow-white back hoofs stood out in stark contrast to his otherwise solid colored body. Captain stretched his neck across the barbed wire fencing, shoved his muzzle into his master's shoulder.

"Hey now, there's no need to get pushy. I'm out here to feed you, big daddy." He stuck a finger in the face of the big red stallion. "Come to think of it, you should be damned grateful I'm even here. I could have stayed in Lake

Coburn for the night. Fortunately for you, it didn't turn out that way."

He entered the feed shed through the gate and filled a bucket with sweet oats to treat the best horse he'd ever owned. Hell, the stud fees alone could pay the note on this place at five hundred bucks a pop and this was only his first year at stud. Once word got out that his offspring were as fast as the daddy, they would rise considerably.

He filled the trough with feed. "Yep, you eat up, Captain. You'll need your strength, because first thing tomorrow morning, I'm bringing you to meet another lady friend." He scratched between Cap's ears and smiled to himself. "Must be nice to get paid for doing what you love to do." He'd seen him in action enough to know he needed very little urging, which was a plus for the thoroughbred mare's owners. He had the proper tools to get the job done as God intended. Lucky for Cap, there were still a few mare owners out there willing to try it the old fashioned way.

"I mean, hell, I loved being a U.S. Marine. I did most of the time, anyway. That is, when I wasn't being shot at, or shriveling up from dehydration in the desert heat, or seeing shit that turned my stomach." The Stallion's huge brown eyes settled on him, seeming to wait for his closing statement. "I know, right? How pathetic is it that it was the best time of my life?" Captain shook his great head back and forth as though trying to communicate with him.

"Are you trying to tell me I have better things to look forward to?"

The horse froze; his huge eyes locked on his, then jerked his head.

Tex laughed and slapped Captain on the neck. "From your horse mouth to whatever God you believe in, Cap."

Chapter 14

Fear the Reaper

Ben sat cross-legged in one of two patches of vegetation on a hill, looking across at the all-too-familiar compound ahead of them. Pinned in by the same river and canal that would be impossible to cross with gear if they had to perform an E an E. The thought had him groaning in frustration, and then issuing a low curse. "Man, I hate this place."

D-dub gave a snort. "Seems to be the consensus—Afghanistan sucks."

"I mean this position. There's nowhere to run except straight into the worse fucking choke point in a fifty mile radius."

His buddy shrugged. "Life's a bitch and then we die."

Ben jerked his head up to glare at the fellow sniper. "Not me, I got a girl waiting on me, and a shit load of ice cold beer to drink." He shook his head and peered into the scope of his M110 SASS. "I refuse to die in this shit hole."

The patrol base located two miles north of Ben's team had been getting brutal peppering of Taliban fire. Their mission to find the shooters and stop them had revealed nothing. For the past three weeks, the bastards had refused to show themselves again.

The Aerostat blimp assigned to their area of operation had recorded frequent comings and goings from a small mud hut nearby, indicating a weapons cache. Two snipers from the second team sat on a hill above the hut, with suppressed M4's, ready to light up any Taliban members attempting to go for weaponry or ammo. Ben and Matt had surveillance on the village below. The remaining four members, situated in another abandoned compound at the bottom of the hill behind them, watched their backs and kept good communications with main.

It had been another long-ass, three weeks since he'd spoken to Haley or any of his family. Always for the same reason—the SAT phone being at another PB by the time his team made it in from missions. They had to be worried sick. Especially since one of the guys in their battalion recently hit an IED and ended up as a double amputee. Due to Facebook, once the family got the news, word about the wounded traveled fast.

Shots rang out to the north, a lot of them, grabbing everyone's attention. Main came on the hook reporting shots fired at the base. Through the weeks, the teams had pushed the missions further south to find the Taliban. The current problem? They were possibly too far south to see the shooters.

"You see anything, Bones?"

Ben peered into the scope of his rifle set up on the tripod. "Nothing, yet." He scanned the fields and nearby villages again. Detecting movement to the south, he checked his scope. "Hey Matt, I got a guy in a brown man-dress, looks to be mid-twenties, standing in the middle of the field. He's talking into a radio, looking towards the PB being fired upon. He's either spotting for the shooters or giving the orders. Call it in."

As the shooting escalated, Ben pulled out his small radio and spoke to his Team Leader. "Hey Sarge, this son of a bitch seems to be giving the orders. Request permission to engage."

The TL came back instantly. "Sending request."

Corporal Bonin waited, his senses increasing to heightened levels, his heart pounding in his chest as the rush of adrenaline kicked in. The thudding grew louder in his ears, too loud; so loud, that surely his target down there could hear it, too. But he didn't. Probably because he was shouting in the radio as he looked out toward the fired-upon patrol base.

He waited for word from the TL, never taking his eyes from the asshole down below. Three years of training, more training, and repetition of training, of blood, sweat, and tears . . . it all came to a head as he waited for permission to engage.

Ben looked down his scope, held his reticle steadily on the Taliban fuck. The suspect continued to point in the direction of the distant patrol base and spoke animatedly into the radio. The firing grew heavier in the distance, accompanied by an even louder blast. The man raised a fist in the air. Ben's stomach turned, hoping none of his brothers had been hurt. Hopefully, no kid lost another parent today.

Ben used his range finder to get an exact distance. Anticipating the okay, he turned to Matt. "405 meters." They set their scopes to 400 meters. The guy was walking away from them now, his back perfectly exposed, and heading toward a water pump shack to the right of the village. "Matt, you hold at his lower chest. I'll hold to his upper. That way if one of us is off, we'll know whose shot is whose and we can make our own adjustment for reengagement." The mirage in the field didn't show much wind activity. Matt and I adjusted our scopes to accommodate a slight south to north windage.

What the hell was taking Main so long to respond? Here we were, ready to drop this guy and they were taking their sweet time.

The radio crackled with a sudden reply. "Main said you have permission to engage."

His body pumped adrenaline at a ridiculous rate, as his training kicked in. It was almost as though he'd transformed into the spectator, watching his subconscious-self take control of the situation.

"Okay, Matt. You ready?"

"Yeah."

"Safety off, condition one?"

"Yes."

"Ok, we are going to do a frame shot, and I'll count down to the T of two."

"I'm ready."

"Five...four...three...two."

Two shots released. Ben quickly recovered from the recoil to catch the impact of the rounds. One round skimmed over the fuck's left shoulder, another brushed his left hip. The guy looked like he'd shit himself, completely unaware of where the shots had come from. He jumped to the wall of the water pump shed, crouching down with his back against the wall. He was facing north now, and still completely exposed. He'd turned sideways though, cutting the target size by half. Ben aimed low and right off of his hip and sent another round that had the asshole dragging himself behind the building. He knew he'd hit him but would have to wait to see how serious the shot was.

Another individual came from the village to carry him off as ten more men emerged from huts in the village. A field worker approached the abandoned compound at the base of the hill and looked over the wall. The worker stared at Ben and Matt's location for a minute. He walked about 10 paces, pulled out a small mirror and began signaling the group of men gathering in the village.

"Matt, we got a spotter."

"Where?"

"Right behind the compound at the bottom of the hill."

"Okay, I see him."

"Zero out your scope."

"Got it."

"On the T of two...ready?"

"Ready."

"Five...four...three...two."

Ben would never forget the distinct sounds of impact. Two soft whispers from their suppressed rifles and an instant later, two loud thumps. They'd been taught that if two rounds impact at the same time, the body cannot handle the stress and shuts down immediately. No shit. The target fell face forward into the mud, completely limp.

The gathering of men in the village hopped on their dirt bikes and started driving toward the suspected weapons cache. The second team, situated with the automatic M4's, rained lead down upon them. They fell, tried to run, and screamed for their lives. The last one tore off across the field. A few shots from an M4 later, and he fell like his brothers. Deathly still and lifeless.

"And that is why all Scout Sniper signs are *Reaper*," Matt murmured beside him.

"Roger that. Fear the Reaper, you sons of bitches." Ben's own words, scratched on a slip of paper in a moment of boredom, suddenly filled his mind as he gathered his gear and prepared to haul ass the two miles back to base.

". . . Death is our brother and he spares our souls for the exchange of another . . . We are the reaper."

Within a minute he had well over a hundred pounds of gear packed and strapped on. The two teams converged, and Ben led them out, running as fast as he could, considering the extra weight on his back. He approached the small dirt bridge, hated the thought of crossing that son of a bitch . . . that same fucking choke point situation again. As usual, no other option showed itself. The canal was too deep to cross with their gear and the eight of them had to RTB in a hurry, or else they'd all be at risk. The small abandoned compound to the left made him uncomfortable as all hell. It stared down at the bridge, its deep dark holes used as windows, glared out like soulless, black eyes. They knew to approach this particular compound with caution since it was commonly used by the Taliban to fire upon Marines. He got to the bridge with his team close behind him, already winded from the sprint.

Extremely wary of an ambush situation, he began making his way across the bridge. He ran as fast as he could while keeping his rifle pointed at the compound and continuously scanning the area. Despite the bridge being a mere twenty yards from end to end, it took an eternity to cross the damn thing. Ben made it to the opposite side, no big comfort when seven more team members still had to cross. The optimum time to spring an ambush would be when the middle man was crossing. He'd been told not to hold back to provide cover, but to move out, and *fast*.

So Ben hoofed it north toward the safety of the patrol base. He chanced the first backward glance. Two guys had crossed and were hauling ass behind him. Ten seconds later he cast the second glance back. Another crossed and no shots fired, always a good thing. Ben faced the front and stepped up the speed. Five shots rang out in a quick release. He snapped around, his weapon up . . . fully prepared to see one of his men lying face fucking down in a bloody mess.

Thorny, the second team's radio operator, stood there with his rifle pointed at a dead dog at his feet.

"What the fuck?" TL yells.

"It wasn't stopping!" Thorny yelled back at him. "He was coming at me fast."

"Keep moving," Jeff shouted.

Ben started trucking it again, thinking that dog looked like the same one that had threatened to attack them the previous night. Afghani dogs were mean, savage-looking creatures, and a large number carried the rabies virus. He didn't blame Thorny for killing that son of a bitch.

He picked up speed, knowing the Taliban would be extremely pissed and out for revenge. The PB was only 2 miles away by road—but roads littered with IED's. He lead his team by way of muddy fields instead, an exhausting alternative which slows them down tremendously.

Ben glanced back once more, verified that everyone had cleared the choke point. The other seven men were lined up ranger file behind him, and all hauling ass. He ran, scanned the horizon in a continuous back and forth motion, scrutinizing every shrub for a possible threat. Eight men running in an open field . . . nothing like being an easy target for American loathing members of the Taliban.

"We got movement at our six."

Ben spun around to check it out. Dozens of people are starting to gather, all dressed in black, and carrying the dead bodies. Voices echo from the speakers of the mosques as a burst of shots rang out. The impact of rounds drew a parallel line in the dirt, to the right of their team's formation. The eight member team whipped around, simultaneously taking a knee, their weapons raised and ready. The shots had come from two Taliban men with one automatic rifle. From the rear, Scotty returned fire at the two men until they hauled butt in the opposite direction. Ben and the rest of the team stood as one, and continued with the task at hand, to get their asses back to the PB.

As soon as the team crossed into friendly lines, the tension between the eight members slid from their shoulders in discernible waves. Their return to base revealed a squad of Marines readying themselves to provide reinforcement, now unnecessary.

After running off of pure adrenaline for two hours, Ben walked up to a hesco wall. He dropped his pack, propped his rifle, and sat his ass down.

Now that his body was physically exhausted, maybe his mind would have a chance to process what had happened.

He wouldn't find out until later that the first man he'd shot that day was the son of a high-ranking member of the Taliban. One whose plans to follow in his father's footsteps had fallen far short of the goal.

"Bones, catch."

He reached up to catch one bottle of water, then a second thrown by his TL.

"Thanks."

"Good work out there today."

Ben nodded. "Hey Sarge, you know if the SAT phone's on our base?"

The man shook his head. "Not at the moment. But I just sent for it. It's been a month since I spoke to my wife." He jutted his chin forward. "Get some rest, Corporal. That's what I intend to do. By the time we wake up, it damned well better be back on our end."

"Roger that, sir." By the time he made it back to his sleeping area, he'd drained both bottles of water and still hadn't quenched his thirst. That didn't stop him from stripping off his gear, and collapsing onto his cot, exhausted, and covered in more than the usual amount of grit.

Ben wasn't able to track down the SAT phone until nearly 23:00 hours, which would have made it around noon in Louisiana and East Texas. He called his mom first, knowing she'd be in the middle of a school day. She answered on the second ring.

"Are you okay, Benjamin?"

"Hey mom. I'm fine."

"Thank you, God."

He smiled, knowing she'd accompany her standard reply by crossing herself. "We haven't been able to get to the sat phones lately. Every time we hit the PB it was somewhere else."

"That's okay, Ben. We all knew you'd call if you could. Haley and I have been keeping tabs with each other."

He heard the school bell ring on her end, accompanied by her low curse. "I know you've got to go, but I wanted to let you know I'm fine over here."

"Okay, son. I love you. We're all praying for you. Are you going to call your dad, or do you want me to let him know you called?"

"Let him know, please. I'll Skype him when I'm back at Delhi."

"And Haley?"

"I'm about to call her."

"Good, she's been sick with worry."

He heard her pause, waited for the follow-up.

"She's a wonderful girl, Benjamin. She cares about you a lot, and that's good enough for us."

"Thanks mom. That means a hell of a lot to me. I love you."

"I love you . . . We all do, sweetie. You take care of yourself."

"Always."

"See you soon, son."

"See you soon, mom," he said, in keeping with the cardinal rule never to say "goodbye".

He pushed the end call button and dialed Haley's cell phone number immediately. His stomach grew squeamish as it rang several times with no answer. Ben ended the call, found a partial wall section to prop himself up on. Resting his head against the wall, he dialed again, taking a moment to pray she'd answer this time. A saying of his Pa Pa's came back to him, something about there being no atheists in foxholes. Nor within the confines of Afghanistan patrol bases, apparently.

One ring, two rings, three rings—

"Ben! Don't hang up!"

His head popped up, her voice sounding like music to his ears. Maybe he'd caught her in the shower again? No, he heard the sound of traffic in the background.

"Oh my God, I was in the middle of a crosswalk, but I'm back at my car, now. Talk to me, baby."

"Damn, it's good to hear your voice."

"I've been so worried, Ben. We all have. We've all been following the story of the Sergeant in your battalion . . ."

"A different unit. I'm sorry, babe, I know. Every fu— flipping time we'd RTB the SAT was gone. I knew y'all had to be worried sick. I'm sorry."

"Stop apologizing for something out of your control. We all know. Sometimes no news is the best news, Ben. If Ms. Monica or Mr. Paul had received another kind of phone call . . ." Her voice cracked.

"I'm fine, Haley." She paused, obviously to pull herself together. When she spoke again, her resolve had returned.

"I know you are, but I was going through withdrawals from not hearing that sexy voice of yours."

It made his day to hear her teasing. God knows it beat the hell out of tears. "I hear that. Did I catch you on your lunch break?"

"Yep, I don't have another class for an hour. Are you still in possession of all your body parts?"

"Mm . . . the important ones."

"Benjamin—"

"Yes, I have all my body parts."

"The originals, right?"

He smiled, hearing the laughter in her voice. "Roger that. Listen, they're saying we may have one more mission here before we head back to Delhi."

"One more mission? And then you're done?"

"That's it."

"I can't believe it. All this time, and you're nearly finished. Have you really been there for seven months already?"

"I wish I could say it flew by, but the closer I get to leaving, the slower time seems to pass."

"Please be careful, Ben. Don't do anything stupid over there to get yourself hurt before coming home. Do you know where they're sending you?"

"Probably Dwyer in a week or so. I'll be the first filthy son of a bitch to jump in a shower to wash off this grit."

"I can't wait to have you home."

"I can't wait to have you in Hawaii. Honestly Haley, there's so much I need to tell you. So much I want to say to you."

"I know, Ben . . . me too."

Silence, heavy and thick, lingered between them. It churned with emotions and feelings too important to reveal under the current circumstances.

Haley released a long sigh, but rather than pollute the airwaves with melancholy, her words and tone of voice radiated hope and optimism. "We'll have time to say everything we want to say to each other. I know we will."

Ben closed his eyes wishing he was there with her to kiss away her loneliness. "Soon, babe. So soon."

"Hey Bones, you nearly done?"

He lifted one hand at the Marine waiting his turn for the sat phone. "I need to let you go, Haley. Are you okay?"

"I know. I'm fine, don't worry about me."

He smiled, knowing good and damn well she was fighting back tears for him. "That's my girl. It's only five more months until I'm out for good. And what's five months, babe?"

"Compared to forever? Not a damn thing. I'll talk to you later, babe."

He laughed and stood, saying the two words that would end the conversation. "Roger that."

Five days later, he led his team back to base from his very last deployment mission with the United States Marine Corps. He made the cross back into friendly lines grinning from ear to ear. As missions go, this one had been somewhat anticlimactic. Three longs days of surveillance and waiting hadn't produced a damn thing. The Taliban group they'd hoped to intercept at a village two kilometers east of them never made an appearance.

"Thanks man." Ben accepted the fresh bottle of water thrown at him. He made his way to his corner and dropped his gear before cracking open the H2O to down it. He sat for ten minutes straight, contemplating the road ahead of him.

"Hey Bones."

He turned to his TL. The man looked unusually chipper for some damn reason.

"We got our transport out of here scheduled for Tuesday morning. Are you sure you don't want to re-enlist, Corporal Bonin? We could use more career men with your abilities."

Ben shook his head. "I've got other plans, some that include hot and cold running water, all damn day long."

His Sergeant grinned at him. "What? All of a sudden, you're too good for baby wipes like the rest of us?"

"You got that right. Five months or so from now I'll be back in the land of chicken and sausage gumbo, crawfish etouffee, ice cold beer, and the prettiest girl in southwest Louisiana."

"Hell, I might have to take a road trip down to your part of the country."

Ben held up one finger to make a point. "But first, she's coming to spend a week with me in Kaneohe Bay."

The sergeant issued a low whistle. "All that celebrating, Hawaiian style. Good for you, man."

Ben grinned at his Marine brother in arms. "It's got to be good for both of us, or it won't count for shit."

A low snort accompanied the other man's reply. "You got that right."

As his TL turned to leave, Ben called out to him. "Hey, is the phone here?" A big thumbs up from Sarge had him jumping up. Haley deserved to know he'd made it back from the last mission safely. A quick "Hey, babe, I'm okay," and if God was willing, the next time they spoke he'd be looking right into that beautiful face of hers via Skype session. The thought added a little extra zip in his step as he went off to wait his turn for the phone.

Sniper platoon arrived at Forward Operation Base Delhi in high spirits, ready for a little down time. First stop was the equipment clean-up and check-in at the armory. He walked out of there with the usual—his M-4 rifle, M-9 pistol, and night vision goggles, along with his considerably lighter backpack. All thoughts of hitting the showers vanished as the aromas coming from the mess tent had his stomach growling in anticipation of real food.

Badge fell into step beside him. "That doesn't smell like MRE's to me, Bones."

MRE's, another part of military life he wouldn't miss. Although Delhi offered a better selection than he'd had at the patrol base, still nothing to bust a wad over.

"It smells like Italian, Badge." He nudged his buddy with his elbow. "Maybe they're treating us today."

Night meals were usually the fully cooked meals flown in and reheated by the cooks, far superior to the standard MRE. As luck would have it, today's lunch offering was spaghetti with real meat sauce. He was hungry enough for a decent meal not to wonder about what kind of meat was used in the sauce. He and Badge got in line, and by the time they found a spot to sit and eat, Ben had already shoveled two rolls into his mouth. He wolfed down a massive amount of spaghetti, along with some kind of fruit cobbler. It disappeared from his plate before he'd taken the time to think about what kind of fruit it contained.

"Oh man, that shit was good. What kind of cobbler was that?"

Ben sat back, patting his full belly, his appetite sated for now. "I have no idea. By the time I realized how good it tasted, it was gone." He looked at Badge and grinned. "I'm foreseeing some midnight food raids in the future."

The two of them made their way back to the tent. Ben dropped his gear on his bunk and sat on the wooden box used as a seat. Inspecting his bag of dirty laundry, he put aside a relatively clean set of work-out clothes and gathered the remaining pile of stink into one sack. He stood up and lifted his bag to his shoulder and addressed his buddy. "Man, I'm gonna hit the showers. I can't stand myself anymore. I'm dropping my laundry off first. You want me to bring yours?"

"Nah, I'll bring mine over in a while. Hope there's warm water for you."

"It'd be nice, but at this rate I don't really give a shit."

He detoured to the full service laundry area, a rarity in the Afghan desert.

The man in charge took the bag from him and grinned. "You want extra starch in those boxers today?"

Ben shook his head, giving him the standard answer. "The usual amount will do."

Still clutching his semi-clean sweats, he hit the showers with a vengeance. It wasn't easy ridding himself of the two week build-up of sandy grit and grime, but he did his damnedest. It suddenly hit him that from now until he left the Corps, he'd be able to shower almost any damn time he wanted to.

Step one of post deployment life. Ooh Rah.

He emerged from his shower, a real shower, red-skinned from scrubbing. A full belly and being half-ass clean . . . two things he could definitely get used to.

On the walk back to his tent he approached the MWR center. The only people he wanted to communicate with were all sleeping soundly at the moment. But he did step inside and connect to a computer long enough to shoot Haley a quick message on Facebook, telling her he'd Skype around 4:30 p.m. her time. He knew from experience this place would be packed from about 6:00 until 10:00 p.m. He still preferred waking up around 2 a.m. to make his calls in relative peace, with nobody waiting on him to finish. Once he'd messaged her, the search for something to do in his down time became all important.

As luck would have it, there was a game of poker brewing in his platoon's tent by the time he walked inside, just the distraction he needed to make the time pass a little faster.

Ben wiped the sleep from his eyes and slipped into his shoes to make the trek to the M-dub shack. Today's temps had hovered around the mid-seventies, and it wasn't much cooler than that now. At least that's what the thermometer hanging outside the tent indicated. Two more weeks, give or take a few days, and he'd be back in Kaneohe Bay with sand and surf to keep him company. Even better, he'd have Haley there with him. May 5th couldn't get here fast enough.

He entered the shack, pleased to be alone, and took a seat to fire up a Skype session, first with his mom. Within seconds, he'd connected and his mother sat there, her face lit up at the sight of him.

"Benjamin . . . How's my baby boy?"

He frowned then chuckled. "Mom, really?"

She flapped her hand at him and made a face. "You will always be my baby boy. If I can put up with worrying about you over there, you can put up with a little embarrassment from your mother."

He nodded and smiled at the woman who'd supported him throughout this journey of his. "Okay mom. How's everything going over there? Those kids driving you crazy yet?"

"Oh, you know, everyone's got the end of the year itch. The weather's nice and warm, and those kids are tired of being cooped in a classroom."

Ben cracked a grin at his mom. "I bet the teacher does too. Admit it, mom. Toledo Bend is calling your name."

She leaned forward and grinned. "You know your mother too well, Benjamin. Hell yeah, I'm ready for long, glorious days of fishing at the Bend. Mrs. Chapman is suffering from severe end-of-school-year burn out." She waved it off. "Enough about me. How are you? You're obviously back at Delhi or we wouldn't be Skyping. How long before your next mission?"

He leaned toward the monitor, knowing he was about to make her day. "No more missions, mom. I'm done. My company will be here at Delhi for a couple of more weeks to show the incoming company the ropes. Then we'll drive to Dwyer and be there until they can fly us out."

Monica Chapman covered her face with both hands for a moment, and then wiped a tear from her eye. "I suspected you were done, Ben. I didn't want to jinx it by saying it out loud." She blinked several times and took a deep breath. "So, this is step one of the journey home. How does it feel?"

"It feels freaking awesome."

After several minutes of playing catch up on family members back home, Monica relayed a message from his dad and step-mom. "Oh, I spoke to Paul and Paula the other day. She said to tell you that she's perfected her Bloody Mary recipe for you."

"That sounds good. Tell her I said thanks, and I can't wait to give it my seal of approval." He grinned to himself, continuously thankful that his divorced parents were on such friendly terms with each other, as well as his two step-parents.

"How's Haley doing, Benjamin? Does she know you're finished with the missions?"

"As far as I know she's fine, and she will soon. I called you first."

"Oh, I know what that means. I'll talk to you later, okay son? I love you, and eat something. You're too thin."

"I will. Love you too, mom. Talk to you later."

He ended the session and checked his watch, knowing Haley would anxiously be awaiting his call. He clicked her name on the contact list. In seconds her beautiful face appeared, beaming, her eyes bright with anticipation. "Hey beautiful." He braced himself, eagerly anticipating the sound of her voice.

"Hey, baby." She took a deep breath before asking. "Are you done with being shot at for a while, Marine?"

He grinned at her. "As far as I know, I am."

She let out a whoop of excitement and raised both arms in the air. "Yes!"

He couldn't stop grinning at her reaction. "Did I make your day, babe?"

She nodded, covered her mouth with her hands, as her emotions got the best of her. She lowered them, revealing a broad smile as she blinked back tears. "Thank God."

Chapter 15

Making Memories of Us

Twenty-one Skype sessions and several phone calls later found a much beefier Corporal Ben Bonin boarding a large aircraft that would carry the Weapons Company of the 3/3 on the last leg of the Afghanistan journey. They'd arrived at Camp Dwyer two days earlier, and were flying to Manas air base on the border of Kyrgyzstan and Kazakhstan.

As promised to himself, his girl, and his mom, Ben had packed on fifteen pounds of muscle by eating massive amounts of protein no less than five times a day, and lifting weights religiously while at FOB Delhi. Back in shape, and anxious to start his trip back to the states, the last three weeks had dragged by like the dog days of summer in south Louisiana.

Bad luck being what it was, the fourteen days at Delhi had stretched into eighteen, and the one day holdover at Dwyer had taken three, so far. As a result, here it was, the 2nd of May, and Haley was due to arrive in Kaneohe Bay on May 5th. He should have been the one to greet her at the airport upon her arrival. But, at the rate things were going, she'd be waiting for him. Even though his sniper training had taught him patience, it irked the hell out of him to have his plans thrown off kilter enough to inconvenience Haley. She was flying in alone and staying with the family of one of his Marine brothers, who'd rented a home on the beach. He knew she wouldn't be alone, but any time spent without her in his arms was a reason to be disappointed.

The plan was to fly from Dwyer to Manas air base, then American Samoa, and on to Hawaii. In hindsight, that had sounded simple enough. More than three and a half years as a Marine, however, had proven that the Corps had its own definition of simple, and it was anything but. A sixty-hour combination of waiting, processing, plane changes, refueling, airplane maintenance, crew changes, and delayed flights finally paid off. Weapons Company had finally arrived in Kaneohe Bay.

Ben stared out the window of the plane as it finally taxied to a stop at the hangar. Antsy as hell to get a glimpse of Haley, he searched for a sign of her through the tiny window at the back of the plane. He couldn't help himself, even knowing it was foolish to do so at this point.

The plane emptied from the front, with the highest ranking officers exiting first to greet their families inside the huge building wrapped in sheet metal. As anxious as he was, the twenty minutes it took to make his way to the front made him want to scream. Finally, he stepped through the plane's opening into the warm Hawaiian sunshine. He made his way slowly across the tarmac, one Marine in a crowd of many, and barely kept from shoving people out of his way. He saw dozens of Marine brothers and sisters, all anxiously waiting for their own family reunions. He faced the front, looking out over the sea of cammie uniforms and concentrated his efforts on the barely visible crowd of civilians.

He saw the sign first . . . GIRLFRIEND of CPL BEN BONIN . . . written in thick, black lettering on a bright yellow poster board. He kept his eye trained on it, waited until slim fingers raised it enough to clear the crown of light auburn hair. If a four star general had ordered him not to call out her name, he doubted he'd have been able to stop himself from doing that very thing.

"Haley!"

The sign lowered the same moment a big guy stepped aside and he finally caught his first glimpse of her face. There she was. His girl, looking every bit as beautiful as the day he'd left her. She caught her first sight of him and screamed his name. He tried to make his way to her through the crowd, but in the end it was all her. His Haley shoved, pushed, and scooted her way through the sea of people until a path opened, allowing her to launch herself into his open arms.

The airfield's hangar had steadily filled all morning long with family members waiting for their loved ones. Weapons Company was flying in together on a plane the military had chartered for this occasion. Chattering among the family members rose to a fevered pitch as someone announced the plane had landed on the strip. Several minutes later it finally taxied to a stop beyond their line of sight. She knew the highest ranking officials unloaded first; tried not to be annoyed when they all took their sweet time greeting their own families. *Move along, dammit!*

A full ten minutes later, the officers began to veer off, finally making room for the other types of Marines, the NCO's like hers. They approached the entrance as one conglomeration of digital Marpat cammies, high and tight haircuts, and close shaves. A huge group of back-pack-wearing, rifle-toting, pistol-packing Marines, all sporting lei's of some type of shells painted in patriotic colors.

"Oh my," she breathed, at the awe inspiring impressiveness of the group of men and women, alike. All had sacrificed so many of their own freedoms to serve their country in one way or another. Haley prayed every single one of them had someone waiting who appreciated their contributions as much as she and Ben's family did. She thought of her own parents, who'd put her on a plane, alone, for her very first flight. Both her mom and dad had cried, terrified of sending their only daughter on a four thousand mile flight, most of which was over open waters of the Pacific Ocean. Yes, they'd sacrificed too.

For the next ten minutes she stood on her tip toes, her neck craned, straining for a glimpse of him. She stepped forward, holding up the sign as high as she could in hopes that Ben would see it and come to her. After what seemed like an eternity she finally heard his voice.

"Haley!"

She turned her head to the sound of the voice, and caught her first sight of the man she'd boarded three separate planes to see.

"Ben!" The sign fell from her fingertips as she pushed her way through the sea of Marines toward him. Finally, the crowd parted. He extended his gun free arm and she turned into a human projectile, launching herself at him, too choked up with emotion to utter more than a single cry.

"Ben . . ."

No words, nothing could have described that first feeling of being wrapped in her Marine's embrace, pulled so tightly to him her toes skimmed the cement. All background noise faded, dimming in comparison to his presence. She tried to pull back to kiss him but he held tight, as though afraid to let her go, his face buried in her hair. The thought that this man, after all he'd been through, couldn't hold her tight enough thrilled her to her core. Finally he relented, pulled back and kissed her. The Ben that had no compunction kissing her in front of his family, had even less doing so in a large crowd of fellow Marines. That first kiss lasted long enough for her sense of surroundings to return to normal.

He finally pulled back, touched his head to hers. "We did it, Haley."

Haley couldn't stop smiling. "We did."

The depth of sincerity in his eyes grew more intense as he spoke the words that took her breath away. "I missed you, baby. Do you know how crazy I am about you?"

She nodded. "I do." Her heart swelled with pride, knowing she'd brought her Marine to the brink of admission. She *felt* loved by this man, even though he couldn't seem to say the words she longed to hear from him. Haley cupped his face in her hands. "I missed you too, Benjamin, so very much." He kissed her then—a desperate, clinging kiss, brimming with emotion. When it ended, he buried his face in her neck.

"Oh God, you feel so good." He lifted his handsome face to gaze at her, giving her a look heavy with promise. "And you're here."

"Of course I am." She touched his face again, unable to get enough of him. She lifted to her toes for another taste of his mouth, and then buried her face in his broad chest, filling her senses with the feel, the smell of him. Her body hummed like a tuning fork at his nearness. "Can we go?"

He groaned and pulled back. "We've got to board the busses. First stop is the armory to turn in weapons, then my barracks for accountability and orders. I'll have 96 hours with you, babe, four entire days before I'll have to go back to my unit for transitional briefings and duty. Were you able to get some sight-seeing in before I got here?"

"Yep, and now the only sight I'm interested in is this one, right here." She tapped his chest and grinned.

His heated gaze shot sparks of anticipation in every direction. "Mm hmm, but we've got to get out of here, first. Where's your ride?"

She turned, pointing to the family she'd driven over with. "That's the Blighe family." They made their way over to them.

Ben was introduced to D-Dub's parents, exchanged handshakes. "Thanks for taking care of my girl."

"No problem, she's a joy to have around." Mr. Blighe nodded toward his own son, standing there beside him. "I asked her if she doesn't have a friend for Dennis. He could use a good woman."

D-Dub flexed his bulked up arms. "And deprive the rest of womankind of this?" He shook his head. "Nah, I'm okay with being a single man for a while." He cocked his head toward Haley as he extended his hand in her direction. "Unless this little beauty ever decides to switch plans for an upgrade. Lance Corporal Dennis Wade Blighe, ma'am, but my friends call me D-Dub."

Haley laughed as she accepted the man's handshake. "Nice to meet you, D-Dub, I'm Haley Broussard, and oh boy, have I heard a lot about you."

He gave her a clearly visible wink. "What do you say, Haley? Want to take a walk on the wild side?"

She laughed and latched on to Ben's arm as he swung it possessively over her shoulder. "Thanks for the offer, but I'm satisfied right where I am." She tilted her head to better hear Ben's murmured comment.

"If you're not now, you will be soon."

She peeked up at him, feeling the heat creep up her neck into her cheeks.

The sight of Haley's cheeks flushed with what he suspected was more than embarrassment, had nearly done him in. Their call to board the busses came as she lifted that beautiful, brown-eyed gaze to his.

"I'll meet you back at the base." He kissed her again, finally let go, anticipating getting his fill of her, if possible.

He and D-Dub boarded the waiting bus as Haley departed with the Blighe family.

They met up again at the armory, separated by sturdy fencing that couldn't keep them away from each other. Fingers linked through the chain fencing, they talked, and kissed, and planned as he waited to turn in his equipment.

One more trip to the barracks for an accountability meeting and the official announcement of the ninety-six hour furlough from the base, and he was free to leave.

He had D-Dub's family drop him off at the car rental place down the street from the Hilton where he'd made his and Haley's reservations. Haley left him once more to get her things from the beach house.

An hour and a half later, he met her with a kiss in the hotel lobby, freshly showered and dressed in casual civvies consisting of a pair of shorts, and a light blue polo shirt.

He grabbed her luggage from her and pulled it toward the elevator with one hand, using his opposite to pull her close. He kissed her again in the semi-crowded elevator. They communicated their thoughts with looks and soft caresses rather than words. She leaned in close to him seconds before the gentle whoosh of elevator doors opened onto the 6th floor.

"This is our floor," he said, his hand at her lower back to gently guide her out the door.

"This is a beautiful hotel."

"You being here makes it even more beautiful." He pulled her close as he rolled her luggage to a door at the end of the corridor.

She looped her arm around his waist and leaned into his side. "Thank you."

"Thank you for being here. You have no idea how much it meant to have you here waiting for me."

"Ben—"

"Wait, babe. Let me say this before we go inside." Ben swiped his room card to unlock the door, and then placed both hands on her shoulders. He stared into twin pools of liquid brown, took a deep breath, and tried to put all his feelings for her into mere words.

"From the first moment I laid eyes on you I knew you were something special. When that prick had his hands all over you, I saw how it fired you up. Even though I tried to talk him out of it, I was glad he took a swing at me. I wanted to punch him for disrespecting you the way he had. And then, when you spent the next two weeks by my side—God, never in a million years, did I think you would have pushed everything aside for me the way you did."

He sighed, and shook his head. "I held you in my arms while you cried toward the end of my leave, knowing I couldn't do a damn thing to keep you from hurting. That was difficult. That's when I knew I'd do whatever it took to get back to you. The thought of you being here, waiting for me . . ." He collected his thoughts to finish. "Even during missions, sitting inside a hide site with very little water, no electricity, no comforts of home, and no word from you. You can't know how much it meant, knowing you were at home, waiting for me. You were there for me."

He touched his head to her forehead. "But it's not something I wanted to say over a crappy phone or during a sketchy Skype session. I wanted to tell you like this." He straightened, before cupping her face. "Holding your beautiful face in my hands." He took a half step forward, pressing his body close to hers. "Thank you, Haley." He kissed the saltiness of her tears from both cheeks before tasting her sweet lips again.

She stretched up on her toes, wrapped her arms around his neck and deepened the kiss. She finally pulled back, giving him the look he'd longed to see for seven long months. "If you don't get me out of this hallway,

Benjamin, we could end up on Waikiki Beach's police blotter for indecent exposure."

He grinned, loving the adorable dimple her sexy little smile exposed. "Yes ma'am." He grasped the door knob, swinging it open slowly to gauge her reaction.

She gasped at his efforts to make the suite a haven for the two of them. A quick trip to the hotel's florist and gift shop had produced several fragrant candles and a bouquet of roses. He'd lit the candles and set them around the room to cast dancing, romantic shadows while emitting luscious fragrances throughout the room. Her gaze landed on the trail of deep red rose petals he'd carefully laid in patterns across the floor. She sent him a questioning glance.

He nodded. "Follow the trail."

She walked through the door, following the first trail of blood red rose petals to a chair at the opposite side of the room. A folded note said READ ME. She picked up the piece of paper and read from it.

"Time apart can sometimes break a heart . . ."

She followed a second trail of petals to the entertainment center, and a second note tucked under a dish of luscious ripe strawberries. She swallowed and read. *"But for you and me, it's easy to see . . ."* Again, she followed the trail to the desk and picked up the third note, folded and standing on a tray that held a bucket of chilled champagne, complete with two crystal flutes. *"We are meant to be together . . . forever . . . and ever . . ."*

She wiped at the steady stream of tears and followed the last trail of petals to the king sized bed. She stood for a moment, staring at the crisp white duvet, marred only by three words, I LOVE YOU, painstakingly spelled out with more red rose petals. "Oh. My. God."

He leaned over her shoulder, grinning. "Guess I should have spell checked, because that's supposed to say "I love you".

She turned slowly, her face covered with the most mysterious expression he'd ever seen on a woman. Her eyes crinkled with laughter as they lit upon the remaining roses set in a vase on one nightstand. "Ooh Rah, Marine."

He rolled the suitcase inside and stood there, staring at her. "Yeah? What do you think?"

"I think—no, I *know* that I love you, too."

Haley hung the "Do Not Disturb" sign on the handle before closing and locking the door. She turned, her sexy little mouth grinning as she spoke.

"And someone is about to get very, very lucky."

Two hours and one visit from room service later, they lay stretched out on the bed, drinking champagne, and eating strawberries dipped in chocolate and hazelnut spread.

"These are so good. I can't believe you remembered how much I like this." Haley licked chocolate spread from her fingertips and beamed at her Marine.

"I remember everything about you, but I'm starving. I'll need something more substantial if you expect me to keep up this pace." He began to nibble at her neck, causing her to giggle and pull away from him.

"*That's* not going to get rid of your hunger pangs."

"It's kind of like having dessert before the main course." He sprang up from the bed, pulling her up and into his arms. "Come on, let's get dressed and get out of here for a couple of hours. What are you hungry for?"

She shook her head, pushing herself away from the headiness of his nearly naked body, covered only by the thin layer of his boxer briefs. "I'm not the one who's been stuck eating MRE's. You choose."

"Steak, I want a big, juicy T-bone, and I know where to get one. I want to grab another shower, though . . . just because I can," he said, winking at her. He walked to the bathroom door and turned to her, his left brow cocked in anticipation. "You coming in with me?"

Haley stared at the hard ridge of muscles along his neck and shoulders, highly defined abs, and sexy pads of muscle above his hip that made her want to lose her flipping mind. She tightened the belt on her fluffy white robe. "Not if you plan on leaving here anytime soon." No way in hell could she keep her hands off *any* of that beefy display. "You go ahead, but I need to know how to dress."

"Casual dress, babe. There's an IHOP down the street that serves the best T-Bone around here and we don't have to get all fancied up." His eyes sparkled with laughter as he sent her a seductive wink. "Make sure it's easy to remove, and wear your bikini under it. I want to take a quick dip in the Pacific afterwards, if it's alright with you."

Haley released a low sigh as the door closed, hiding him from sight. She knew he'd done that more for her sake, than his own. Being military, the man didn't have an ounce of shyness left in him. But, even with two hours of lovemaking under her belt, learning every square inch of that muscular body of his . . . the idea of that kind of contact with him still made her want to hide under the covers. She loved him even more for taking her feelings into consideration.

"Oh, my goodness," she breathed, reaching for a suitcase. She unzipped it, pulling out one of three bikini bathing suits she'd brought along, a brightly colored sarong, and a low cut yellow tank top, trimmed with lace. She attacked her shoe bag next, and chose a pair of sandals. She put the rest back and shoved the bag out of the way.

By the time Ben emerged from the bathroom, wearing a towel draped loosely around his hips, Haley had finished touching up her make-up. She grabbed her clothes and headed for the bathroom, doing what she could to avoid the sight of his barely covered body. Shaking her head, she closed the door on his low chuckle. He knew exactly what the sight of him did to her.

Ten minutes later, she emerged, completely put together, to find him standing out on the balcony. She stepped up beside him, taking in the view before her with a reverent sigh. "It's so beautiful."

"Yes, it is."

She turned, seeing his gaze plastered on her. "You like, Marine?"

One side of his mouth lifted in that sexy as hell grin that made her want to kiss it right off of his face. He shook his head. "I love, babe." He reached out, catching her behind the neck to pull her gently toward him. "I love every single bit of it." He lowered his mouth to hers for another long, heart-melting kiss.

Haley's insides heated as she looped her arms around his neck. She breathed him in, wishing she could crawl inside him for the next five months. She wanted to stay there with him, safe, and loved, until it was time for him to come home to her for good.

No doubt, they'd have ended up back in bed, had his stomach not taken that moment to remind them why they'd crawled out in the first place. She pulled away from him, pressing her hand to her abdomen to still the quivering his nearness caused in her.

"Sustenance," she groaned. "Let's get you fed so you don't pass out from starvation. You've got a long night ahead of you."

"Roger that."

The two of them headed down to the lobby where valet parking had brought his rental around, a bright red, two-seater Jeep Wrangler.

He laughed at her squeal of excitement. "I take it you're pleased?"

"It's perfect." She turned to him. "Can we take off the cover?"

He nodded. "We'll do that tomorrow. Let's go find something to eat."

They left the local IHOP, stuffed with steaks and omelets, and drove straight to the public beach. They parked the Jeep, and one loosened knot later, Haley's sarong bit the dust along with her tank top. She stood in her bikini, blushing at the lecherous look on Ben's face.

He gave his head a slow shake as he shoved his shirt and shorts onto the back seat. "My God, you are some kind of beautiful, you know that?"

She beamed up at him. "I feel beautiful when I'm with you, so thank you." Haley traded out her sandals for surf shoes and placed her bag in the back section of the Jeep. She turned to him, accepting the hand he held out to her. Hand in hand, they walked to the beach and entered the warm waters of the Pacific Ocean. A thought came to her as a wave washed over her thighs, making her lips part with a delighted laugh.

"What are you thinking?"

She swallowed the lump in her throat as she attempted an explanation. "I was thinking that this is one more first for us, you know? Our first ride in a Jeep together, our first swim in the Pacific Ocean together, our first . . . time . . . together." She smiled into his handsome face, knowing he'd understand.

He lifted her easily in his arms. "Our first, but definitely not our last."

She grinned and kissed his forehead. Then leaned in to whisper seductively in his ear. "Definitely not." She nibbled at his earlobe, delighted at her big, strong Marine's uncontrollable shiver.

He groaned, walking further out into the surf. "And here comes another first."

"What's that?" she asked, lifting her head in time to see a large wave rolling toward the shore.

"Our first wipe out." He turned his back to the wave as the two of them got dunked unceremoniously.

Haley came up coughing and sputtering as Ben's delighted laughter accompanied his next comment. "Man, you don't know how bad I missed this shit!"

"I believe you." She pushed her hair from her face. "I feel a little like a ragdoll being tossed around in these massive waves, though."

"It's the power of mother nature at her finest. I've got something to show you tomorrow that I know you'll love." He brought her nearer to shore where it was calmer.

The two of them walked along the beach, frolicking in the waves until the shadows lengthened in the late afternoon sun. He tightened his grip on her waist then lifted her into his arms. He kissed her again, and she wondered if she'd ever get enough of it.

"Mm, bring me back to the room, baby. Please?" She tucked her face into his neck, nipping gently at his skin, again causing a shiver to pass through him.

He released a low, guttural groan. "If you don't stop that we won't make it back to the room."

"Put me down, Ben."

"Why? You don't weigh a thing." As soon as he set her on her feet, she took off running toward the Jeep. Within seconds he'd caught up to her, scooped her up from behind, and carried her the rest of the distance to the rental. He deposited her in the sand and unlocked the door. They dressed hurriedly and he got them back to the hotel as quickly as the traffic would allow.

Hand in hand, they slipped into the already occupied elevator. Ben picked a back corner to lean against, tucking Haley close to his body, his arm wrapped protectively around her. Heat from his body seared her through the thin material of her tank top. Her stomach fluttered at the contact—they couldn't get to the 6th floor fast enough. As soon as the doors opened she rushed forward.

"Excuse us, please." None too gently, she pushed her way to the opening, pulling Ben behind her.

He got to the door first, room card at the ready and swiped it. The light flashed green and a second later he'd pushed open the door and pulled her through behind him.

The enticing scent of rose petals and scented candles launched a full blown assault on Haley's senses. By the time Ben had secured the door and turned, the sarong and tank top were already on the floor in a heap. He pulled her into the bathroom with him and reached over to turn on the taps. Her eyes widened as she stared at the large, luxurious, glass enclosed shower.

"Babe? Are you all right with this?"

"I-I'm not sure."

He gave her an understanding smile. "You want to shower first? I'll wait."

She shook her head. "No, you go on."

Ben nodded. "Okay. I won't be long."

Haley closed the door behind her, resting her head against it. She heard the snap and zipper of his shorts, then the sound of his clothes dropping to the floor. She listened, knowing exactly when he stepped into the spray of jets, could hear the water slapping at his hard body. A low groan accompanied the knowledge that she *had* to be in there with him. She opened the door and stepped inside, closing it behind her soundlessly. In a few scant seconds her bikini hit the floor and she'd slipped inside the shower.

He froze as she placed her hand on his broad back, and then turned slowly toward her, his eyes questioning and hopeful.

She smiled at him and nodded. "It's one more first for us, right?" The smile he gave her melted her heart.

Ben took the bottle of shampoo provided by the hotel and poured the contents into one hand, worked it into her long hair until it was thick with luxurious lather.

Haley closed her eyes, letting his long fingers gently massage her scalp.

"Ready to rinse?"

She nodded and stepped into the spray of warm water. She let it rinse away all traces of shampoo, and then allowed Ben to apply the conditioner. One more thorough scalp massage and she stepped under the spray again. By the time she'd rinsed, Ben was waiting with a washcloth thoroughly lathered with Haley's shower gel. Rather than making him ask, she closed the gap between them, holding his gaze with her own. Slowly, his hand moved along her skin, spreading the perfumed, silky lather over her body.

She closed her eyes and sighed, luxuriating in the feel of his hands on her. He turned her gently to wash her back, applying gentle pressure. She leaned forward, placing her hands on the glass wall to keep her balance as his hands moved over her. When his arms wrapped loosely around her she turned to face him. Drawing his head down for a kiss with one hand, she turned off the water with the other. Haley jerked a towel from the wall holder and placed it over the built-in shower seat. His curious gaze turned to one of pleasant shock when she pushed him gently back upon it.

He sat, looking up at her as she approached. "What's this?" he asked, as she lowered herself to straddle him.

She sent him a seductive smile and a wink. "Another first . . . Don't worry, Marine. I'll be gentle with you."

Chapter 16

Working on Forever

December 1st

Formally discharged Corporal Ben Bonin checked his phone as soon as his plane landed at the Lake Coburn airport. Still taxiing to the runway, he opened his Facebook page, saw Haley's grinning face and the message:

"On our way to pick up my baby from the airport, and we'll never have to say goodbye again. Benjamin is coming home for good."

He sent her a quick text: *Just landed.*

She immediately sent back a smiley face.

He sat back in his seat thinking about the past half year since he'd last seen her at Kaneohe Bay. He'd fed off the memories of her visit for months. All the things they'd done during that week she'd stayed with him, all the 'firsts' they'd experienced.

They'd snorkeled, kayaked, hiked, clubbed, danced, and done a little cliff diving, played volleyball with the guys, and had seen the sights all over the island of Oahu. They'd made some mighty fine memories, that's for damn sure.

He closed his eyes, thinking of the many times they'd made love during that visit. He remembered the last time, and how she'd barely held it together for him. Telling him goodbye for another five months that, for one reason or another, turned into six and a half, hadn't been easy for either of them. It had helped that they could Skype often, and did so, along with phone calls, Facebook messaging, and texts.

The plane rolled to a stop, and Ben, whose seat had somehow been upgraded to first class, was one of the first people off the plane. He headed down the ramp through the jet bridge into the terminal. He pushed through two sets of doors and rounded a corner to see his mom, step-dad, sister, and Haley standing there wearing bright gold T-shirts, each of them bearing similar, but different, messages. Haley saw him first and sprinted toward him, proving her shirt's message of PROUD GIRLFRIEND OF A MARINE. He braced himself to catch her in midair as she, once again, threw herself at him with the force of a projectile rocket.

"You're home. I can't believe it, you're finally home."

He held tightly to her, spinning her in a circle, not wanting to let go. Eventually he had to, as his sister assaulted him, and then his mom. He hugged each in turn, and then gave his step-dad a hug as he shook his hand. He turned to face Haley, only to have her launch herself at him again. He caught her easily and held on, walking to put a little distance between them and the others.

"Oh God, I missed holding you," he groaned, as he set her on her own two feet. "And I missed this." He cupped her face between his hands to kiss her. He pulled his mouth from hers to stare into the twin orbs of chocolate brown he'd seen in his dreams. "I'm here now." He lifted her chin and dried her tears with the cuff of his jacket. "I love you so much, Haley."

"I love you, Ben. Oh my God, I can't believe this day is finally here."

"It's here. I'm here. We made it through a year of separation, and everything from here on out is gravy, right?"

Haley's face glowed with the happiness she couldn't have hidden if she'd tried to. "That's right." She kissed him again, and then touched her forehead to his. "Can we go home, now?"

He nodded. "Let me get my bag." He walked to the luggage pick-up area to see Mr. Ben pulling his huge duffle from the conveyor belt.

"Is this all you have, Benjamin?"

"Yes sir, that's it."

"Well, let's get the hell outta here, then. I know your dad, step-mom, and brother are dying to see you back home."

The five of them exited the building and walked to his mom's Expedition. They loaded inside and started the fifty minute drive home to Lake Erin. Haley snuggled close to him, and pulled out her phone to send a text out to people waiting at home. His own phone buzzed and he took it out to check for messages. It was Haley's message that popped up on his Facebook page. She'd posted their mantra for the last thirteen months.

"A year is nothing compared to forever . . ."

He had to smile before leaning over to give her another kiss.

His phone vibrated in a continuous onslaught of hits and comments to the message she'd tagged him in. He lifted the phone, and noticed she'd posted a second message. His heart filled with absolute joy as he read the addendum to the original message.

And forever starts today . . . I Love you, Benjamin Bonin!

He pulled her even closer to his body, buried his face in the silkiness of her perfumed hair. "Ooh Rah, Haley."

His girl practically purred with happiness as she lifted her gaze to meet his. Her beautiful eyes sparkled with promise, and a hint of mischief. "Roger that, babe."

MESSAGE FROM THE AUTHOR

Around the middle of 2013, while researching for MEAGAN'S MARINE, I put out feelers on Facebook, asking if anyone knew of a U.S. Marine who could give me information. I could research on the internet but I needed details of a Marine's daily life. I received an immediate response from a very proud mother of a recently deactivated Marine. Corporal Benjamin Bonin, a Scout Sniper with the 3/3, Weapons Company, had come home the previous December. Ben's Mom, Monica Chapman, told her son I'd be contacting him via Facebook messenger. As my need for information grew, the messaging graduated to phone texting and emails. Not only did he give me valuable info for MEAGAN'S MARINE, but he and his girlfriend, Haley Broussard, inspired the idea for a subplot using characters like them in my next book. Haley would be written in as an established character's younger sister. Ben would be her U.S. Marine love interest. Before long, I'd set up a lunch date to meet with Ben and Haley.

Ben's hometown of Lake Arthur, LA is a mere fifteen miles west of my birthplace, Gueydan, LA. As it happened, we knew lots of the same people. By the time we met at the lovely Regatta Restaurant in downtown Lake Arthur for an interview, I was on fairly good text messaging terms with the couple.

I'd done a little Facebook lurking on their walls so I'd recognize them at the restaurant. Armed with my notebook and pen to jot down some notes, I thought I was prepared for our little meeting.

As soon as I entered the restaurant, they stood to greet me. After a few brief introductions, I sat back and gazed at them, realizing that all the snapshots in the world couldn't do the real Ben and Haley justice. That's how perfect they were together.

I sensed an initial shyness in Haley, a sweet, beautiful young lady with sparkling brown eyes and a bright smile. I realized soon after striking up a conversation with Ben—a handsome, athletically built young man—that his man-of-few-words demeanor wasn't a result of shyness, but rather the quiet, self-confidence he exuded. As I watched the two of them together, I could tell these two people knew exactly what they wanted out of life—and it began and ended with each other.

They constantly touched, communicated with looks, and soft words, sometimes finishing each other's sentences. At other times they broke into quiet laughter, because neither could answer one of my questions.

I asked Haley what it was like having Ben eight thousand miles away, and in danger, for so many months at a time. She turned those big, brown eyes on her Marine and reached for the hand he held out to her.

"I tried to keep busy, but when I couldn't do that, I tried to sleep as much as I could. That's the only time I didn't miss him."

Honestly, I think Haley thought I was only there for Ben's viewpoint. But this is a romance that would be read by mostly women. I needed her thoughts and feelings as well. I learned that while Ben was away, she dealt with her nerves in different ways: she ate pounds of sunflower seeds, never let go of her phone, checked for messages constantly, and picked at her cuticles and nails. She waited anxiously, hoping for a short but sweet phone call at the end of each mission. Those only occurred if the Satellite phone was in their area of operation once his sniper team returned to the patrol base. She lived for those *other* calls...when his unit headed back to Forward Operating Base Delhi for some R&R. That's when they got the chance to Skype their families. He'd set his alarm for 2 a.m. and crawl out of bed and head over to the MWR (Morale/Welfare/Recreation services) shack, where he could Skype Haley and various members of his family in relative peace. Afghanistan time is about 10.5 hours ahead of Louisiana.

As we talked, I took notes when I remembered to, and by the time I left there, I was certain of two things: Ben and Haley would have their own book, and I wanted those two faces on the book cover. That's not a difficult thing to happen when you've been friends with a fabulous photographer for over twenty years. Enter Joan Granger, of Simple Memories Photography in Welsh, LA.

I gave Ben enough time to hit the gym so he could get back into "Marine" shape. No regrets there . . . It was ridiculous how good he looked. I told them what I wanted them to wear to the shoot but added "Bring extra changes of clothes, because when Joan gets a look at y'all she's going to go ape-**** crazy taking pictures. I know she will." She did, of course, and I stood back and let her do her thing.

She got so many wonderful shots, angles, and poses of those two I nearly lost my mind trying to choose ONE for the cover. In fact, I couldn't. I've decided to have the same version of the book with two different covers, one for regular and one for large print.

So, after nine months of working on this book, I'm finally ready to publish. Before all of you out there who know Ben and Haley jump up to say "That's not what happened!" let me explain. Ben and Haley are real people, some of the things that happened in the story really happened. This book, however, is a work of fiction, based loosely on true occurrences. I worked their characters into a story with a pre-existing timeline.

I was terrified of writing a love story that spans a year, especially when the couple is separated by eight thousand miles for most of that time. It turned out to be much easier than I'd imagined, thanks to Ben and Haley and their inspiring stories.

I'd like to add that Benjamin's contributions, in the form of journal style entries, were so well written I could practically have put them in the book as they were. Unfortunately, I had to spread some of the info out over various scenes to avoid what we call an 'info dump'.

I can only hope that you, the reader, are as satisfied with the results as I am.

Thanks for your time, and allowing me into your homes via the written word.

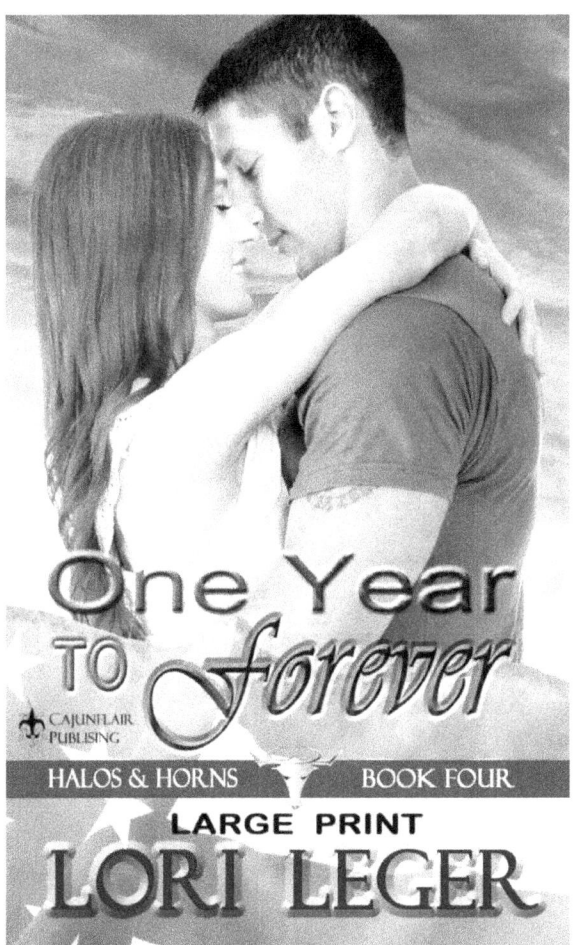

One Year TO forever

CAJUNFLAIR
PUBLISHING

HALOS & HORNS   BOOK FOUR

LARGE PRINT

LORI LEGER

(Large Print cover) Cover photography by
Joan Granger, owner of Simple Memories Photography,
Welsh, LA

Ben & Haley

All snapshots courtesy of Haley Broussard
The Kaneohe Bay reunion . . . Absolute joy.

It doesn't get much better than this, does it?

Ben and Haley enjoying the beautiful beaches

More beach...

Haley and Miss Red Dakota

Haley and Dakota doing their thing . . .

Photos by Charlotta Benoit

(C. Benoit Photography)

(C. Benoit Photography)

(C. Benoit Photography)

ABOUT THE AUTHOR

Lori Leger is a wife, mother, doting grandmother, and Mistress of Procrastination. She lives in Louisiana with the love of her life, her very own Studley-do-Right. He's earned his spot in the Keeper Husband's Hall of Fame by allowing her to walk away from an eighteen plus year career as an Engineering Technician in Road Design to stay home and write.

She adores writing stories set in her beloved southwest Louisiana, where good Cajun cooking, helping your neighbors, and saying y'all is as normal as hurricanes, heat, and humidity. She figures as long as she's not tunneling through ten feet of snow to get to her car, it's a perfectly acceptable trade-off.

Lori has ten full-length novels, and one novella published in three series: La Fleur de Love, its spin-off, Halos & Horns, and her latest, the Prime of Love series. She has also contributed to, as well as published, short stories in each of the five Seasons of Love anthologies, an author collaboration series. She's compiled four of the short stories about one particular couple, Cathryn and Zachary, into a single book called Full Circle Love. It acts as a prequel to the Prime of Love series.

She's contributed to the Sweet & Savory Cookbook of Amazon Authors, published by Top Ten Press. Lori also has an article published in the non-fiction book Writing After Retirement: Tips From Retired Writers, published by Rowman and Littlefield Publishers, and edited and compiled by Carol Smallwood and Christine Redman-Waldeyer.

Hanging On To Hope is the Second book in her Prime of Love Series, novels dedicated to mature characters finding love and laughter through the everyday twists and turns of growing older. She has a third planned for the spring of 2016.

www.lorilegerauthor.com
cajunflair@lorilegerauthor.com
lleger641@yahoo.com
www.facebook.com/lorilegerauthor/
Twitter: @lleger641
https://www.goodreads.com/LoriLeger_CajunflairAuthor